GENIS-VELL
CAPTAIN MARVEL

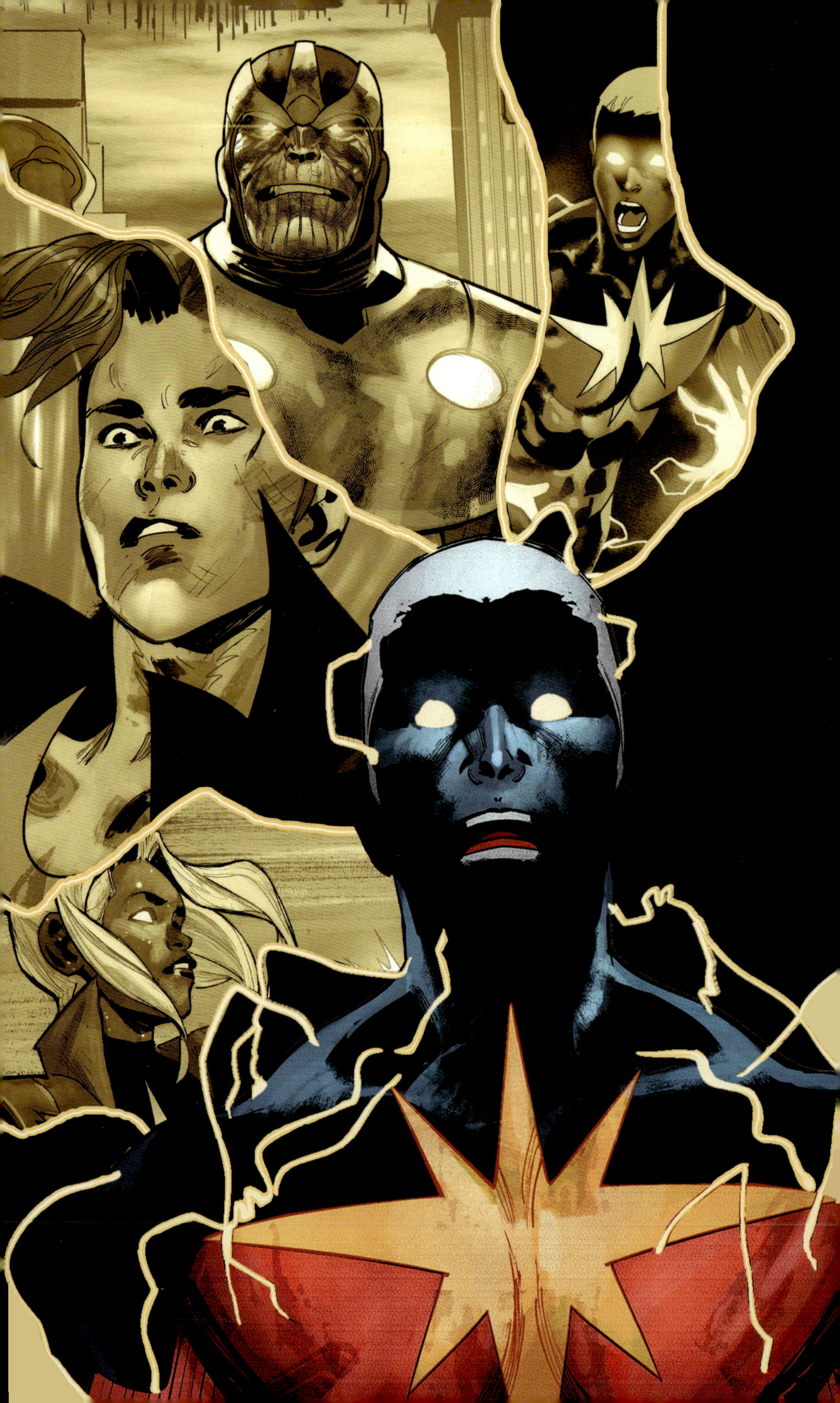

GENIS-VELL, son of the original Kree hero Captain Mar-Vell, followed in his father's footsteps by bonding with Earthling **RICK JONES** via the cosmically-powered Nega-Bands. When the bands were clanged together, the two would swap places between our world and the Microverse. Together, they soared the cosmos as the hero **CAPTAIN MARVEL**!

Years after their connection was severed, both Rick and Genis faced grim deaths alone. But that's all in the past now, as both of them are once again among the living!

GENIS-VELL
CAPTAIN MARVEL

PETER DAVID
writer

JUANAN RAMÍREZ
artist

FEDERICO BLEE
color artist

MIKE McKONE & ANTONIO FABELA
cover art

VC's ARIANA MAHER *(#1-2, #4-5)* **& CORY PETIT** *(#3)*
letterers

DANNY KHAZEM
editor

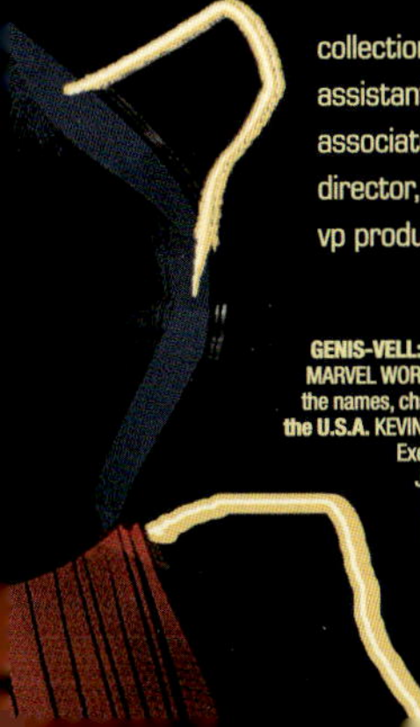

collection editor DANIEL KIRCHHOFFER
assistant managing editor MAIA LOY
associate manager, talent relations LISA MONTALBANO
director, production & special projects JENNIFER GRÜNWALD
vp production & special projects JEFF YOUNGQUIST

book designer SARAH SPADACCINI
senior designer JAY BOWEN
svp print, sales & marketing DAVID GABRIEL
editor in chief C.B. CEBULSKI

GENIS-VELL: CAPTAIN MARVEL. Contains material originally published in magazine form as GENIS-VELL: CAPTAIN MARVEL (2022) #1-5. First printing 2022. ISBN 978-1-302-94672-2. Published by MARVEL WORLDWIDE, INC., a subsidiary of MARVEL ENTERTAINMENT, LLC. OFFICE OF PUBLICATION: 1290 Avenue of the Americas, New York, NY 10104. **Printed in the U.S.A.** KEVIN FEIGE, Chief Creative Officer; DAN BUCKLEY, President, Marvel Entertainment; DAVID BOGART, Associate Publisher & SVP of Talent Affairs; TOM BREVOORT, VP, Executive Editor; NICK LOWE, Executive Editor, VP of Content, Digital Publishing; DAVID GABRIEL, VP of Print & Digital Publishing; SVEN LARSEN, VP of Licensed Publishing; MARK ANNUNZIATO, VP of Planning & Forecasting; JEFF YOUNGQUIST, VP of Production & Special Projects; ALEX MORALES, Director of Publishing Operations; DAN EDINGTON, Director of Editorial Operations; RICKEY PURDIN, Director of Talent Relations; JENNIFER GRÜNWALD, Director of Production & Special Projects; SUSAN CRESPI, Production Manager; STAN LEE, Chairman Emeritus. For information regarding advertising in Marvel Comics or on Marvel.com, please contact Vit DeBellis, Custom Solutions & Integrated Advertising Manager, at vdebellis@marvel.com. For Marvel subscription inquiries, please call 888-511-5480. **Manufactured between 11/18/2022 and 12/20/2022 by SEAWAY PRINTING, GREEN BAY, WI, USA.**

10987654321

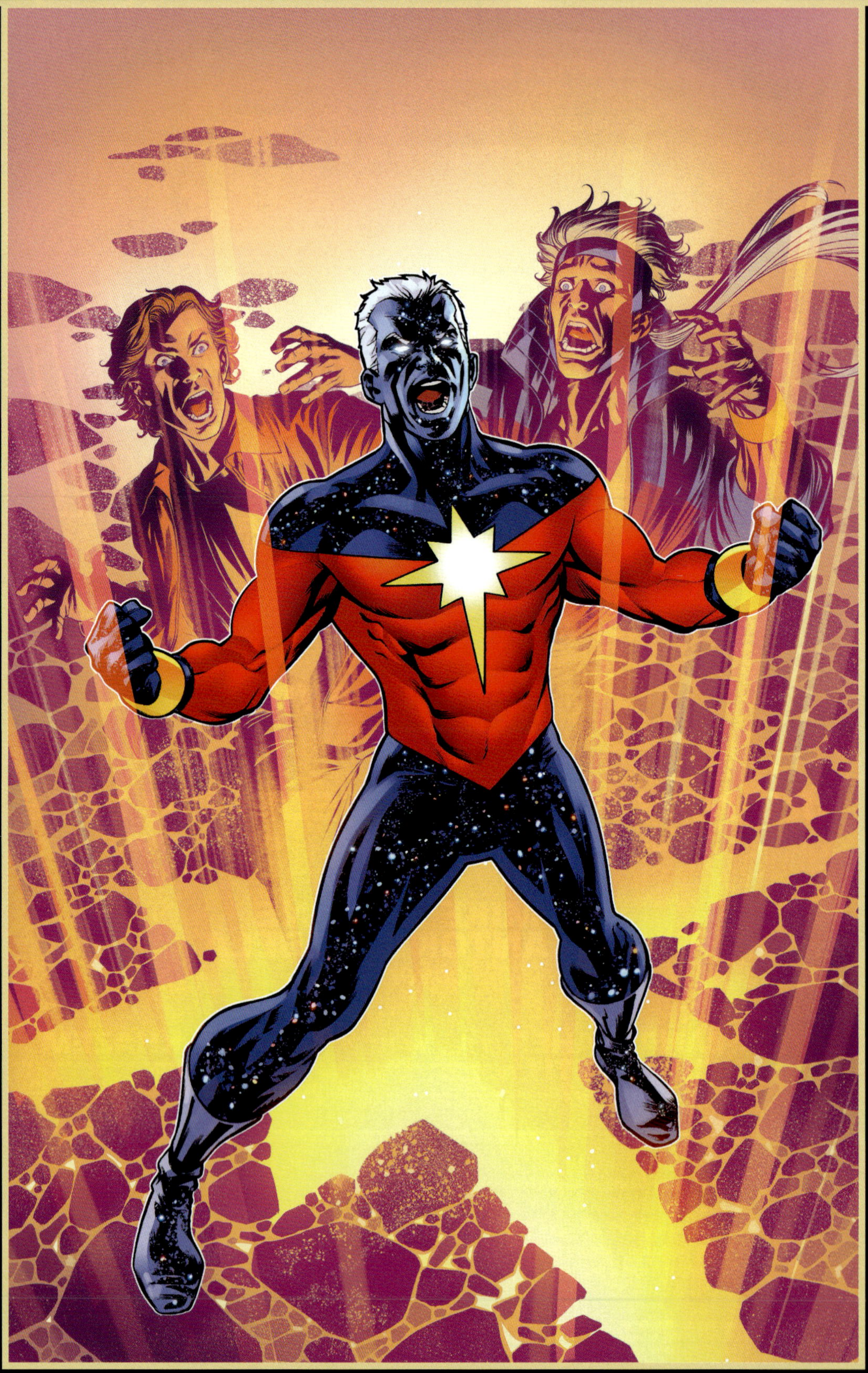

1

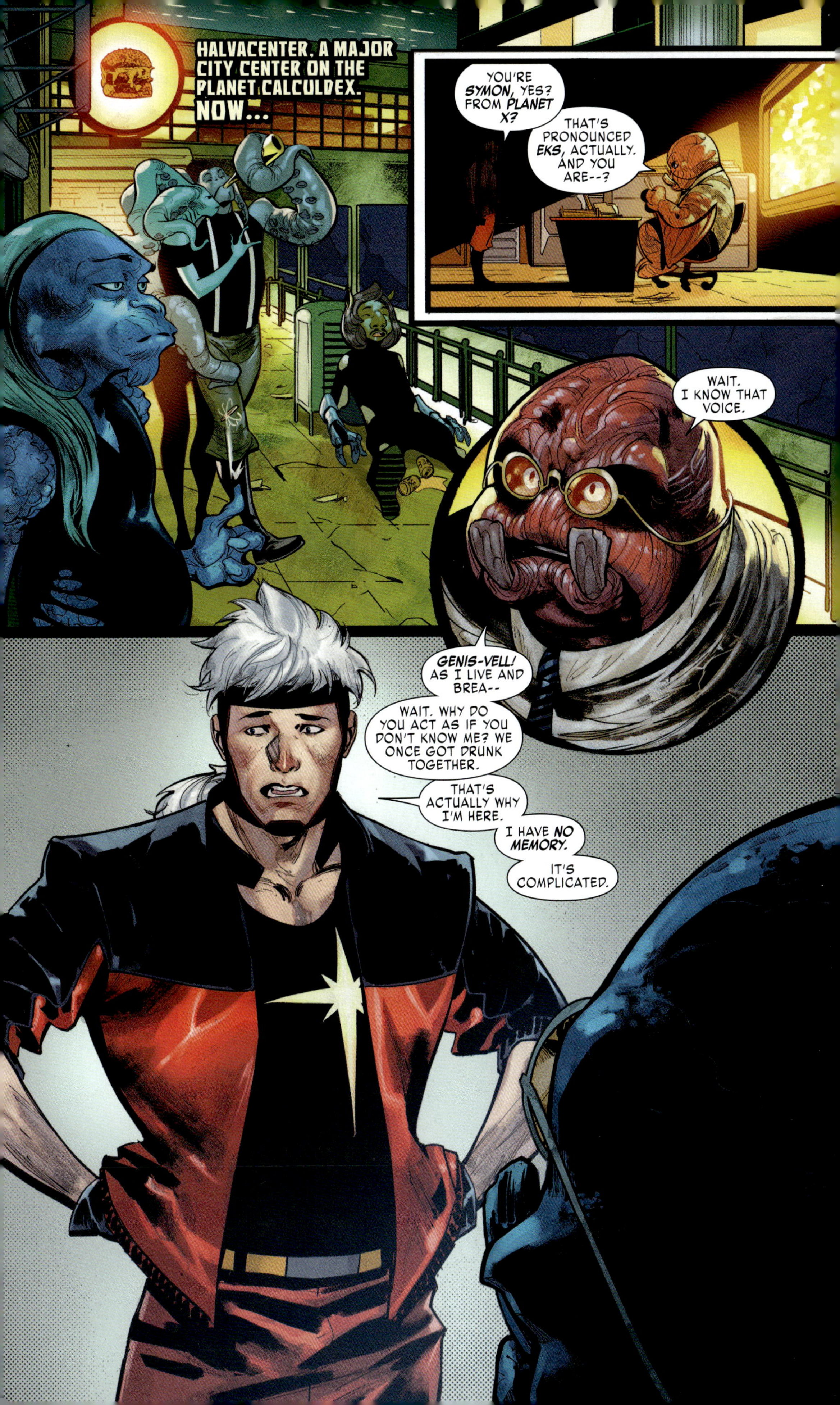
HALVACENTER, A MAJOR CITY CENTER ON THE PLANET CALCULDEX. NOW...
YOU'RE SYMON, YES? FROM PLANET X?
THAT'S PRONOUNCED EKS, ACTUALLY. AND YOU ARE--?
WAIT. I KNOW THAT VOICE.
GENIS-VELL! AS I LIVE AND BREA--
WAIT. WHY DO YOU ACT AS IF YOU DON'T KNOW ME? WE ONCE GOT DRUNK TOGETHER.
THAT'S ACTUALLY WHY I'M HERE.
I HAVE NO MEMORY.
IT'S COMPLICATED.

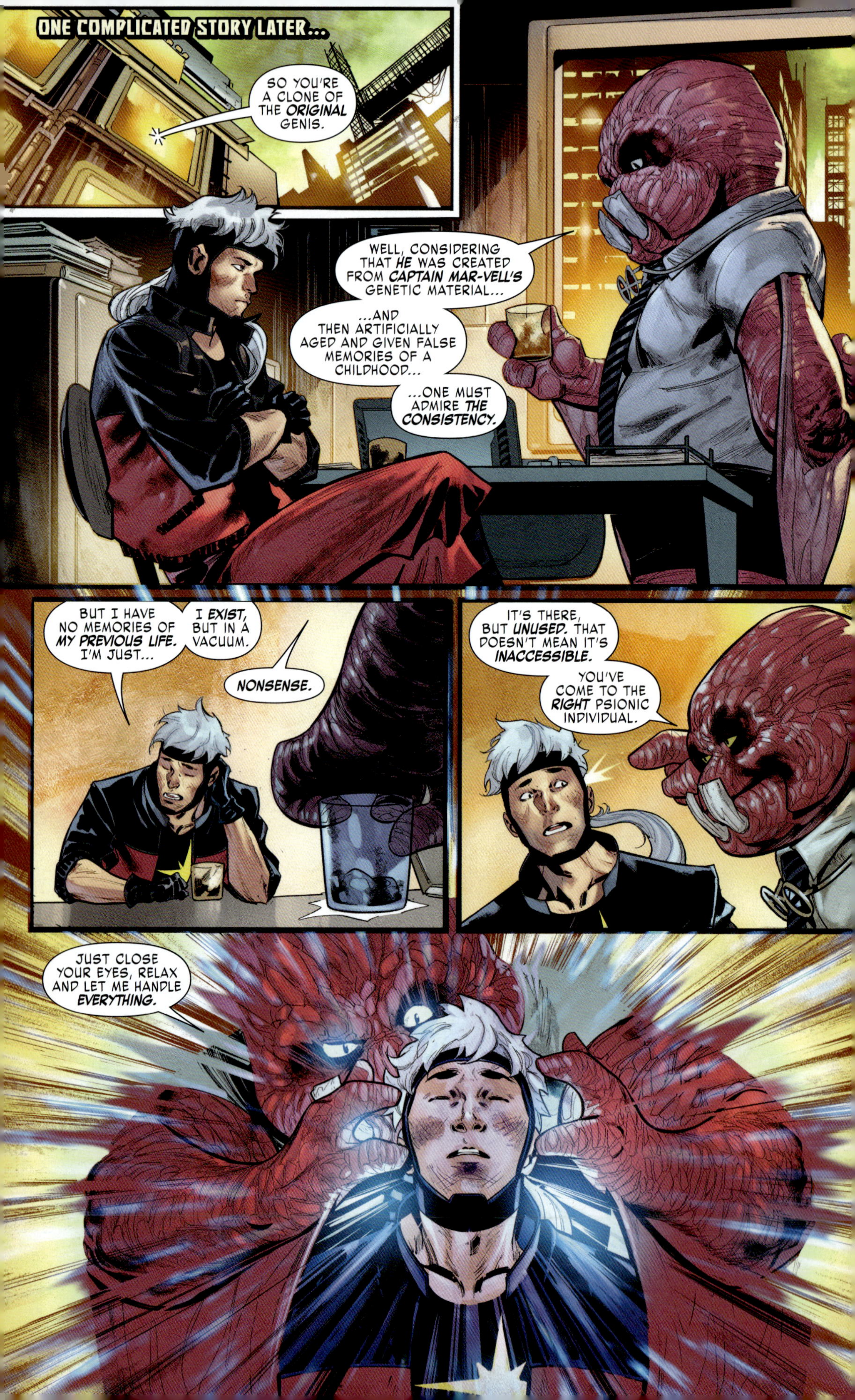
ONE COMPLICATED STORY LATER...
SO YOU'RE A CLONE OF THE ORIGINAL GENIS.
WELL, CONSIDERING THAT HE WAS CREATED FROM CAPTAIN MAR-VELL'S GENETIC MATERIAL...
...AND THEN ARTIFICIALLY AGED AND GIVEN FALSE MEMORIES OF A CHILDHOOD...
...ONE MUST ADMIRE THE CONSISTENCY.
BUT I HAVE NO MEMORIES OF MY PREVIOUS LIFE. I'M JUST...
I EXIST, BUT IN A VACUUM.
NONSENSE.
IT'S THERE, BUT UNUSED. THAT DOESN'T MEAN IT'S INACCESSIBLE.
YOU'VE COME TO THE RIGHT PSIONIC INDIVIDUAL.
JUST CLOSE YOUR EYES, RELAX AND LET ME HANDLE EVERYTHING.

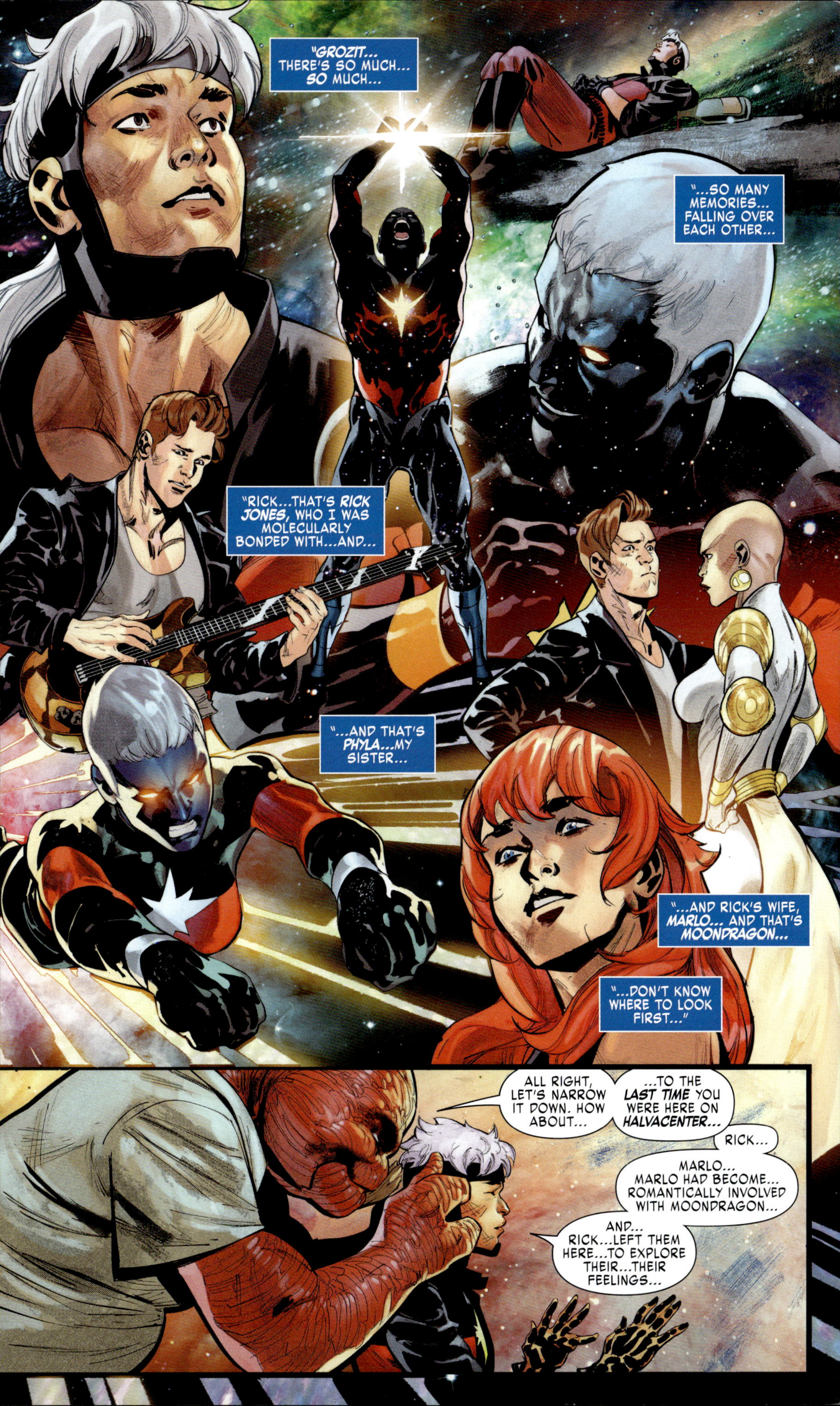
"GROZIT... THERE'S SO MUCH... SO MUCH...
"...SO MANY MEMORIES... FALLING OVER EACH OTHER...
"RICK...THAT'S RICK JONES, WHO I WAS MOLECULARLY BONDED WITH...AND...
"...AND THAT'S PHYLA...MY SISTER...
"...AND RICK'S WIFE, MARLO... AND THAT'S MOONDRAGON...
"...DON'T KNOW WHERE TO LOOK FIRST..."
ALL RIGHT, LET'S NARROW IT DOWN. HOW ABOUT...
...TO THE LAST TIME YOU WERE HERE ON HALVACENTER...
RICK...
MARLO... MARLO HAD BECOME... ROMANTICALLY INVOLVED WITH MOONDRAGON...
AND... RICK...LEFT THEM HERE...TO EXPLORE THEIR...THEIR FEELINGS...

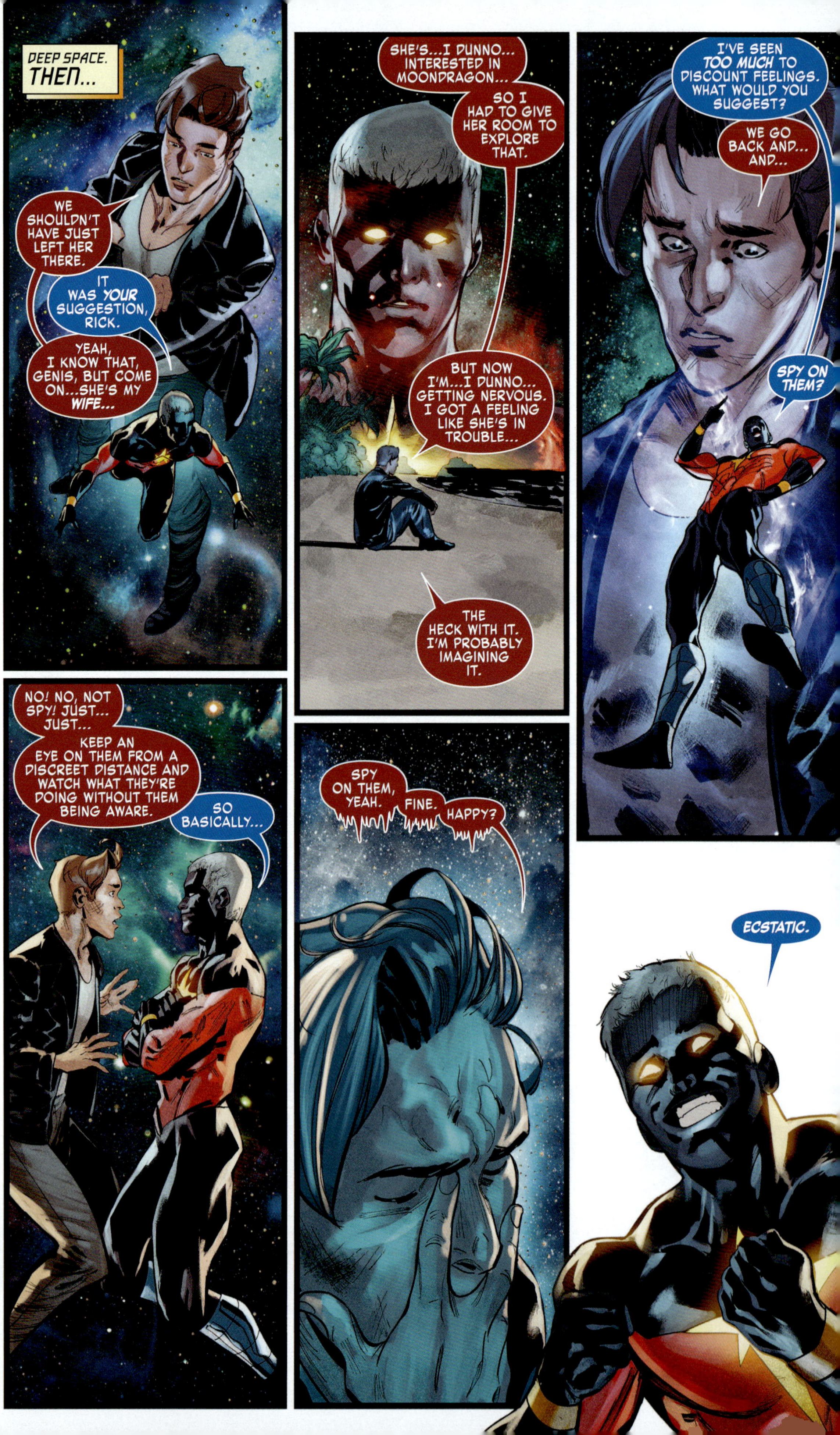
DEEP SPACE. THEN...
WE SHOULDN'T HAVE JUST LEFT HER THERE.
IT WAS YOUR SUGGESTION, RICK.
YEAH, I KNOW THAT, GENIS, BUT COME ON...SHE'S MY WIFE...
SHE'S...I DUNNO... INTERESTED IN MOONDRAGON...
SO I HAD TO GIVE HER ROOM TO EXPLORE THAT.
BUT NOW I'M...I DUNNO... GETTING NERVOUS. I GOT A FEELING LIKE SHE'S IN TROUBLE...
THE HECK WITH IT. I'M PROBABLY IMAGINING IT.
I'VE SEEN TOO MUCH TO DISCOUNT FEELINGS. WHAT WOULD YOU SUGGEST?
WE GO BACK AND... AND...
SPY ON THEM?
NO! NO, NOT SPY! JUST... JUST...
KEEP AN EYE ON THEM FROM A DISCREET DISTANCE AND WATCH WHAT THEY'RE DOING WITHOUT THEM BEING AWARE.
SO BASICALLY...
SPY ON THEM, YEAH.
FINE.
HAPPY?
ECSTATIC.

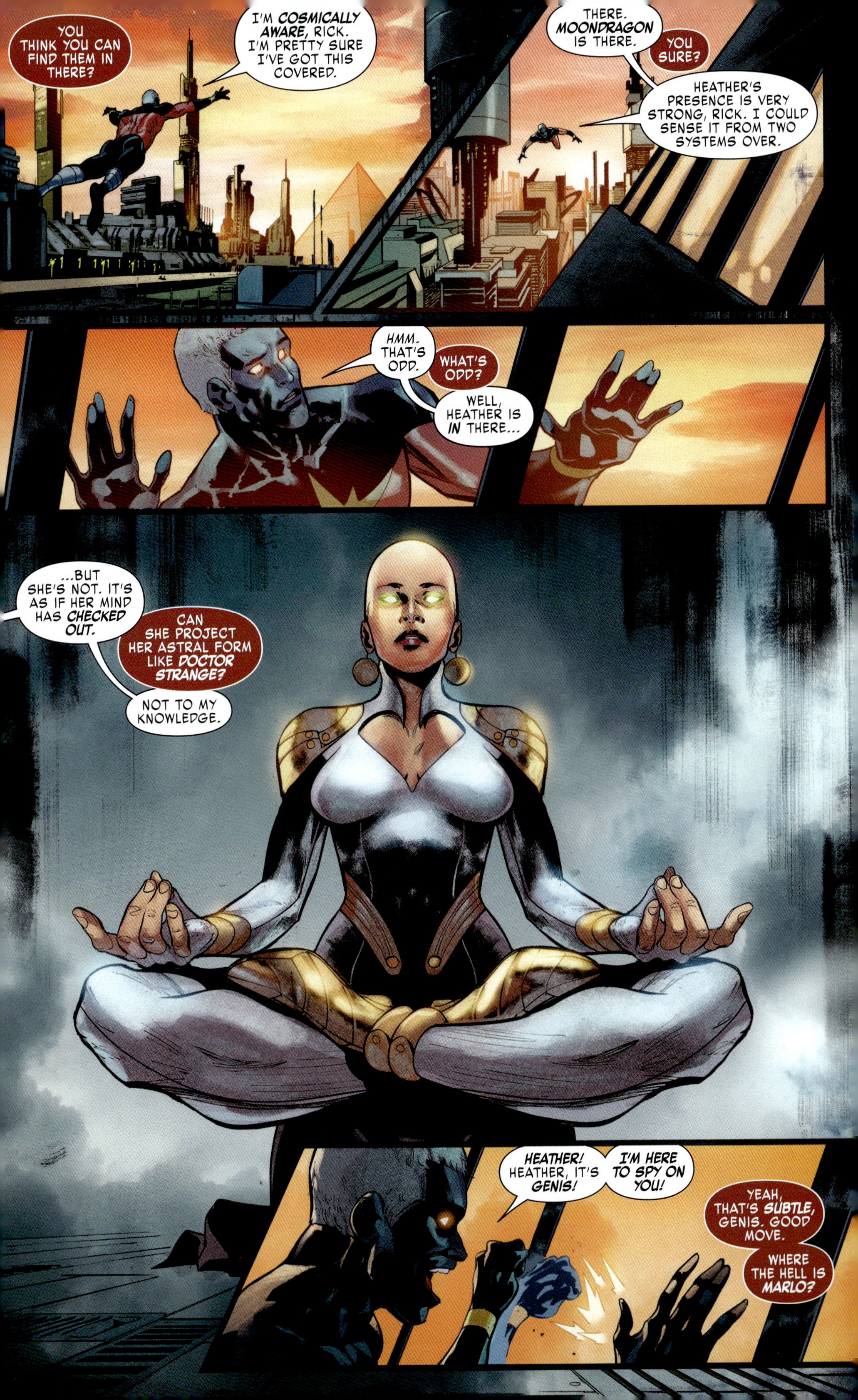
YOU THINK YOU CAN FIND THEM IN THERE?
I'M COSMICALLY AWARE, RICK. I'M PRETTY SURE I'VE GOT THIS COVERED.
THERE. MOONDRAGON IS THERE.
YOU SURE?
HEATHER'S PRESENCE IS VERY STRONG, RICK. I COULD SENSE IT FROM TWO SYSTEMS OVER.
HMM. THAT'S ODD.
WHAT'S ODD?
WELL, HEATHER IS IN THERE...
...BUT SHE'S NOT. IT'S AS IF HER MIND HAS CHECKED OUT.
CAN SHE PROJECT HER ASTRAL FORM LIKE DOCTOR STRANGE?
NOT TO MY KNOWLEDGE.
HEATHER! HEATHER, IT'S GENIS!
I'M HERE TO SPY ON YOU!
YEAH, THAT'S SUBTLE, GENIS. GOOD MOVE.
WHERE THE HELL IS MARLO?

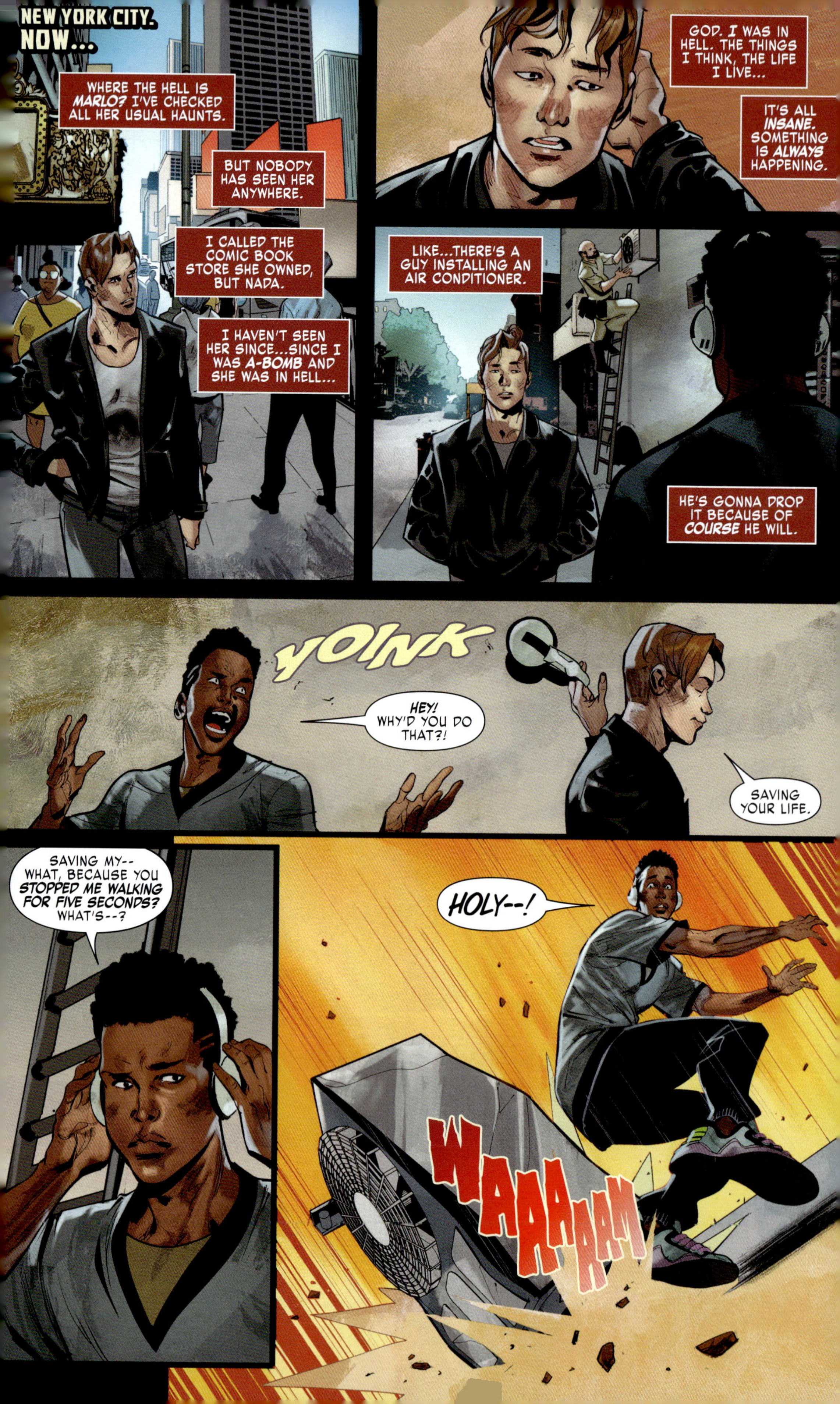

NEW YORK CITY. NOW...
WHERE THE HELL IS MARLO? I'VE CHECKED ALL HER USUAL HAUNTS.
BUT NOBODY HAS SEEN HER ANYWHERE.
I CALLED THE COMIC BOOK STORE SHE OWNED, BUT NADA.
I HAVEN'T SEEN HER SINCE...SINCE I WAS A-BOMB AND SHE WAS IN HELL...
GOD. I WAS IN HELL. THE THINGS I THINK, THE LIFE I LIVE...
IT'S ALL INSANE. SOMETHING IS ALWAYS HAPPENING.
LIKE...THERE'S A GUY INSTALLING AN AIR CONDITIONER.
HE'S GONNA DROP IT BECAUSE OF COURSE HE WILL.
YOINK
HEY! WHY'D YOU DO THAT?!
SAVING YOUR LIFE.
SAVING MY-- WHAT, BECAUSE YOU STOPPED ME WALKING FOR FIVE SECONDS? WHAT'S--?
HOLY--!
WAAAAAM

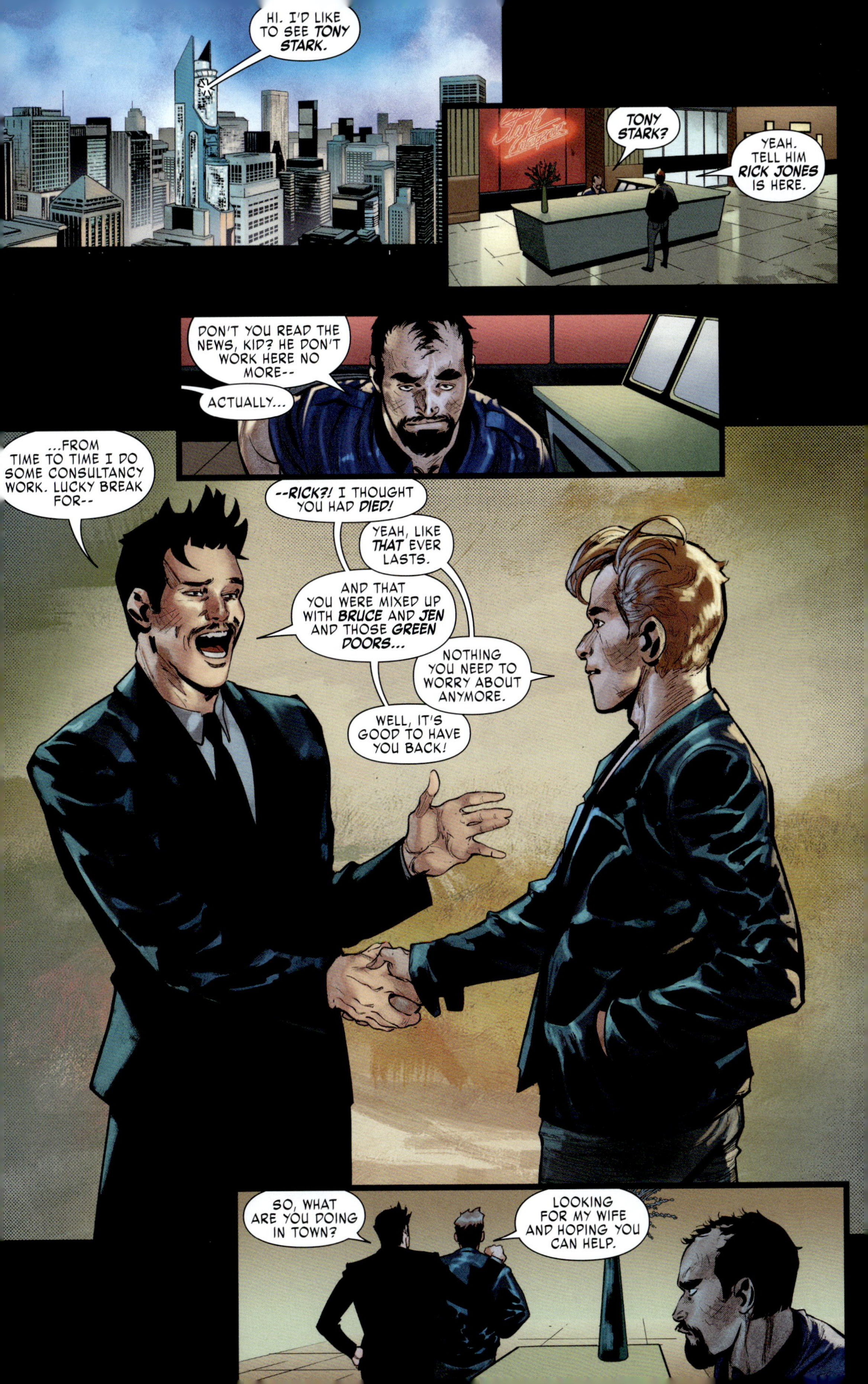
HI. I'D LIKE TO SEE TONY STARK.
TONY STARK?
YEAH. TELL HIM RICK JONES IS HERE.
DON'T YOU READ THE NEWS, KID? HE DON'T WORK HERE NO MORE--
ACTUALLY...
...FROM TIME TO TIME I DO SOME CONSULTANCY WORK. LUCKY BREAK FOR--
--RICK?! I THOUGHT YOU HAD DIED!
YEAH, LIKE THAT EVER LASTS.
AND THAT YOU WERE MIXED UP WITH BRUCE AND JEN AND THOSE GREEN DOORS...
NOTHING YOU NEED TO WORRY ABOUT ANYMORE.
WELL, IT'S GOOD TO HAVE YOU BACK!
SO, WHAT ARE YOU DOING IN TOWN?
LOOKING FOR MY WIFE AND HOPING YOU CAN HELP.

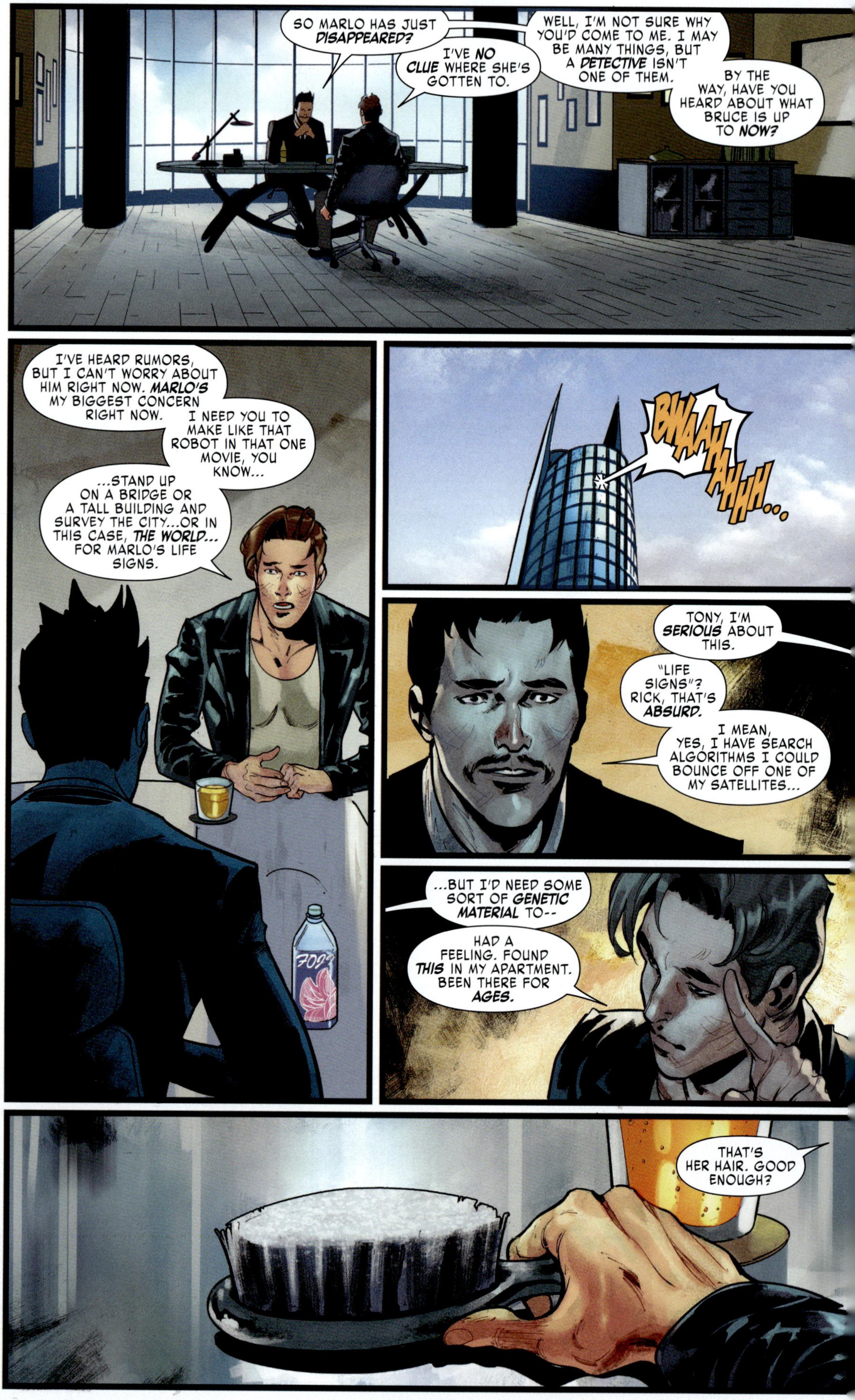
SO MARLO HAS JUST DISAPPEARED?
I'VE NO CLUE WHERE SHE'S GOTTEN TO.
WELL, I'M NOT SURE WHY YOU'D COME TO ME. I MAY BE MANY THINGS, BUT A DETECTIVE ISN'T ONE OF THEM.
BY THE WAY, HAVE YOU HEARD ABOUT WHAT BRUCE IS UP TO NOW?
I'VE HEARD RUMORS, BUT I CAN'T WORRY ABOUT HIM RIGHT NOW. MARLO'S MY BIGGEST CONCERN RIGHT NOW.
I NEED YOU TO MAKE LIKE THAT ROBOT IN THAT ONE MOVIE, YOU KNOW...
...STAND UP ON A BRIDGE OR A TALL BUILDING AND SURVEY THE CITY...OR IN THIS CASE, THE WORLD... FOR MARLO'S LIFE SIGNS.
BWAAHAHHH...
TONY, I'M SERIOUS ABOUT THIS.
"LIFE SIGNS"? RICK, THAT'S ABSURD.
I MEAN, YES, I HAVE SEARCH ALGORITHMS I COULD BOUNCE OFF ONE OF MY SATELLITES...
...BUT I'D NEED SOME SORT OF GENETIC MATERIAL TO--
HAD A FEELING. FOUND THIS IN MY APARTMENT. BEEN THERE FOR AGES.
THAT'S HER HAIR. GOOD ENOUGH?

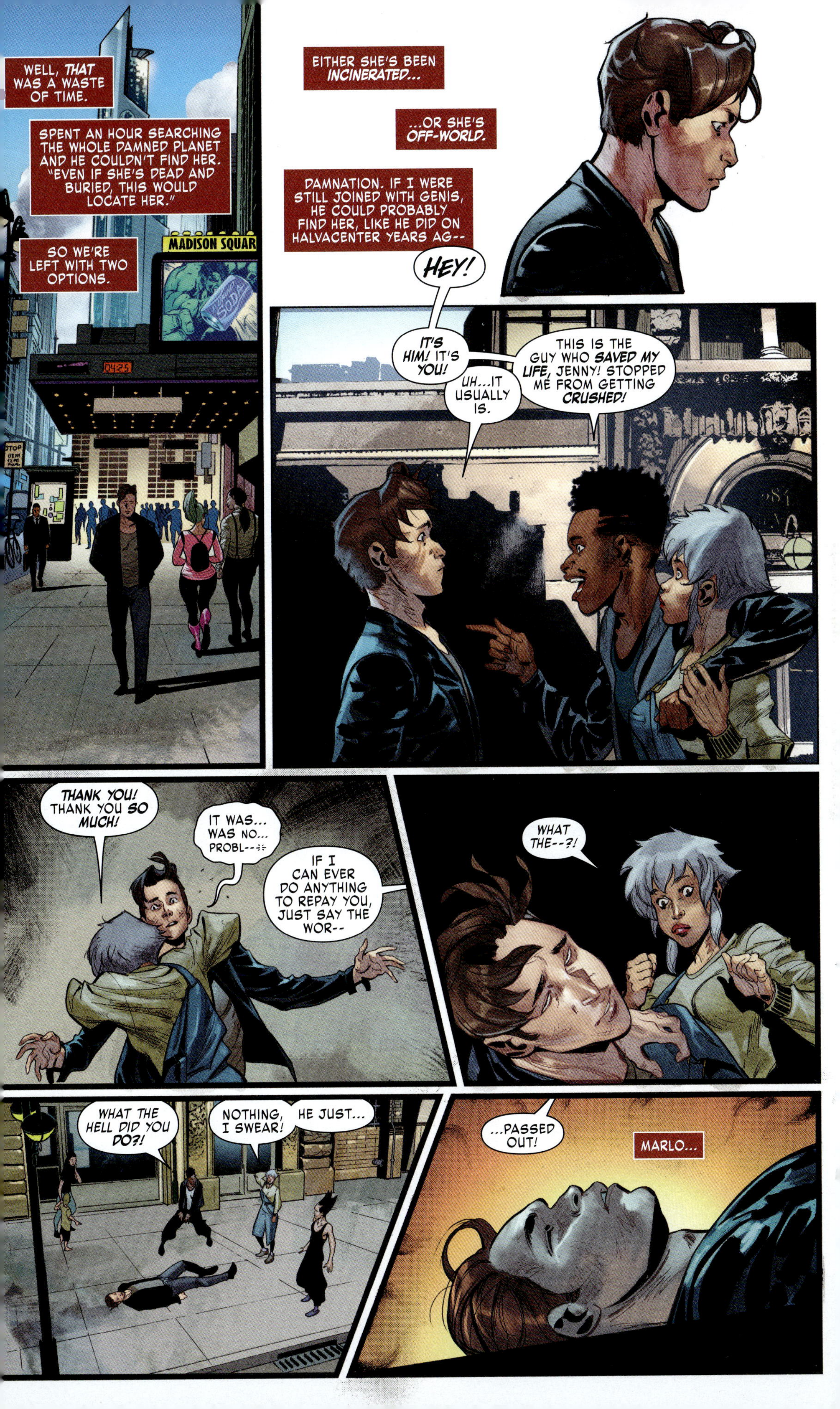

WELL, THAT WAS A WASTE OF TIME.
SPENT AN HOUR SEARCHING THE WHOLE DAMNED PLANET AND HE COULDN'T FIND HER. "EVEN IF SHE'S DEAD AND BURIED, THIS WOULD LOCATE HER."
SO WE'RE LEFT WITH TWO OPTIONS.
MADISON SQUAR
SODA
EITHER SHE'S BEEN INCINERATED...
...OR SHE'S OFF-WORLD.
DAMNATION. IF I WERE STILL JOINED WITH GENIS, HE COULD PROBABLY FIND HER, LIKE HE DID ON HALVACENTER YEARS AG--
HEY!
IT'S HIM! IT'S YOU!
THIS IS THE GUY WHO SAVED MY LIFE, JENNY! STOPPED ME FROM GETTING CRUSHED!
UH...IT USUALLY IS.
THANK YOU! THANK YOU SO MUCH!
IT WAS... WAS NO... PROBL--
IF I CAN EVER DO ANYTHING TO REPAY YOU, JUST SAY THE WOR--
WHAT THE--?!
WHAT THE HELL DID YOU DO?!
NOTHING, I SWEAR!
HE JUST...
...PASSED OUT!
MARLO...

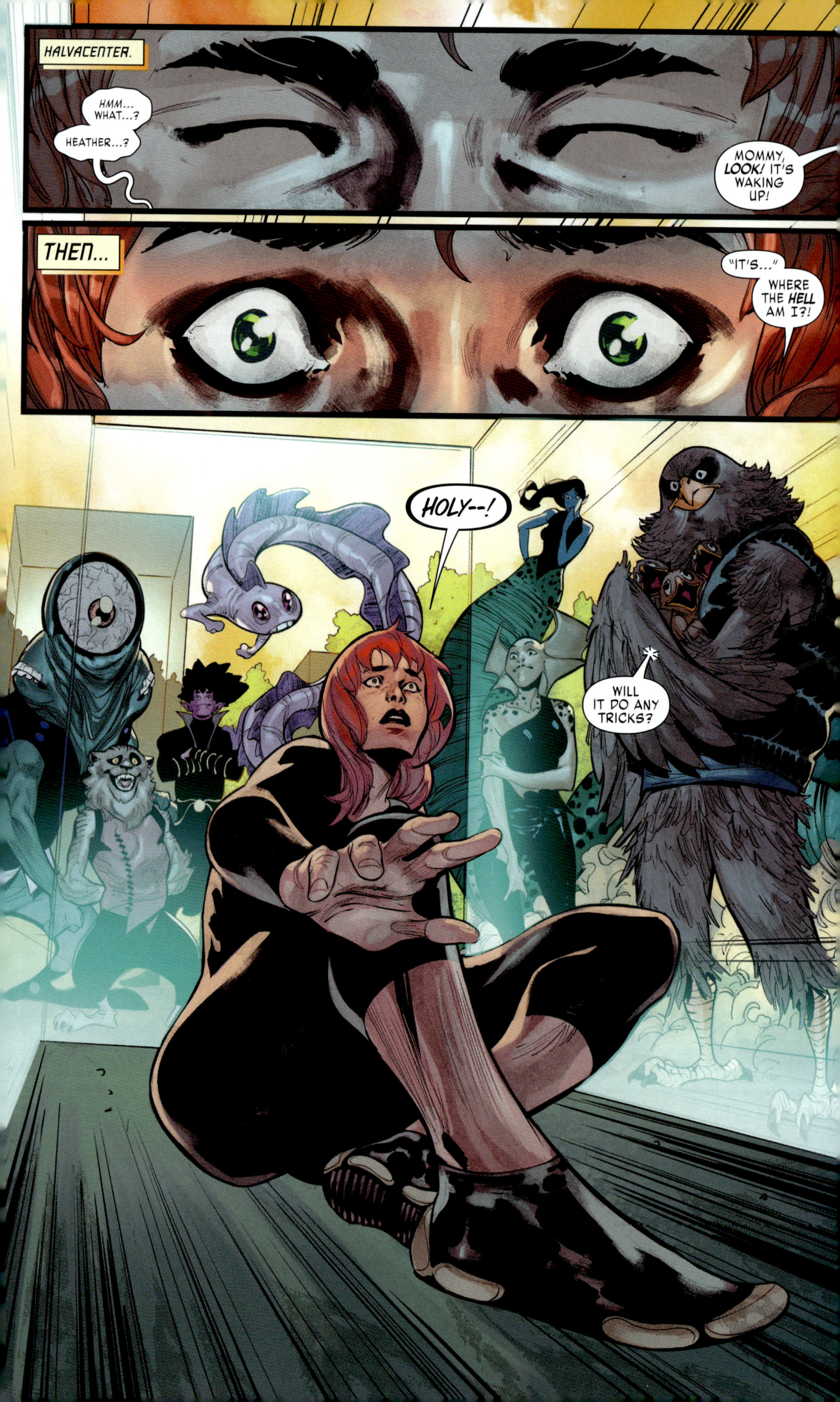
HALVACENTER.
HMM... WHAT...?
HEATHER...?
MOMMY, LOOK! IT'S WAKING UP!
THEN...
"IT'S..."
WHERE THE HELL AM I?!
HOLY--!
WILL IT DO ANY TRICKS?

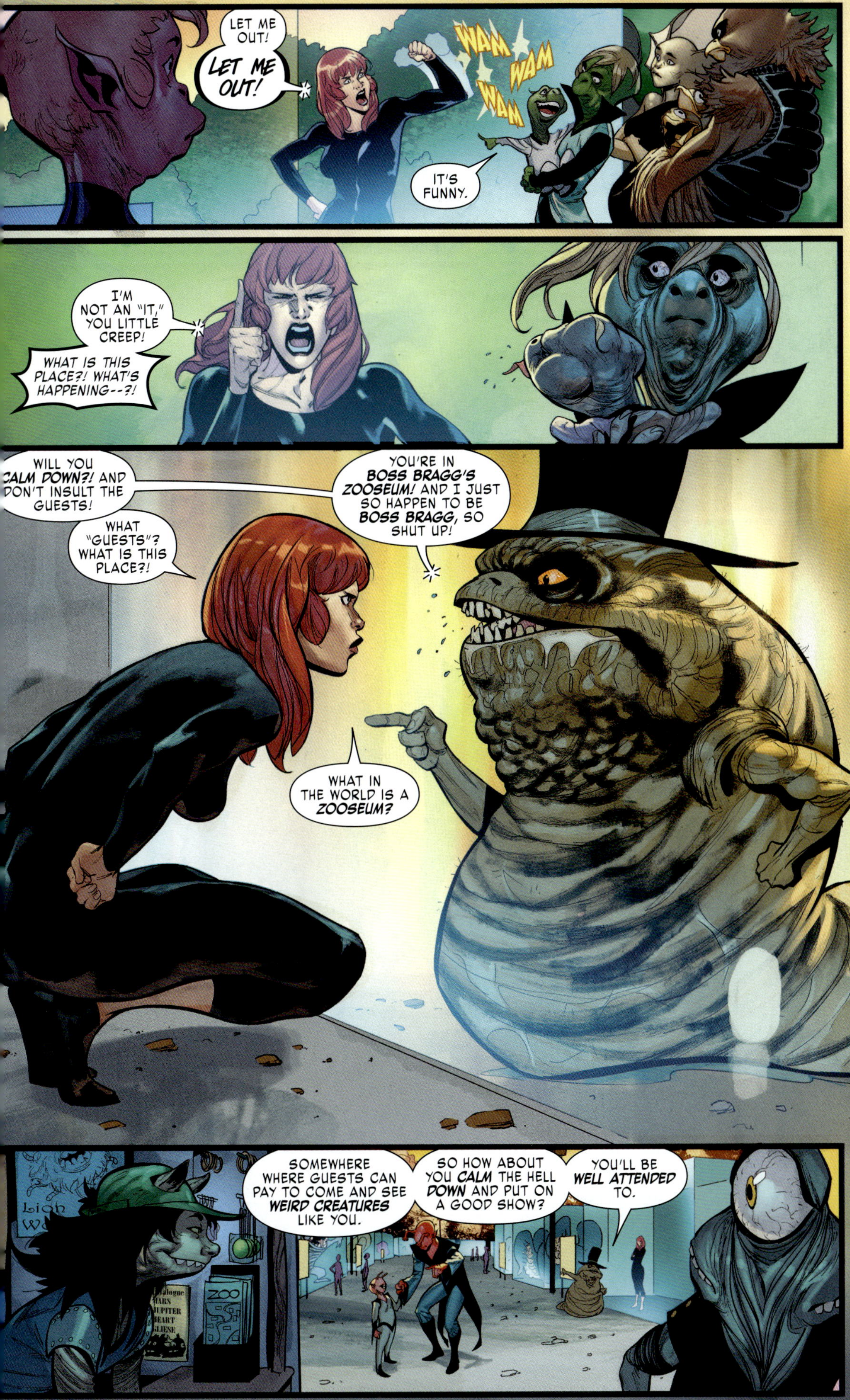
LET ME OUT!
LET ME OUT!
WAM WAM WAM
IT'S FUNNY.
I'M NOT AN "IT," YOU LITTLE CREEP!
WHAT IS THIS PLACE?! WHAT'S HAPPENING--?!
WILL YOU CALM DOWN?! AND DON'T INSULT THE GUESTS!
YOU'RE IN BOSS BRAGG'S ZOOSEUM! AND I JUST SO HAPPEN TO BE BOSS BRAGG, SO SHUT UP!
WHAT "GUESTS"? WHAT IS THIS PLACE?!
WHAT IN THE WORLD IS A ZOOSEUM?
SOMEWHERE WHERE GUESTS CAN PAY TO COME AND SEE WEIRD CREATURES LIKE YOU.
SO HOW ABOUT YOU CALM THE HELL DOWN AND PUT ON A GOOD SHOW?
YOU'LL BE WELL ATTENDED TO.
ZOO

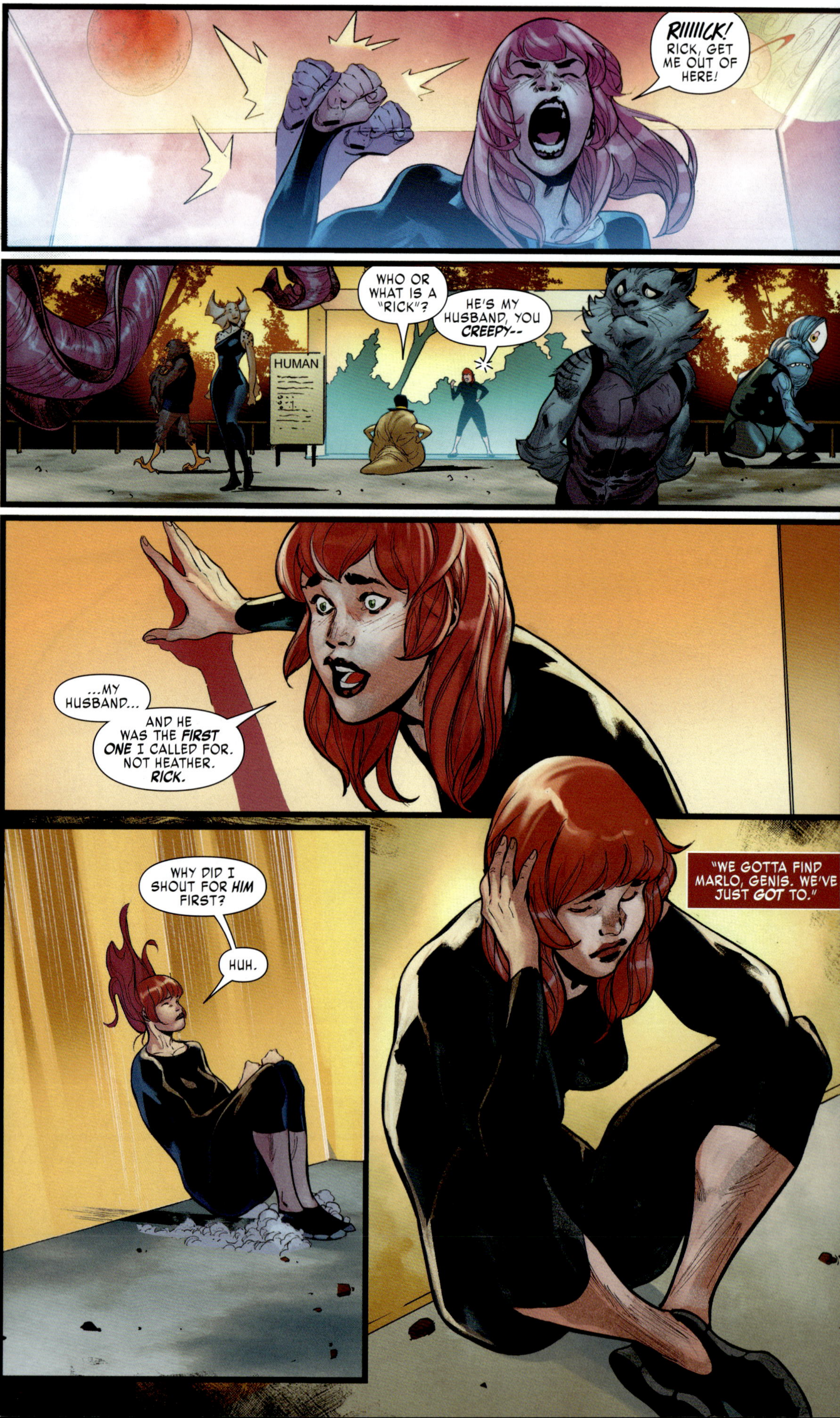
RIIIIICK!
RICK, GET ME OUT OF HERE!
WHO OR WHAT IS A "RICK"?
HE'S MY HUSBAND, YOU CREEPY--
HUMAN
...MY HUSBAND...
AND HE WAS THE FIRST ONE I CALLED FOR. NOT HEATHER. RICK.
WHY DID I SHOUT FOR HIM FIRST?
HUH.
"WE GOTTA FIND MARLO, GENIS. WE'VE JUST GOT TO."

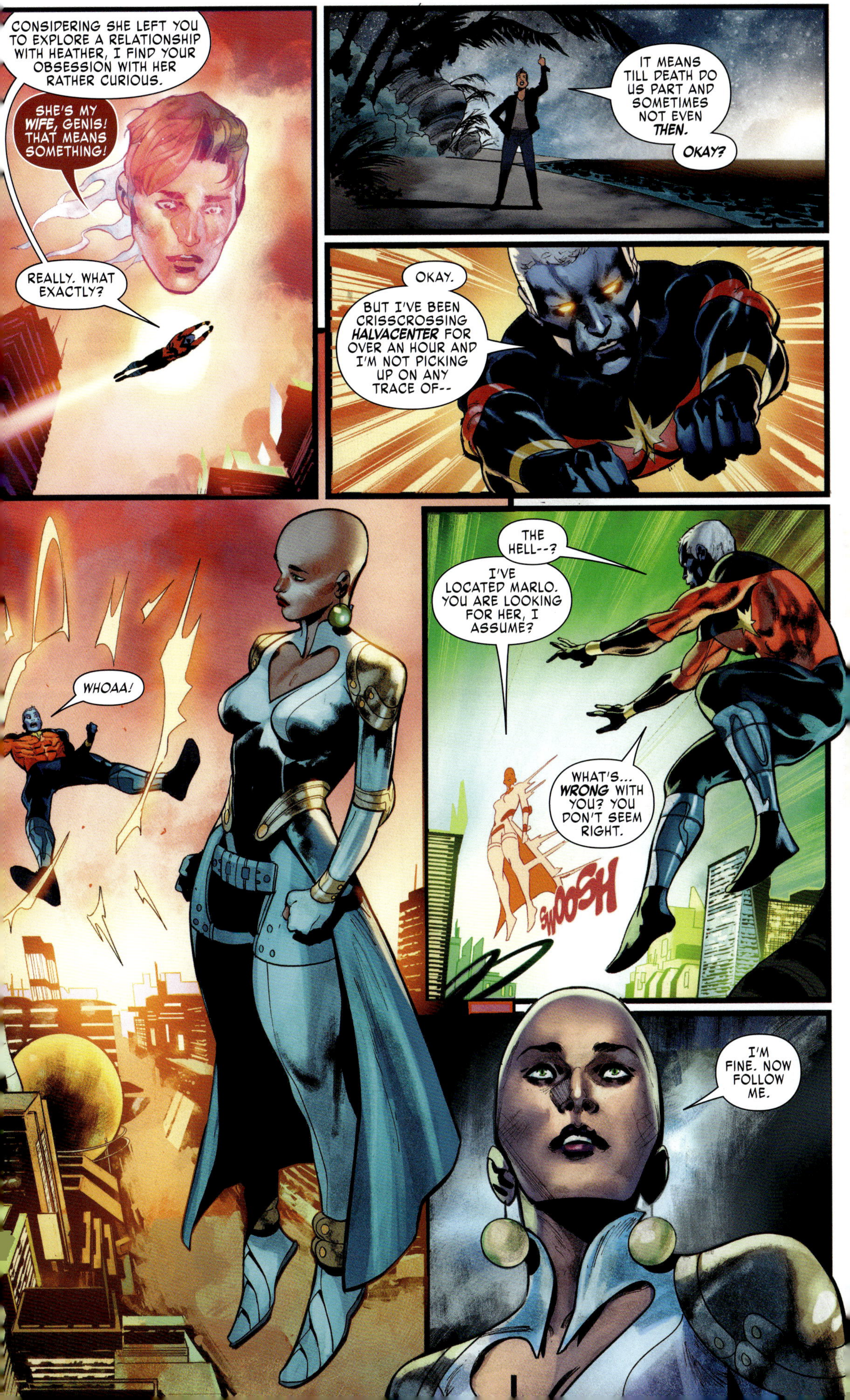
CONSIDERING SHE LEFT YOU TO EXPLORE A RELATIONSHIP WITH HEATHER, I FIND YOUR OBSESSION WITH HER RATHER CURIOUS.
SHE'S MY WIFE, GENIS! THAT MEANS SOMETHING!
REALLY. WHAT EXACTLY?
IT MEANS TILL DEATH DO US PART AND SOMETIMES NOT EVEN THEN.
OKAY?
OKAY.
BUT I'VE BEEN CRISSCROSSING HALVACENTER FOR OVER AN HOUR AND I'M NOT PICKING UP ON ANY TRACE OF--
WHOAA!
THE HELL--?
I'VE LOCATED MARLO. YOU ARE LOOKING FOR HER, I ASSUME?
WHAT'S... WRONG WITH YOU? YOU DON'T SEEM RIGHT.
SWOOSH
I'M FINE. NOW FOLLOW ME.

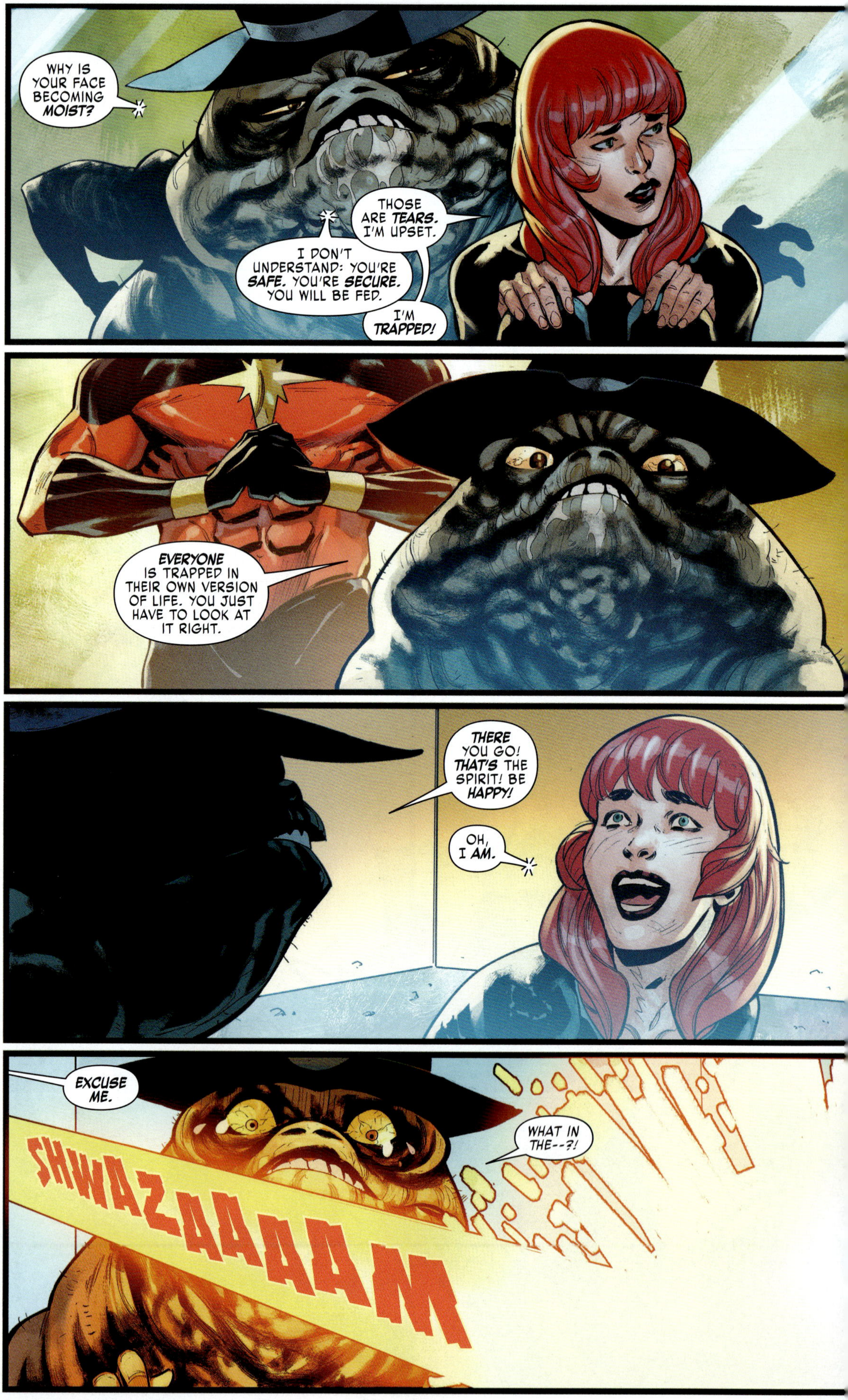

WHY IS YOUR FACE BECOMING MOIST?
THOSE ARE TEARS. I'M UPSET.
I DON'T UNDERSTAND: YOU'RE SAFE. YOU'RE SECURE. YOU WILL BE FED.
I'M TRAPPED!
EVERYONE IS TRAPPED IN THEIR OWN VERSION OF LIFE. YOU JUST HAVE TO LOOK AT IT RIGHT.
THERE YOU GO! THAT'S THE SPIRIT! BE HAPPY!
OH, I AM.
EXCUSE ME.
WHAT IN THE--?!
SHWAZAAAAAM

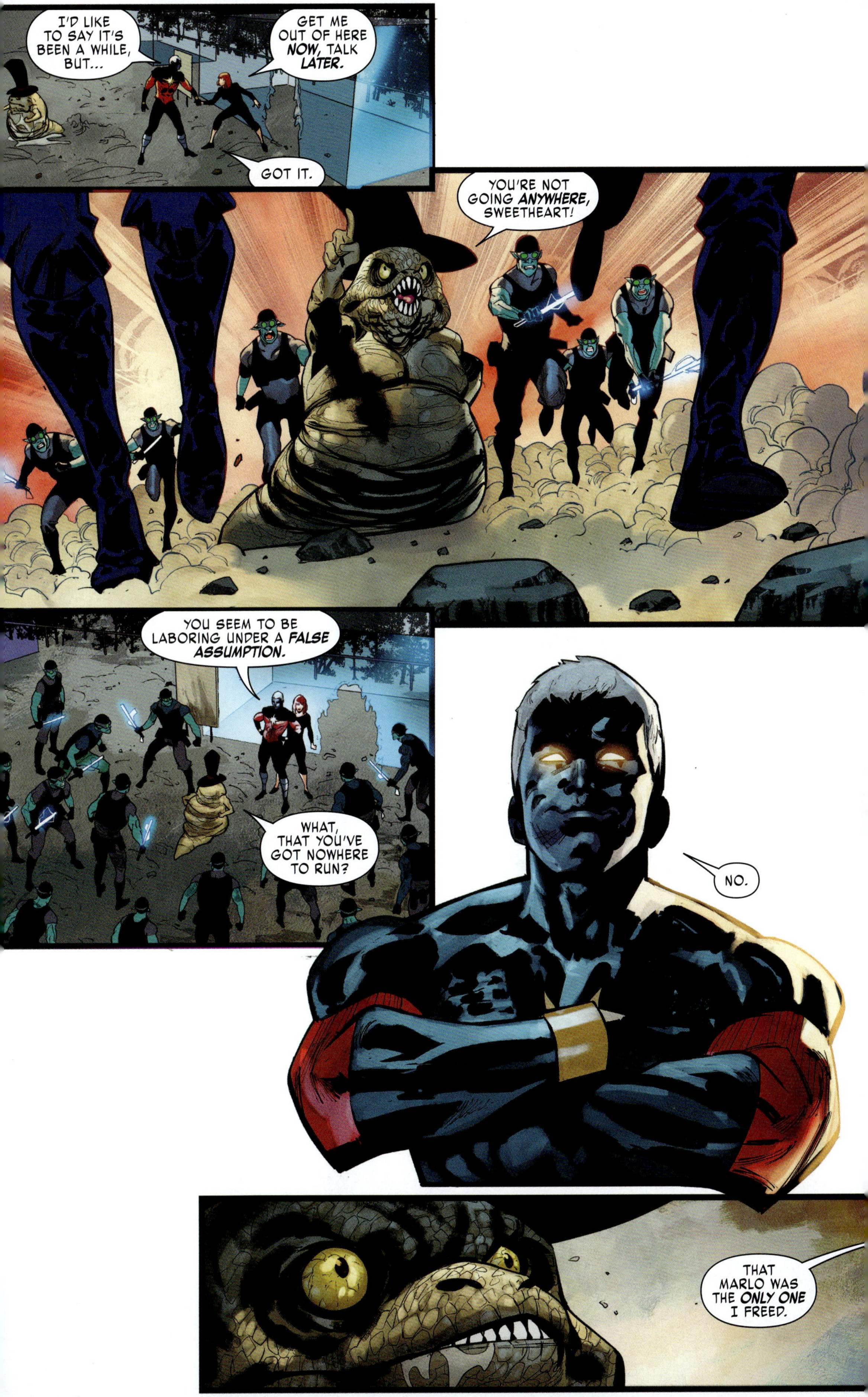
I'D LIKE TO SAY IT'S BEEN A WHILE, BUT...
GET ME OUT OF HERE NOW, TALK LATER.
GOT IT.
YOU'RE NOT GOING ANYWHERE, SWEETHEART!
YOU SEEM TO BE LABORING UNDER A FALSE ASSUMPTION.
WHAT, THAT YOU'VE GOT NOWHERE TO RUN?
NO.
THAT MARLO WAS THE ONLY ONE I FREED.

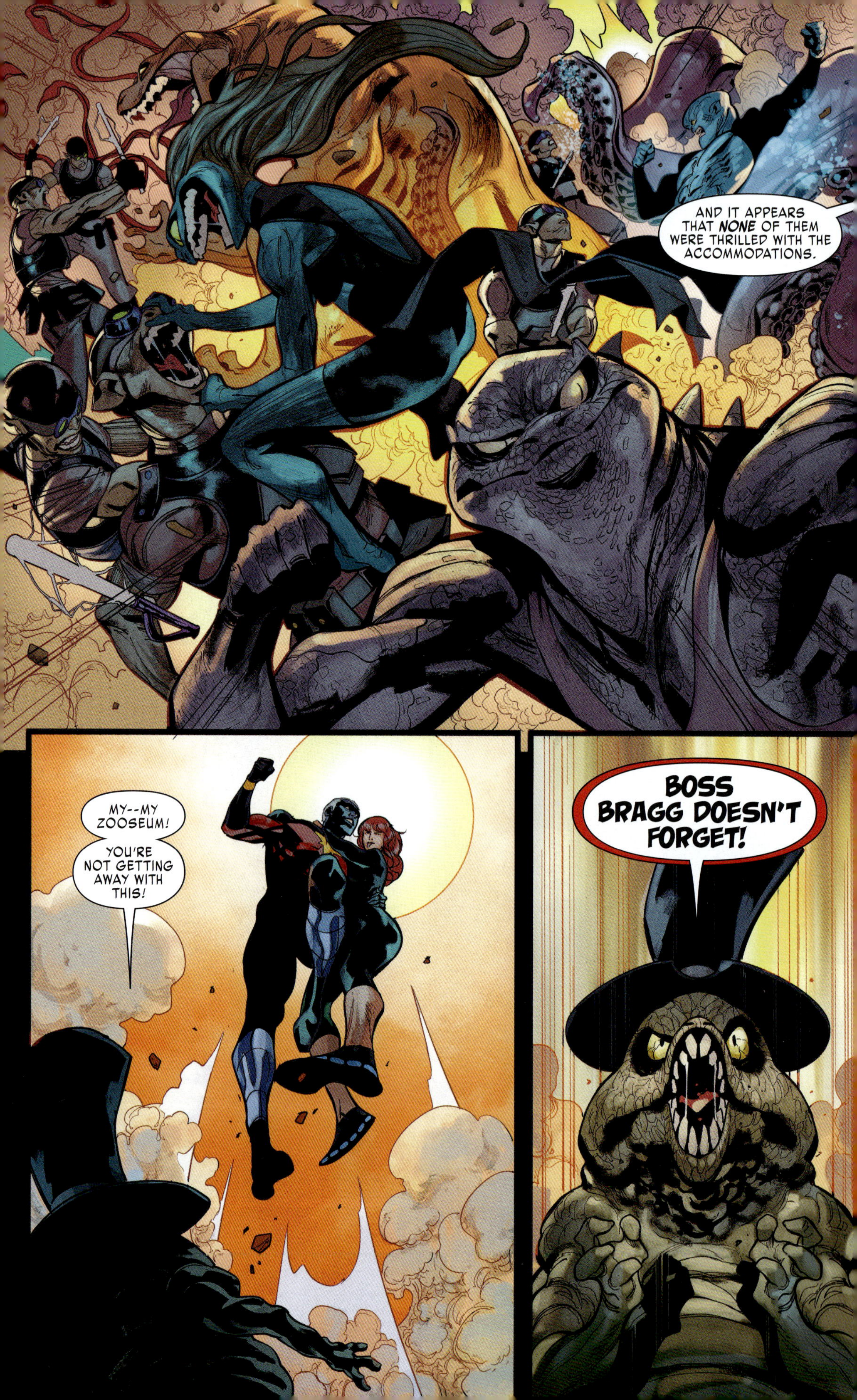
AND IT APPEARS THAT *NONE* OF THEM WERE THRILLED WITH THE ACCOMMODATIONS.
MY--MY ZOOSEUM!
YOU'RE NOT GETTING AWAY WITH THIS!
BOSS BRAGG DOESN'T FORGET!

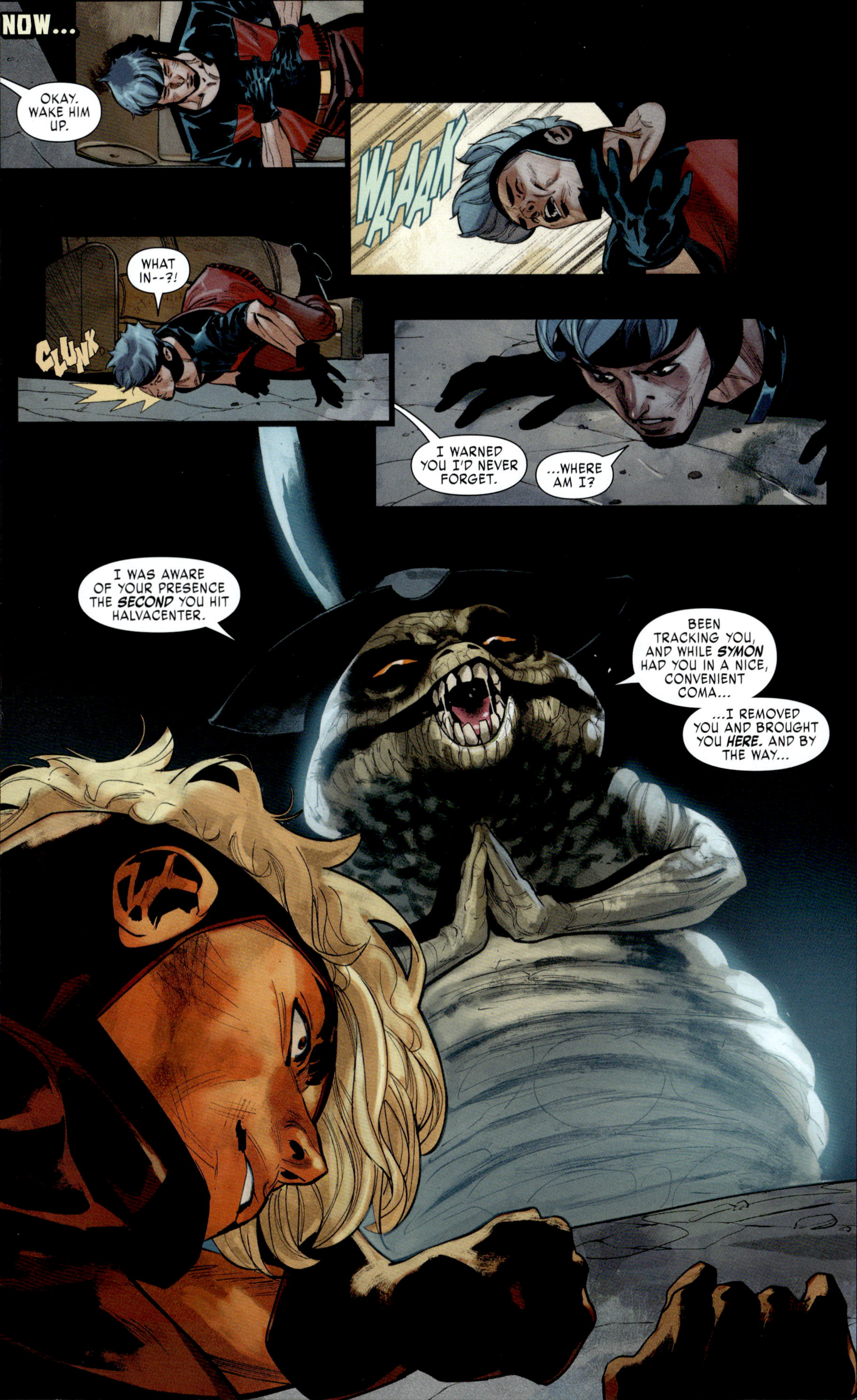
NOW...
OKAY. WAKE HIM UP.
WAAAK
WHAT IN--?!
CLUNK
I WARNED YOU I'D NEVER FORGET.
...WHERE AM I?
I WAS AWARE OF YOUR PRESENCE THE SECOND YOU HIT HALVACENTER.
BEEN TRACKING YOU, AND WHILE SYMON HAD YOU IN A NICE, CONVENIENT COMA...
...I REMOVED YOU AND BROUGHT YOU HERE. AND BY THE WAY...

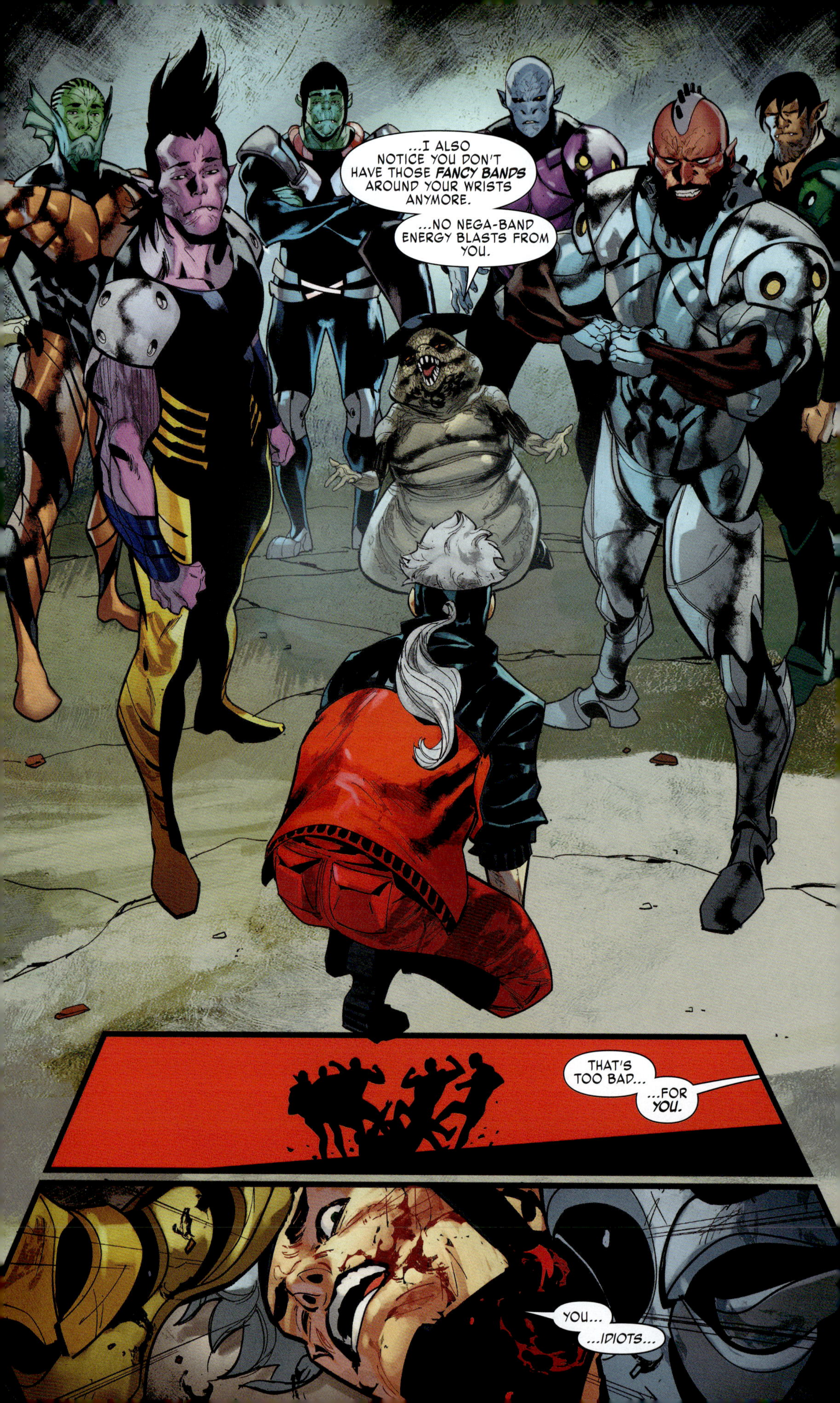
...I ALSO NOTICE YOU DON'T HAVE THOSE FANCY BANDS AROUND YOUR WRISTS ANYMORE.
...NO NEGA-BAND ENERGY BLASTS FROM YOU.
THAT'S TOO BAD...
...FOR YOU.
YOU...
...IDIOTS...

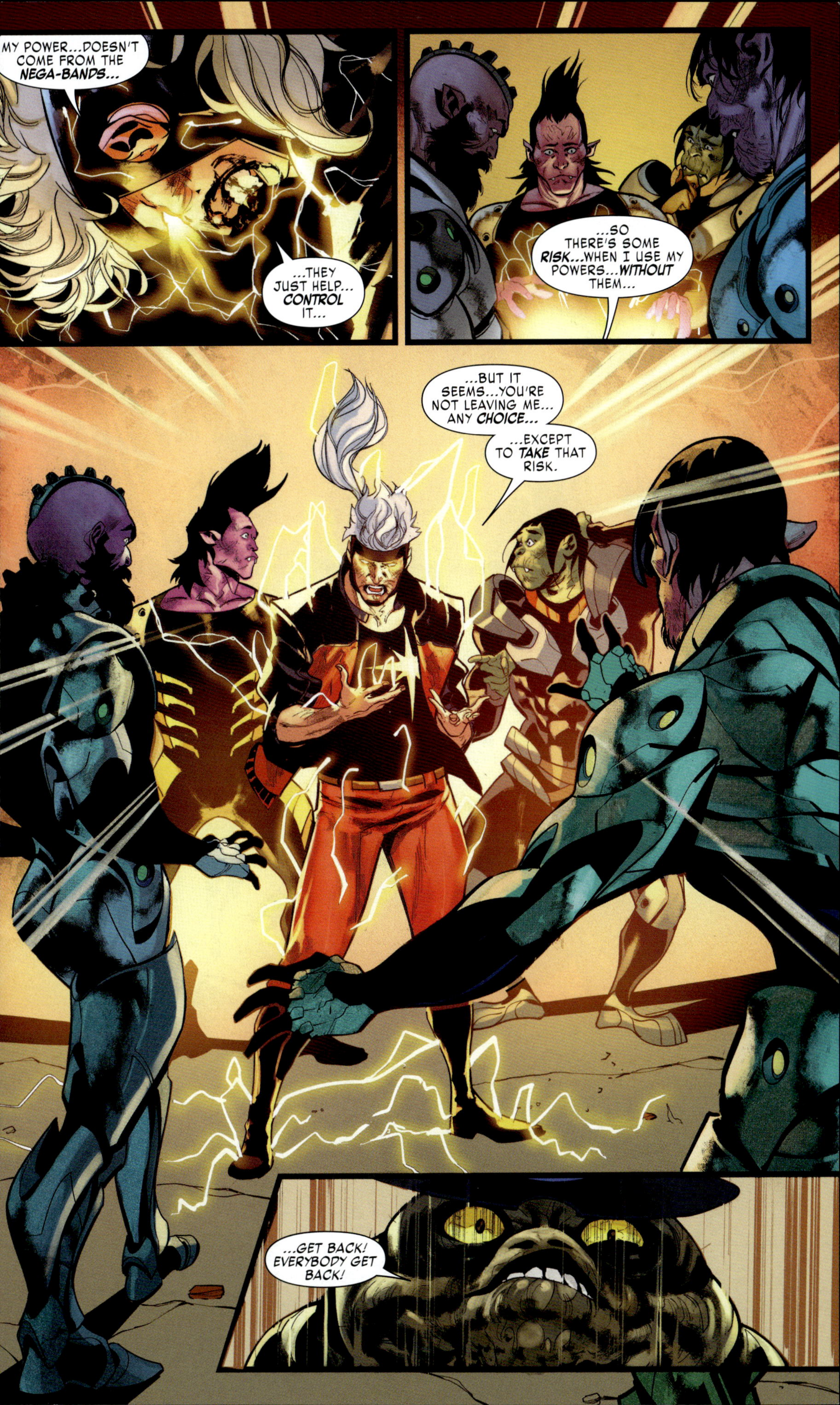
MY POWER...DOESN'T COME FROM THE NEGA-BANDS...
...THEY JUST HELP... CONTROL IT...
...SO THERE'S SOME RISK...WHEN I USE MY POWERS...WITHOUT THEM...
...BUT IT SEEMS...YOU'RE NOT LEAVING ME... ANY CHOICE...
...EXCEPT TO TAKE THAT RISK.
...GET BACK! EVERYBODY GET BACK!

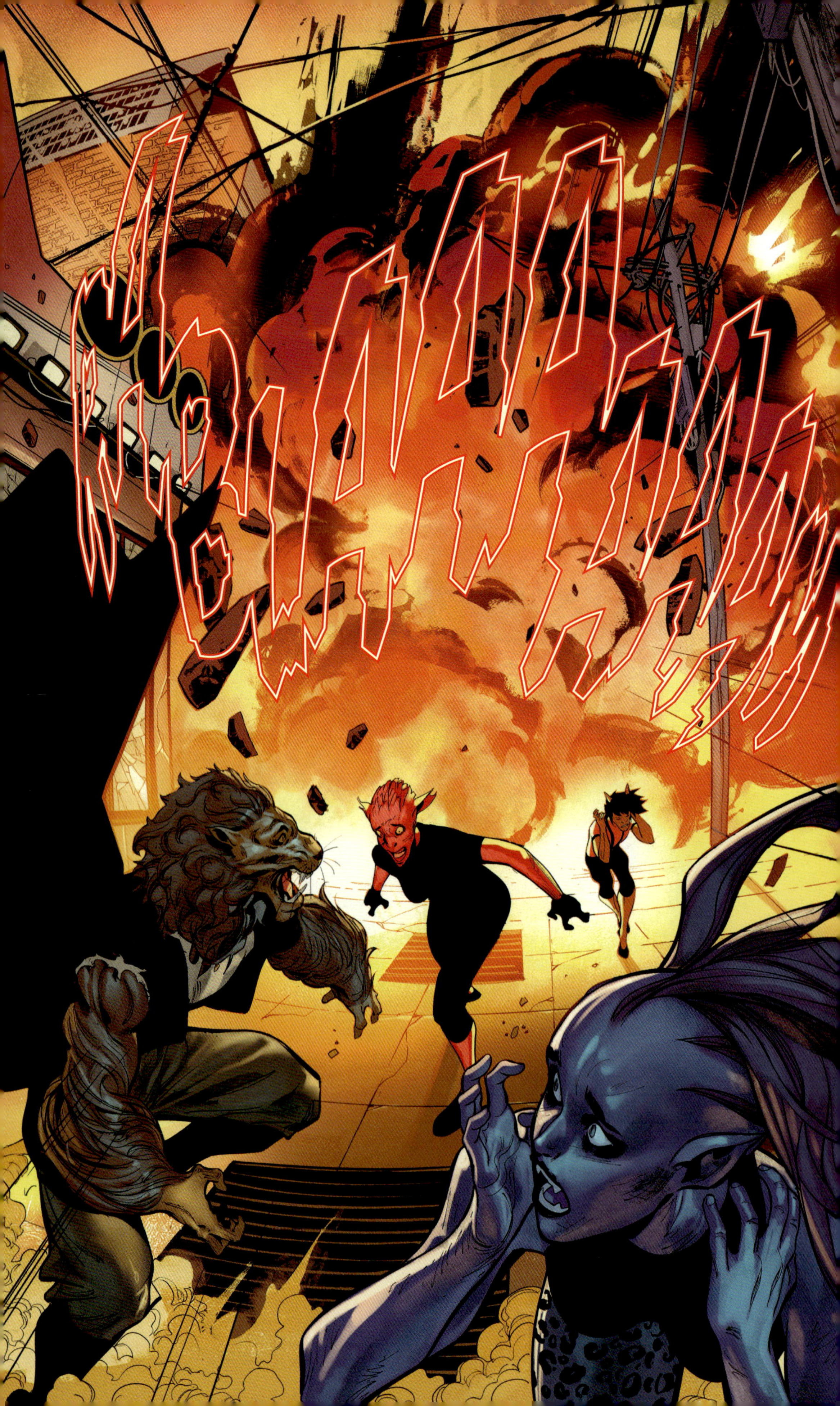

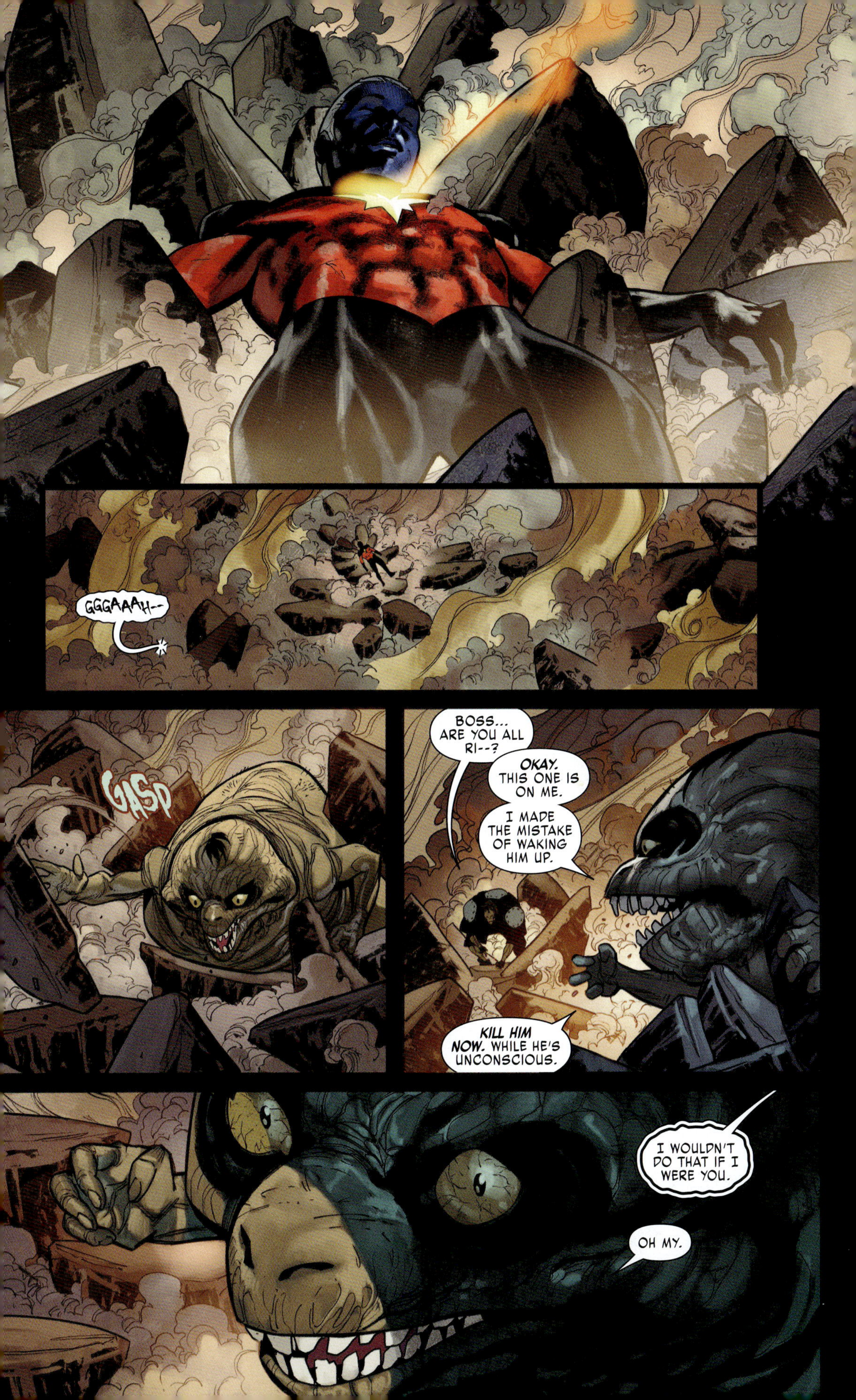
GGGAAAH--
GASP
BOSS... ARE YOU ALL RI--?
OKAY. THIS ONE IS ON ME.
I MADE THE MISTAKE OF WAKING HIM UP.
KILL HIM NOW. WHILE HE'S UNCONSCIOUS.
I WOULDN'T DO THAT IF I WERE YOU.
OH MY.

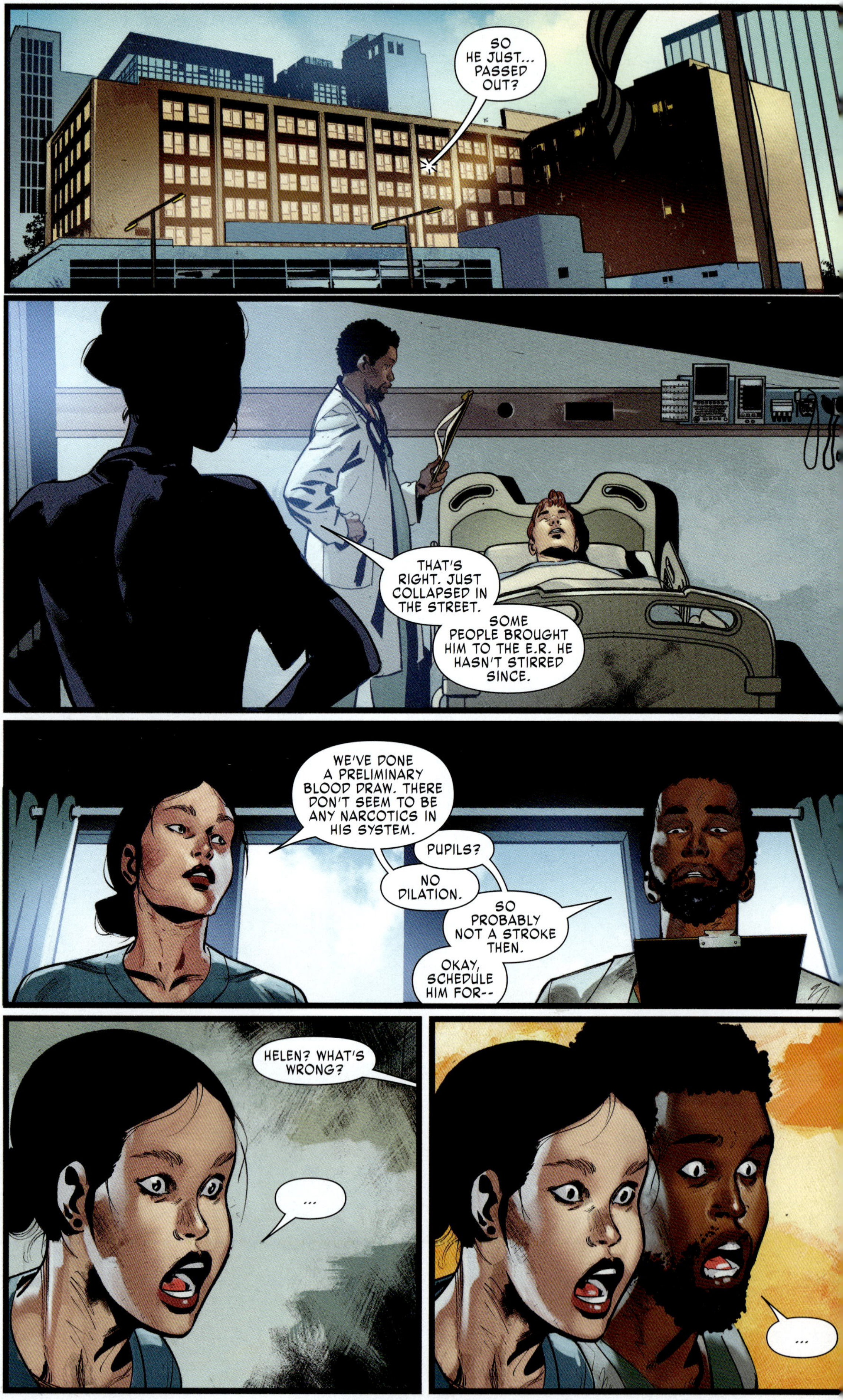

SO HE JUST... PASSED OUT?
THAT'S RIGHT. JUST COLLAPSED IN THE STREET.
SOME PEOPLE BROUGHT HIM TO THE E.R. HE HASN'T STIRRED SINCE.
WE'VE DONE A PRELIMINARY BLOOD DRAW. THERE DON'T SEEM TO BE ANY NARCOTICS IN HIS SYSTEM.
PUPILS?
NO DILATION.
SO PROBABLY NOT A STROKE THEN.
OKAY, SCHEDULE HIM FOR--
HELEN? WHAT'S WRONG?
...
...

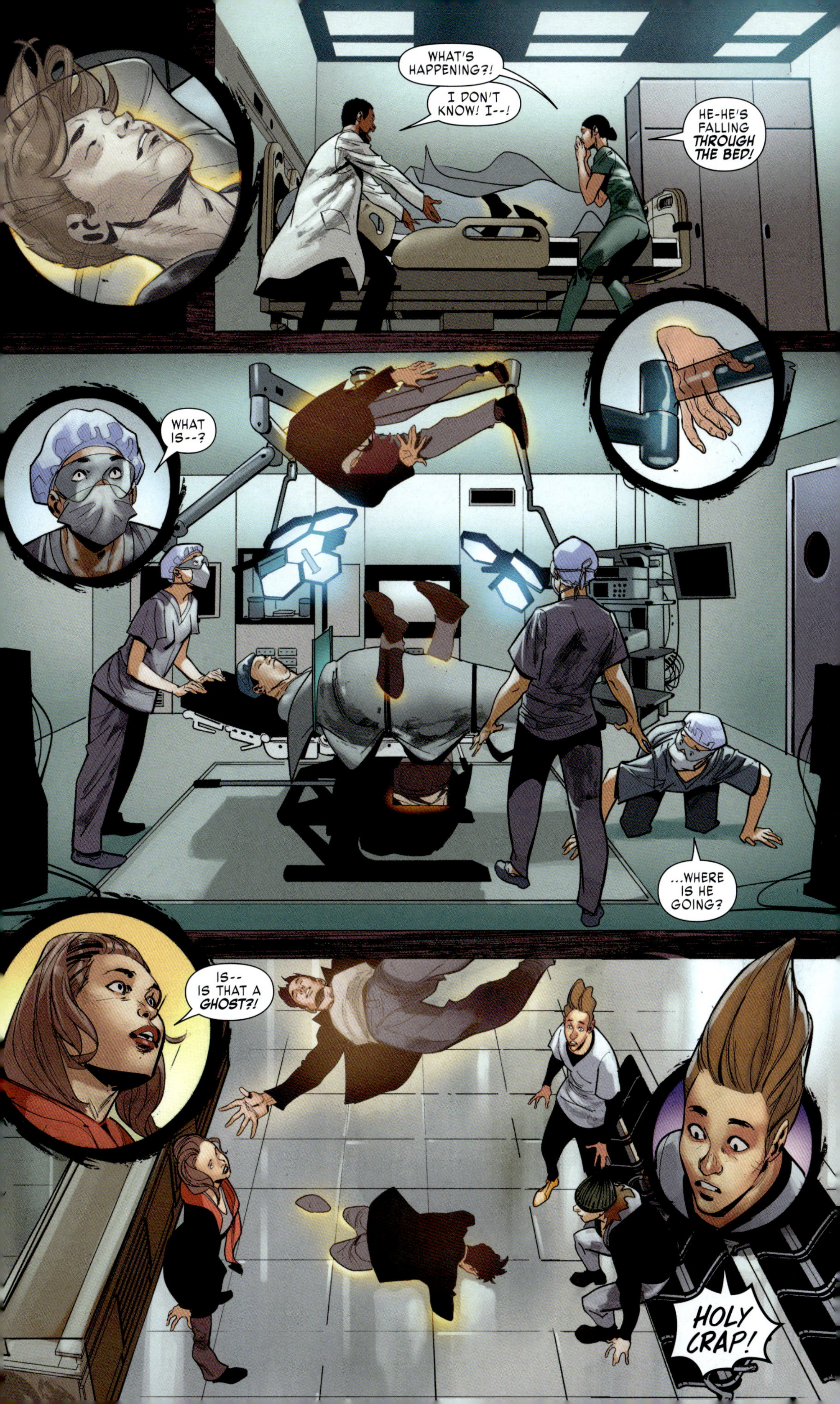
WHAT'S HAPPENING?!
I DON'T KNOW! I--!
HE-HE'S FALLING THROUGH THE BED!
WHAT IS--?
...WHERE IS HE GOING?
IS-- IS THAT A GHOST?!
HOLY CRAP!

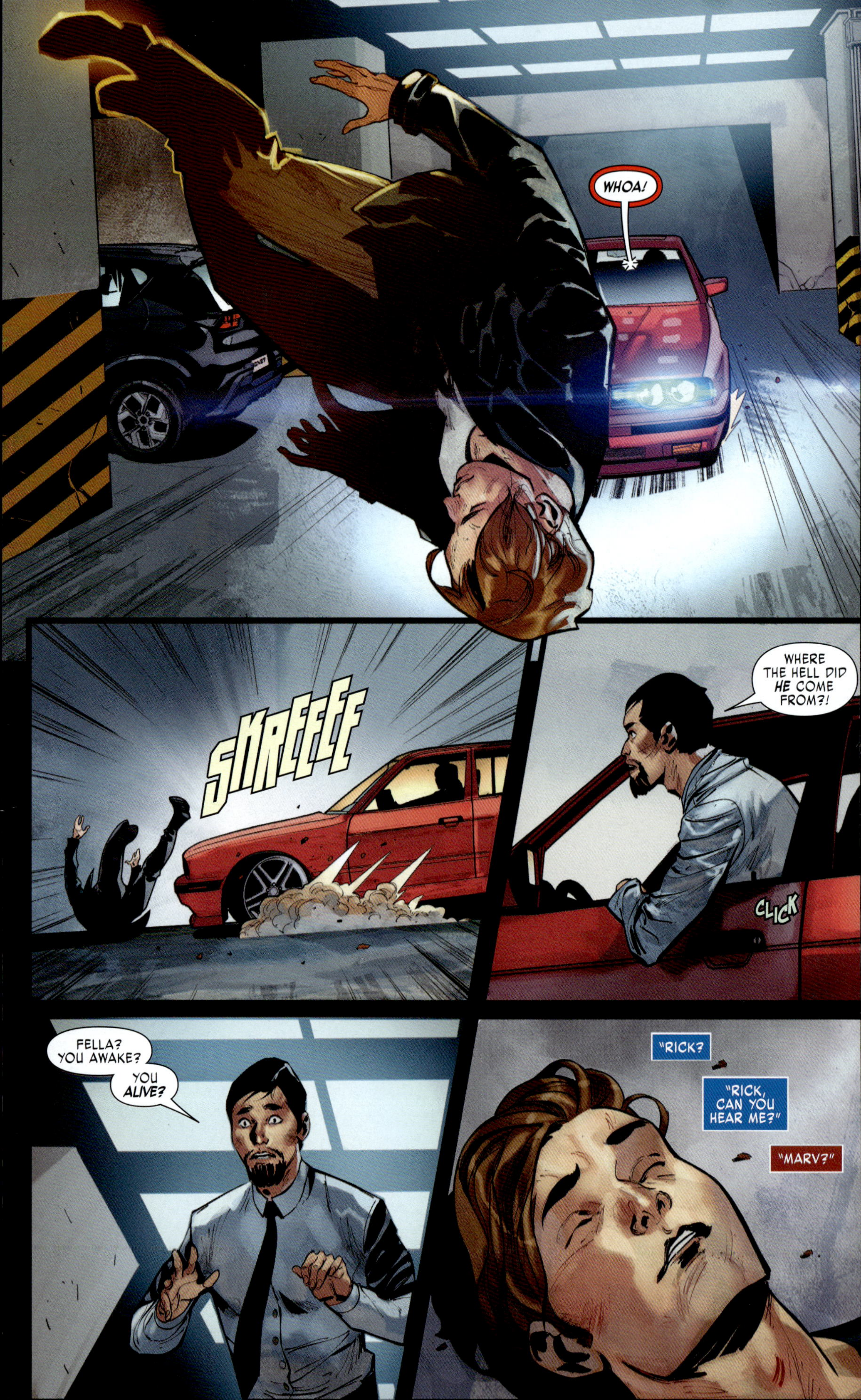
WHOA!
SKREEEE
WHERE THE HELL DID HE COME FROM?!
CLICK
FELLA? YOU AWAKE?
YOU ALIVE?
"RICK?
"RICK, CAN YOU HEAR ME?"
"MARV?"

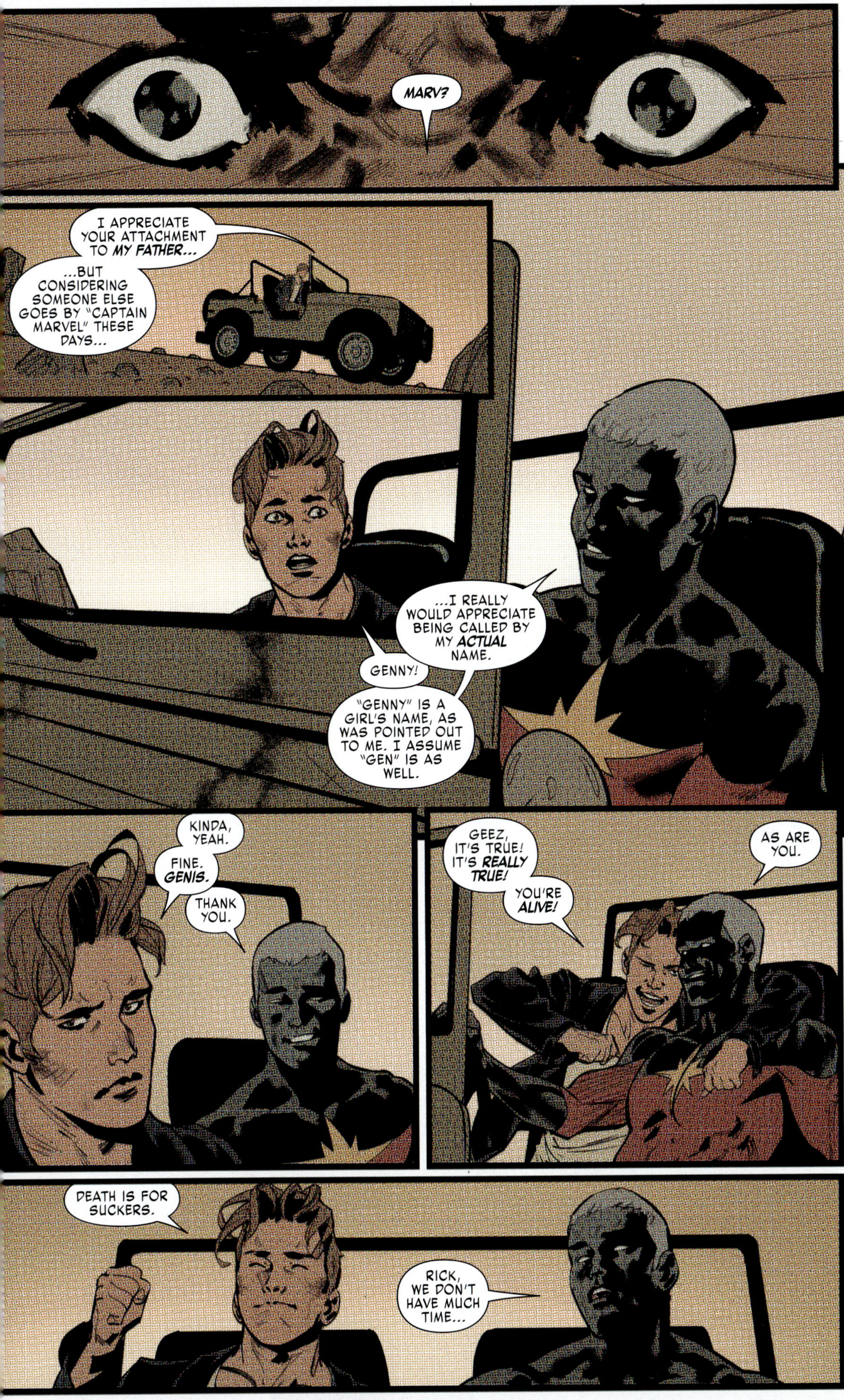

MARV?
I APPRECIATE YOUR ATTACHMENT TO MY FATHER...
...BUT CONSIDERING SOMEONE ELSE GOES BY "CAPTAIN MARVEL" THESE DAYS...
...I REALLY WOULD APPRECIATE BEING CALLED BY MY ACTUAL NAME.
GENNY!
"GENNY" IS A GIRL'S NAME, AS WAS POINTED OUT TO ME. I ASSUME "GEN" IS AS WELL.
KINDA, YEAH.
FINE. GENIS.
THANK YOU.
GEEZ, IT'S TRUE! IT'S REALLY TRUE!
YOU'RE ALIVE!
AS ARE YOU.
DEATH IS FOR SUCKERS.
RICK, WE DON'T HAVE MUCH TIME...

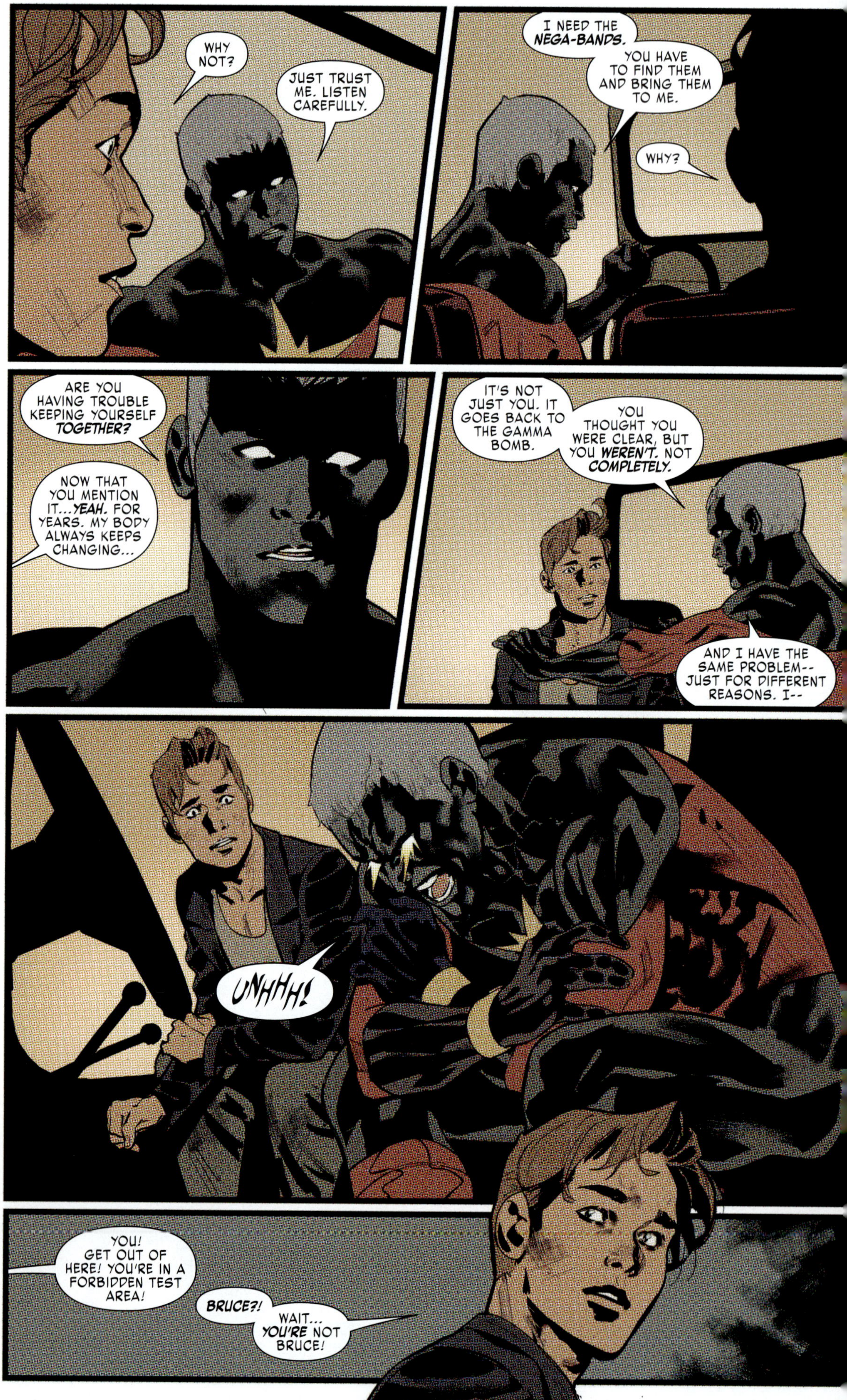
WHY NOT?
JUST TRUST ME. LISTEN CAREFULLY.
I NEED THE NEGA-BANDS.
YOU HAVE TO FIND THEM AND BRING THEM TO ME.
WHY?
ARE YOU HAVING TROUBLE KEEPING YOURSELF TOGETHER?
NOW THAT YOU MENTION IT...YEAH. FOR YEARS. MY BODY ALWAYS KEEPS CHANGING...
IT'S NOT JUST YOU. IT GOES BACK TO THE GAMMA BOMB.
YOU THOUGHT YOU WERE CLEAR, BUT YOU WEREN'T. NOT COMPLETELY.
AND I HAVE THE SAME PROBLEM-- JUST FOR DIFFERENT REASONS. I--
UNHHH!
YOU! GET OUT OF HERE! YOU'RE IN A FORBIDDEN TEST AREA!
BRUCE?!
WAIT... YOU'RE NOT BRUCE!

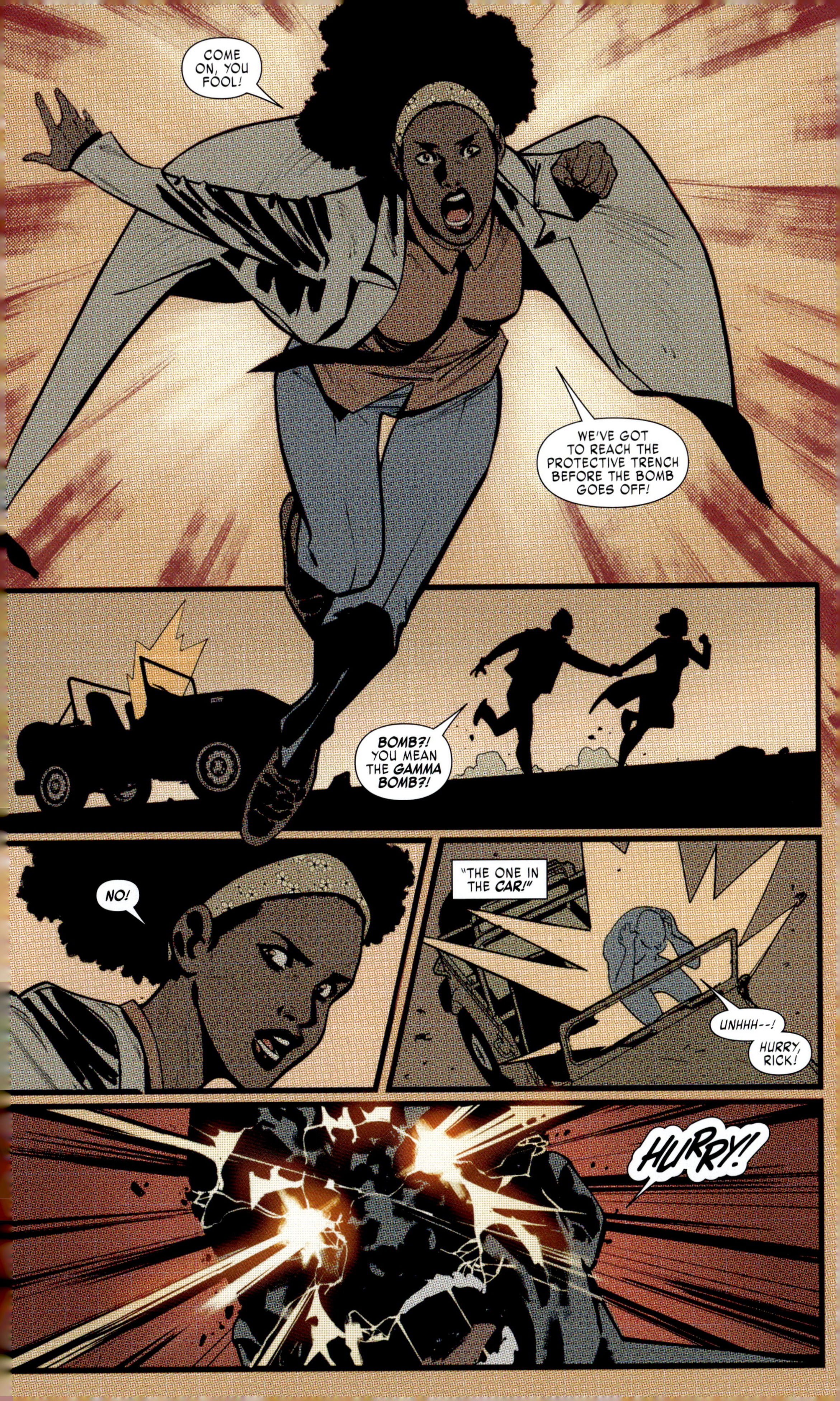
COME ON, YOU FOOL!
WE'VE GOT TO REACH THE PROTECTIVE TRENCH BEFORE THE BOMB GOES OFF!
BOMB?! YOU MEAN THE GAMMA BOMB?!
NO!
"THE ONE IN THE CAR!"
UNHHH--!
HURRY, RICK!
HURRY!

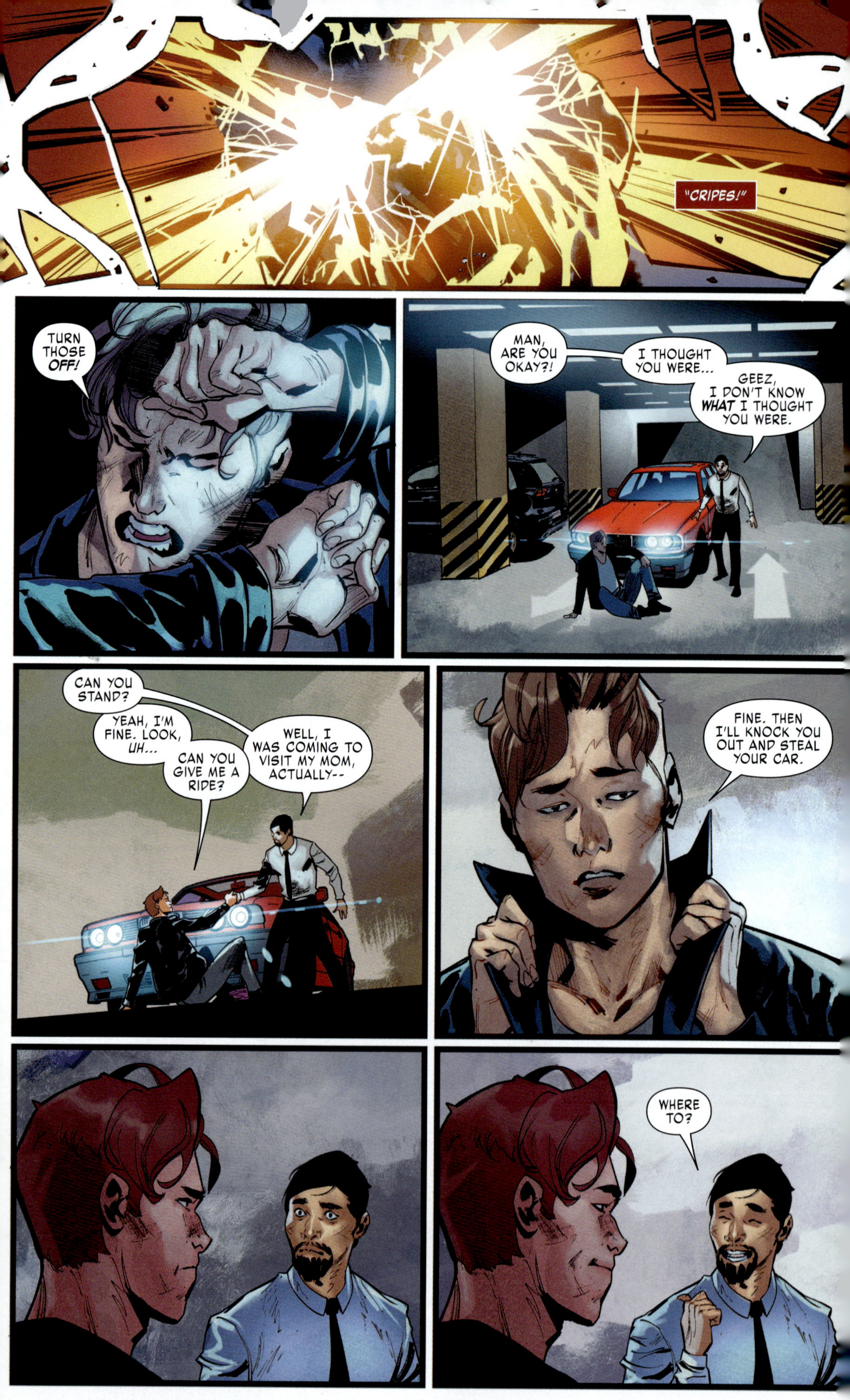
"CRIPES!"
TURN THOSE OFF!
MAN, ARE YOU OKAY?!
I THOUGHT YOU WERE...
GEEZ, I DON'T KNOW WHAT I THOUGHT YOU WERE.
CAN YOU STAND?
YEAH, I'M FINE. LOOK, UH...
CAN YOU GIVE ME A RIDE?
WELL, I WAS COMING TO VISIT MY MOM, ACTUALLY--
FINE. THEN I'LL KNOCK YOU OUT AND STEAL YOUR CAR.
WHERE TO?

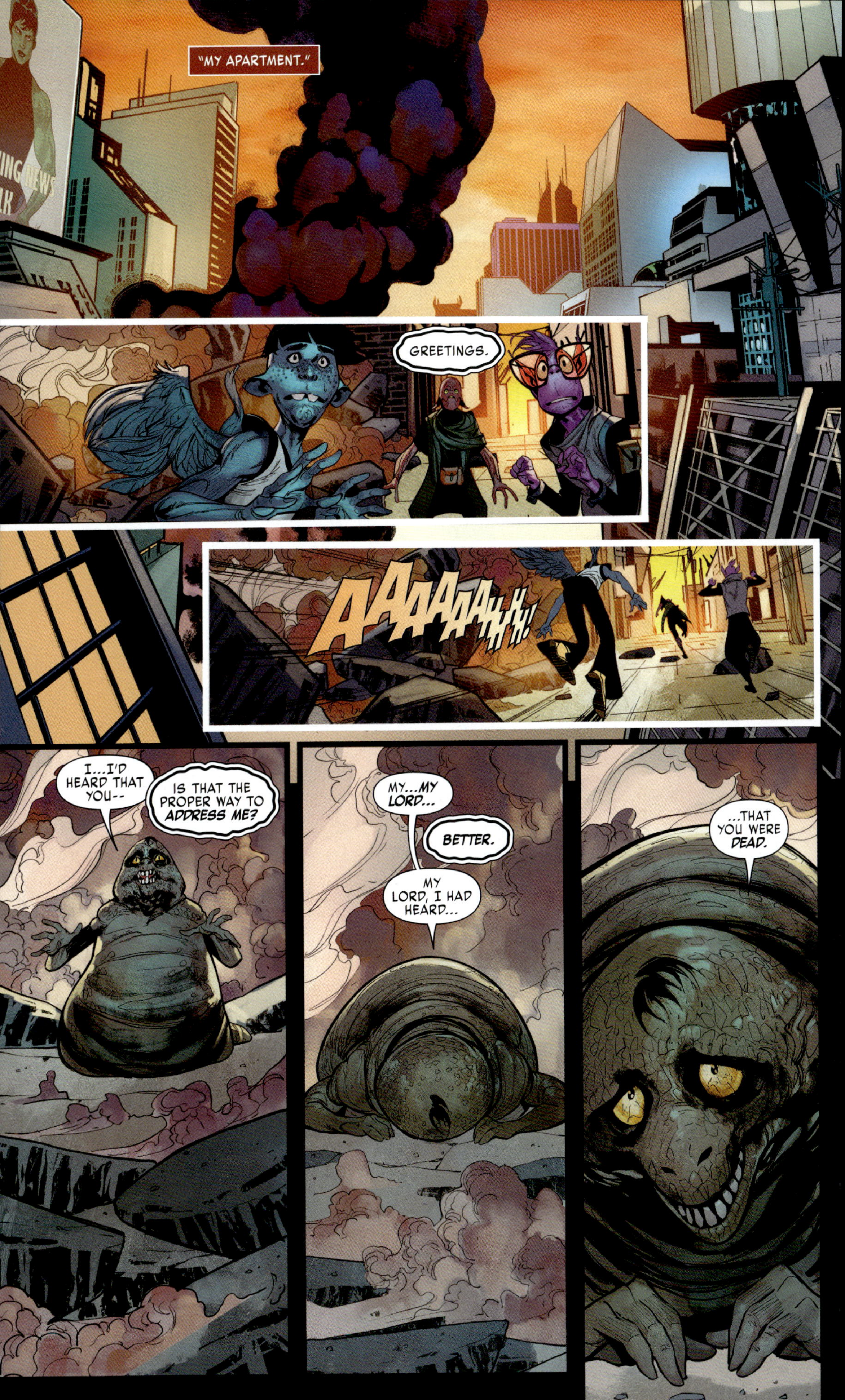
"MY APARTMENT."
GREETINGS.
AAAAAAHHH!
I...I'D HEARD THAT YOU--
IS THAT THE PROPER WAY TO ADDRESS ME?
MY...MY LORD...
BETTER.
MY LORD, I HAD HEARD...
...THAT YOU WERE DEAD.

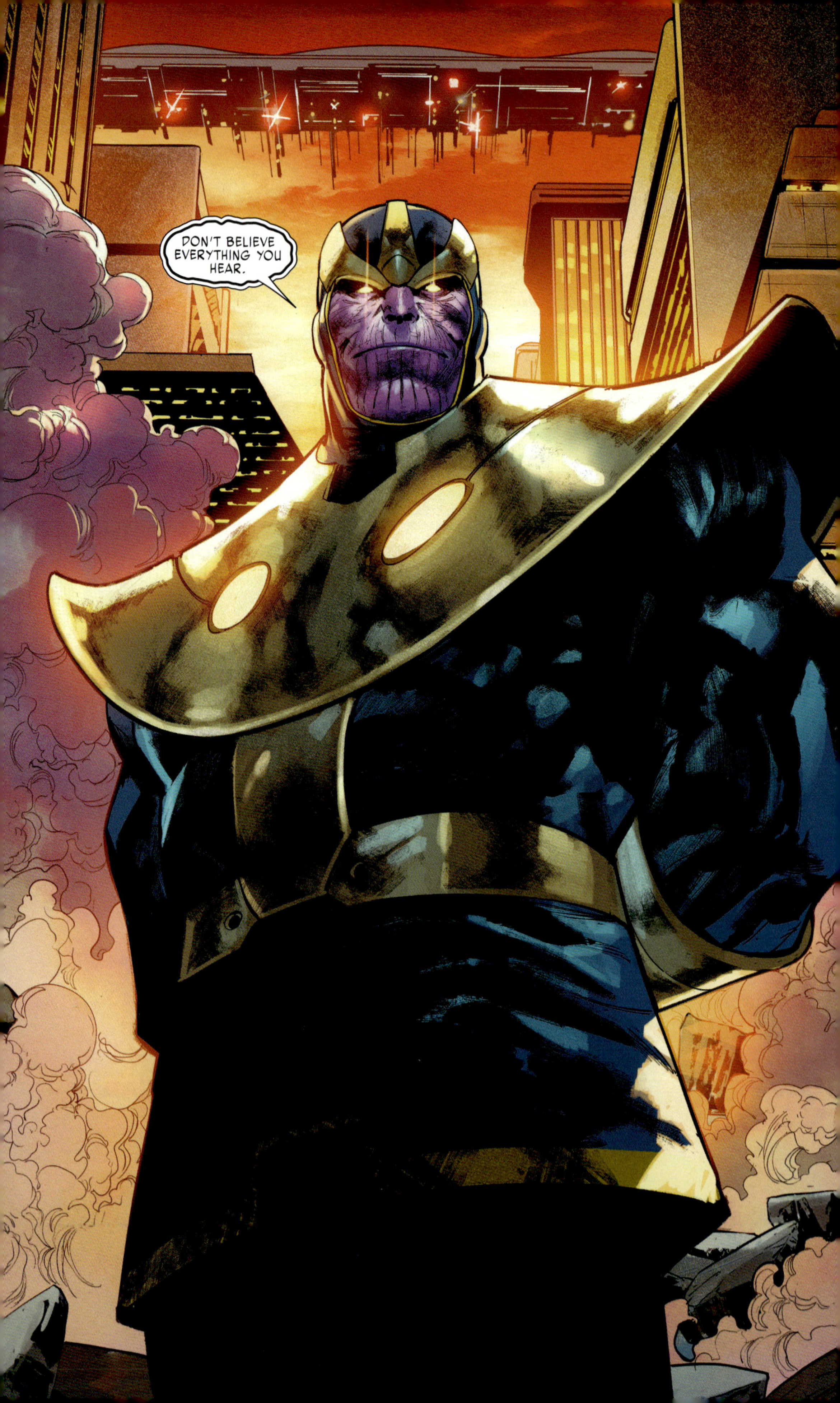
DON'T BELIEVE EVERYTHING YOU HEAR.

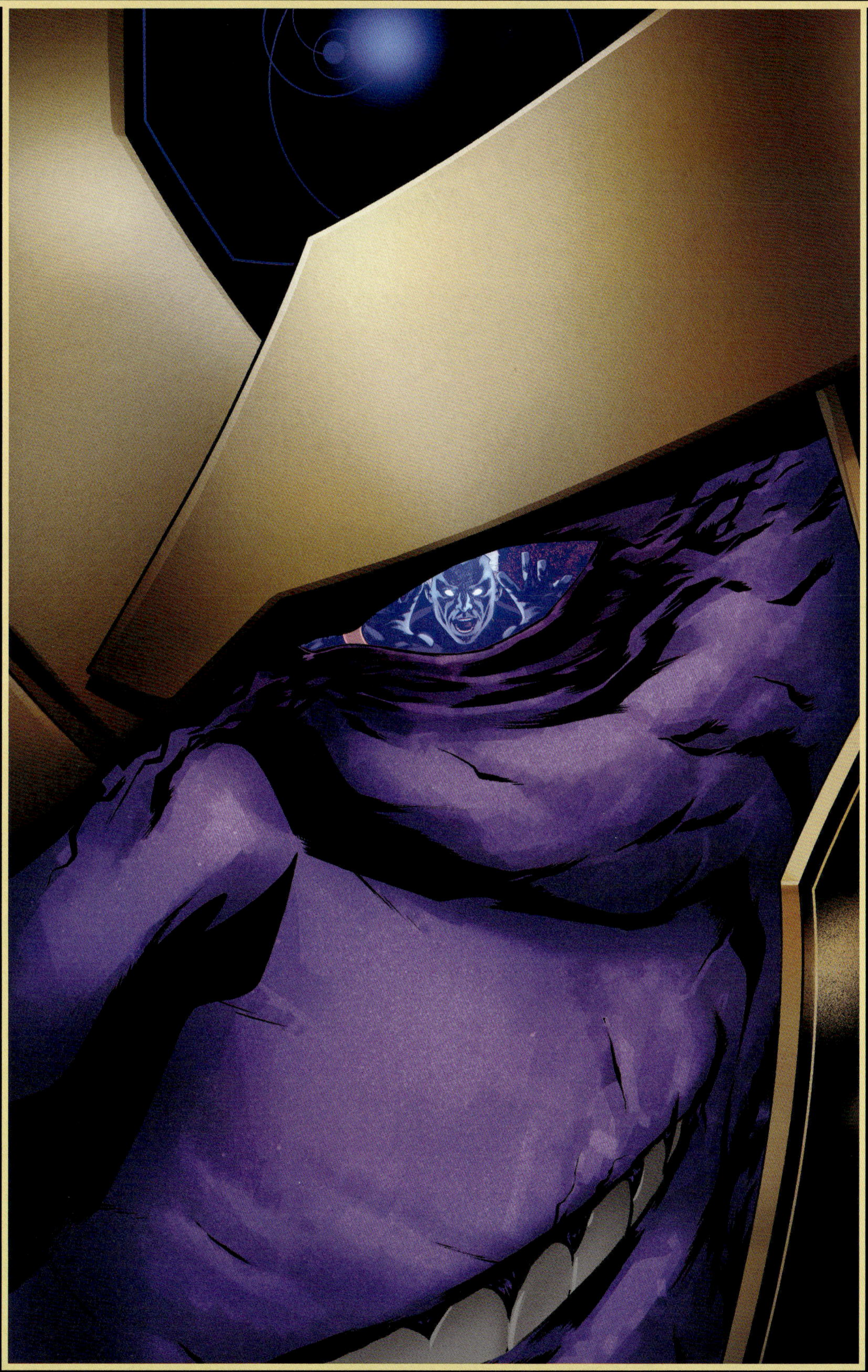

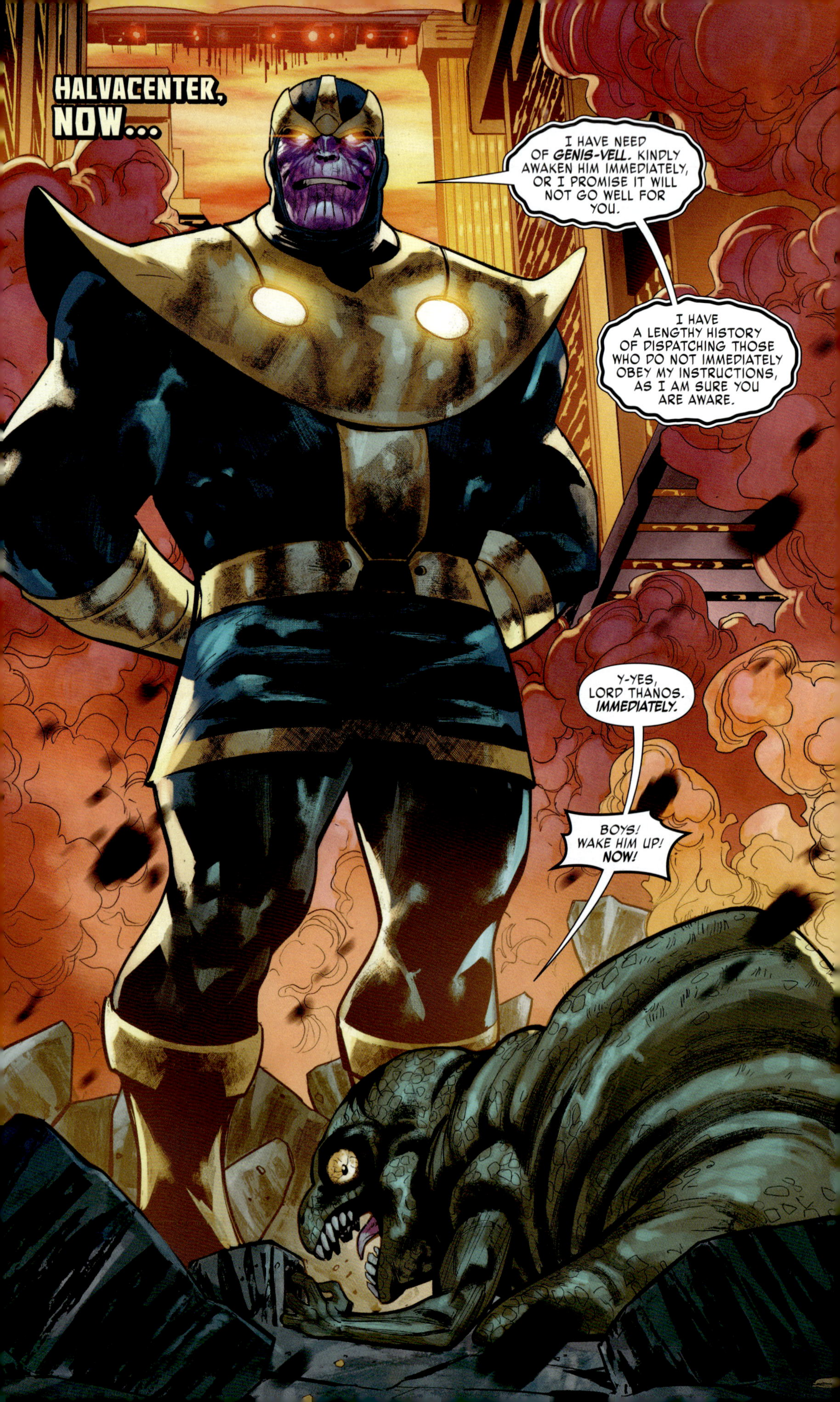
HALVACENTER, NOW...
I HAVE NEED OF GENIS-VELL. KINDLY AWAKEN HIM IMMEDIATELY, OR I PROMISE IT WILL NOT GO WELL FOR YOU.
I HAVE A LENGTHY HISTORY OF DISPATCHING THOSE WHO DO NOT IMMEDIATELY OBEY MY INSTRUCTIONS, AS I AM SURE YOU ARE AWARE.
Y-YES, LORD THANOS. IMMEDIATELY.
BOYS! WAKE HIM UP! NOW!

WAKE UP! HURRY, FOR GOD'S SAKE!
UNNHHH... WHAT? WHERE?
THANOS HAS BUSINESS WITH YOU!
THANOS?
RIGHT IN FRONT OF YOU!
WHERE? I...I CAN'T SENSE H--
EH?
HE MAY BE TEMPORARILY BLINDED BY HIS RELEASE OF ENERGY.
PAY HIM NO MIND. I'LL TAKE HIM AS HE IS.
COME. WE HAVE MUCH TO DISCUSS.
UHM... ALL...ALL RIGHT.
WHEEEWW!
GENTLEMEN, WE GOT OFF LUCKY.

ALL RIGHT...WHO ARE YOU? YOU'RE CERTAINLY NOT THANOS.
HE RADIATES POWER THAT YOU DON'T HAVE.
INDEED. IT'S GOOD THAT BRAGG AND HIS PEOPLE WERE SO CONSUMED WITH FEAR THAT THEY WEREN'T REALLY LISTENING TO YOU.
YOU HAVEN'T ANSWERED THE QUESTION:
WHO THE HELL ARE YOU?
MY NAME...
...IS JAZINDA.
YOU'RE A SKRULL.
INDEED I AM. NOW COME WITH ME. WE HAVE A RESCUE MISSION.
WHO DO WE HAVE TO RESCUE?
DEATH.
DEATH?
YOU KNOW HER?
I'VE MET HER.

HALVACENTER. YEARS EARLIER...
THERE. YOUR ROOM IS JUST AHEAD, MARLO.
AND "MOONDRAGON" IS THERE. WE NEED TO HAVE A CHAT.
WHY DID YOU SOUND LIKE YOU PUT QUOTES AROUND HER NAME?
I SEE MY TIP PAID OFF.
YOUR TIP, YES. MARLO IS BACK SAFE AND SOUND. NOW...
...TELL ME WHO YOU ARE.
OBVIOUSLY, I'M MOONDRAGON.
NO. YOU'RE NOT.
WHY DO YOU SAY THAT?
BECAUSE MY EYES TELL ME THAT YOU'RE HEATHER...
...BUT I GET NO SENSE OF YOUR PRESENCE. I PERCEIVE ONLY A VOID. AN EMPTINESS.
YOU'RE HERE, BUT YOU'RE NOT. SO WHO ARE YOU, OR, MORE ACCURATELY...
...WHAT ARE YOU?
I AM DEATH.
PERHAPS YOU'VE HEARD OF ME.

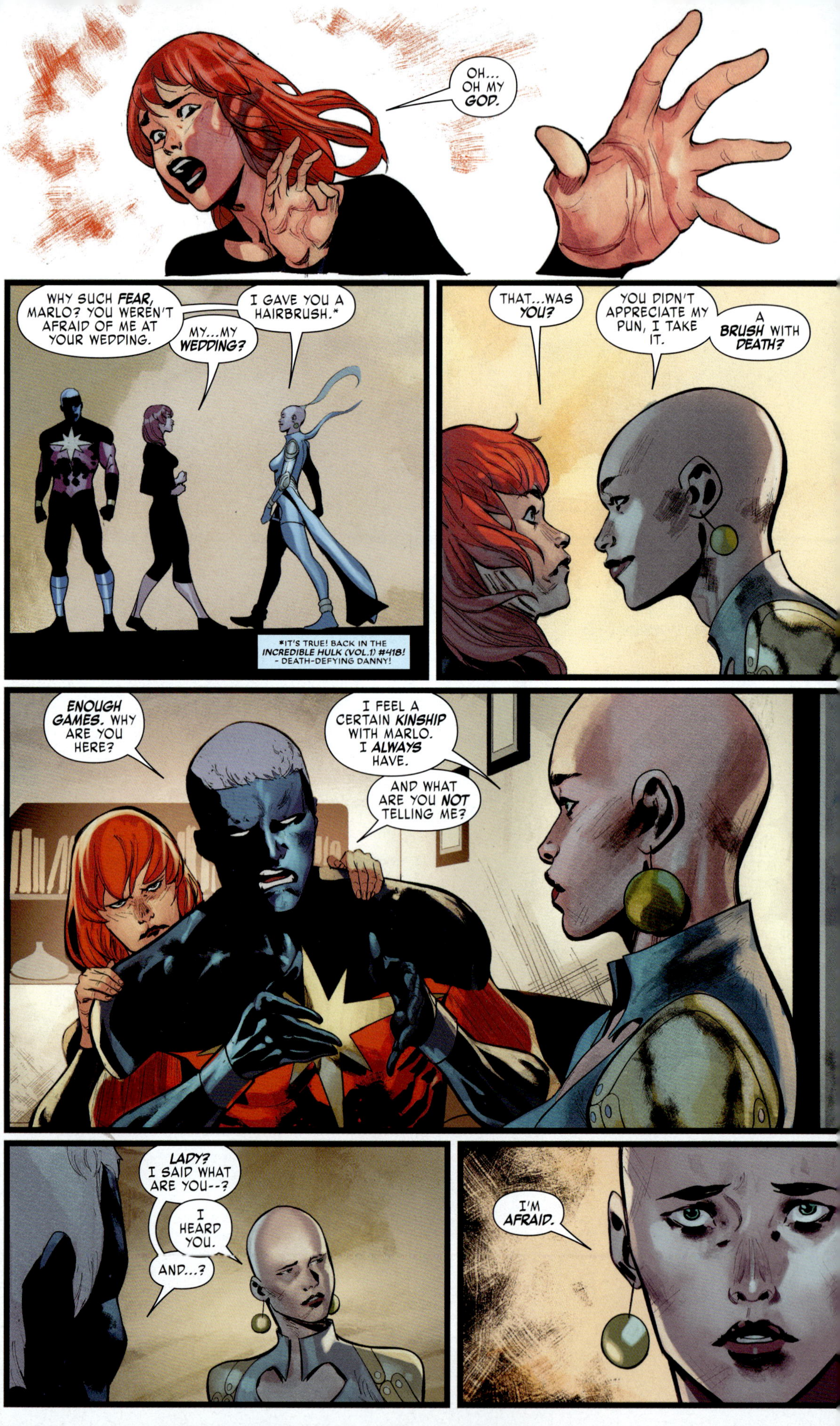
OH... OH MY GOD.
WHY SUCH FEAR, MARLO? YOU WEREN'T AFRAID OF ME AT YOUR WEDDING.
MY...MY WEDDING?
I GAVE YOU A HAIRBRUSH.*
*IT'S TRUE! BACK IN THE INCREDIBLE HULK (VOL.1) #418! - DEATH-DEFYING DANNY!
THAT...WAS YOU?
YOU DIDN'T APPRECIATE MY PUN, I TAKE IT.
A BRUSH WITH DEATH?
ENOUGH GAMES. WHY ARE YOU HERE?
I FEEL A CERTAIN KINSHIP WITH MARLO. I ALWAYS HAVE.
AND WHAT ARE YOU NOT TELLING ME?
LADY? I SAID WHAT ARE YOU--?
I HEARD YOU.
AND...?
I'M AFRAID.

NOW...
SO, SHE WAS IMPERSONATING YOUR FRIEND MOONDRAGON.
SHE'S A SHAPE-SHIFTER. YOU SHOULD BE ABLE TO RELATE TO THAT.
WHAT WAS SHE AFRAID OF?
NO, YOU TELL ME. HOW DO YOU KNOW SHE'S IN DANGER?
HAVE YOU HEARD OF THE GEM OF SY-TORAK?
I HEARD IT WAS STOLEN AGES AGO.
YES, WELL, YOU'RE STANDING NEXT TO THE THIEF.
REALLY?
YES. AND WHEN IT LOOKED AS IF I WAS GOING TO GET CAUGHT, I SWALLOWED IT. AND IT...
...I DON'T KNOW... IT BONDED WITH ME.
WHENEVER I DIE, I COME BACK FROM THE DEAD. NOT ONLY THAT...
...BUT BECAUSE OF IT, I CAN KIND OF...COMMUNE... WITH DEATH HERSELF.
AND SHE LET ME KNOW SHE'S IN TROUBLE.
IN TROUBLE? HOW CAN SHE BE IN TROUBLE?
THE KREE HAVE HER.

MY PEOPLE HAVE HER?
VOX SUPREME CAPTURED HER.
BUT HE'S DEAD NOW.
"YES. AND VOX'S HEAD SCIENTIST, REN-VARR, TOOK CONTROL OF HER.
"A LUNATIC LIKE THAT WASN'T JUST GOING TO LET A POWER SOURCE LIKE THE LADY DEATH ESCAPE."
SO SHE'S ON EDEN.
THEY'VE RENAMED IT "NEW HALA" NOW.
WELL, THE OLD ONE BLEW UP, SO I GUESS THAT MAKES SENSE.
AND THAT'S WHERE WE'RE HEADED NOW?
EXACTLY.
UH-OH.
WHAT'S "UH-OH"?
BRACE YOURSELF! INCOMING!

CHOOOM
CHOOOM
THIS THING HAVE **SHIELDS?**
IF IT DIDN'T, WE'D BE FLOATING IN SPACE RIGHT NOW.
ATTENTION, **FUGITIVE SKRULL.** YOU ARE **UNDER ARREST.** SURRENDER IMMEDIATELY OR PREPARE TO BE **ANNIHILATED.**
THAT'S A **BADOON SHIP!**
YOU **TICKED OFF** THE BADOON?
YES.
I MAY HAVE.
IS THERE ANYONE YOU **HAVEN'T** MANAGED TO UPSET?
WHO?
THE SWISS.
YOU **REALLY** WANT TO DISCUSS THIS, OR DO YOU WANT TO **DISPATCH** THE BADOON?
FREAKING SKRULLS.

I'M NOT THRILLED WITH THIS SITUATION.
MY LIGHT POWERS ARE STILL DANGEROUSLY UNPREDICTABLE. IF I HAD MY NEGA-BANDS, I COULD CONTROL THEM.
BUT I DON'T.
SHWZAAAK
SO I JUST HAVE TO PRAY THAT--
DAMNATION. SO MUCH FOR PRAYERS.
IT'S HAPPENING FASTER THIS TIME.
HE'S IN DISTRESS!
TARGET HIM! BLOW HIM OUT OF SPACE!
AND THIS TIME, IF I BLOW UP...
...I MAY NOT BE ABLE TO PULL MYSELF TOGETHER AGAIN.

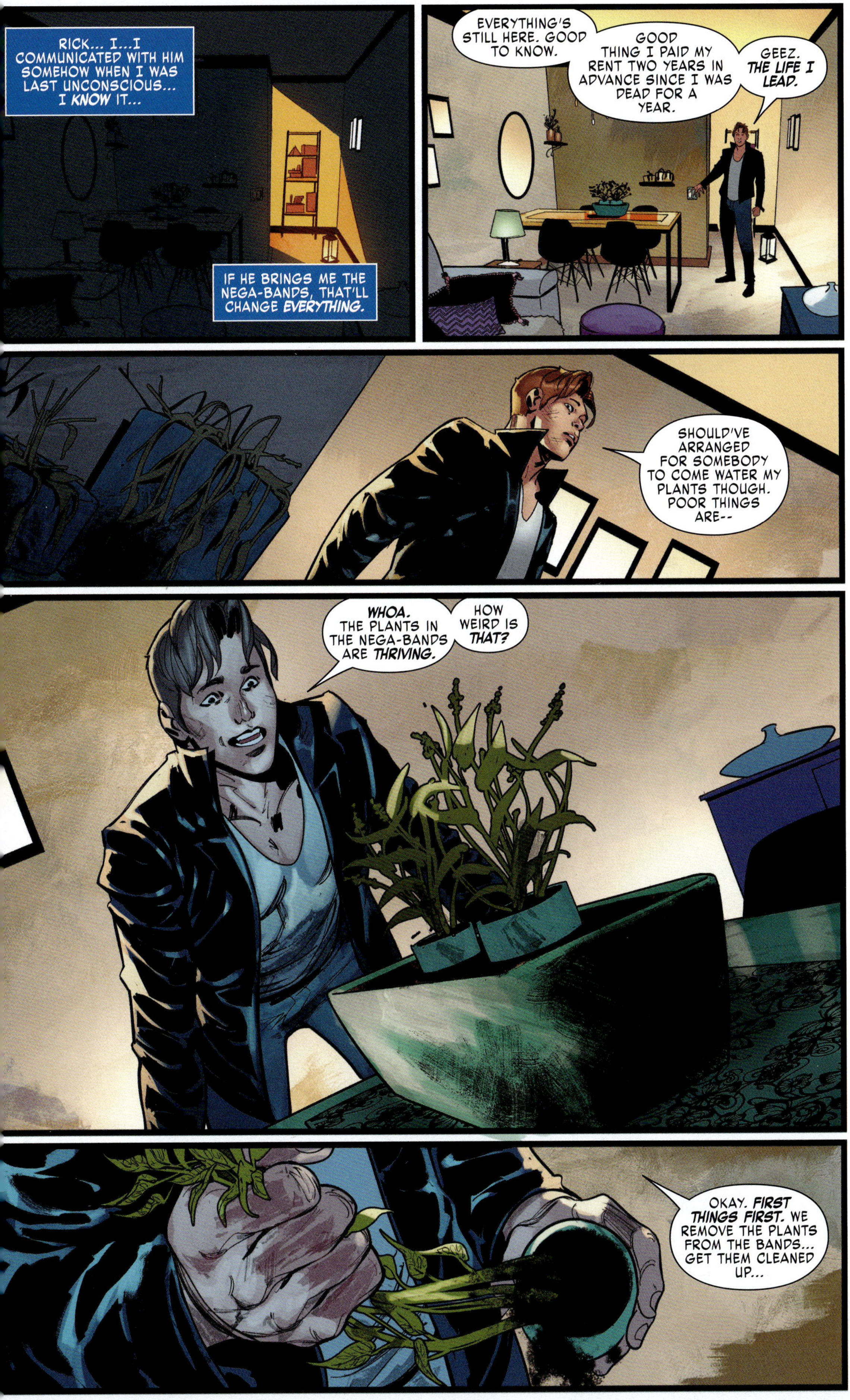
RICK... I...I COMMUNICATED WITH HIM SOMEHOW WHEN I WAS LAST UNCONSCIOUS... I *KNOW* IT...
IF HE BRINGS ME THE NEGA-BANDS, THAT'LL CHANGE *EVERYTHING.*
EVERYTHING'S STILL HERE. GOOD TO KNOW.
GOOD THING I PAID MY RENT TWO YEARS IN ADVANCE SINCE I WAS DEAD FOR A YEAR.
GEEZ. *THE LIFE I LEAD.*
SHOULD'VE ARRANGED FOR SOMEBODY TO COME WATER MY PLANTS THOUGH. POOR THINGS ARE--
WHOA. THE PLANTS IN THE NEGA-BANDS ARE *THRIVING.*
HOW WEIRD IS *THAT?*
OKAY. *FIRST THINGS FIRST.* WE REMOVE THE PLANTS FROM THE BANDS... GET THEM CLEANED UP...

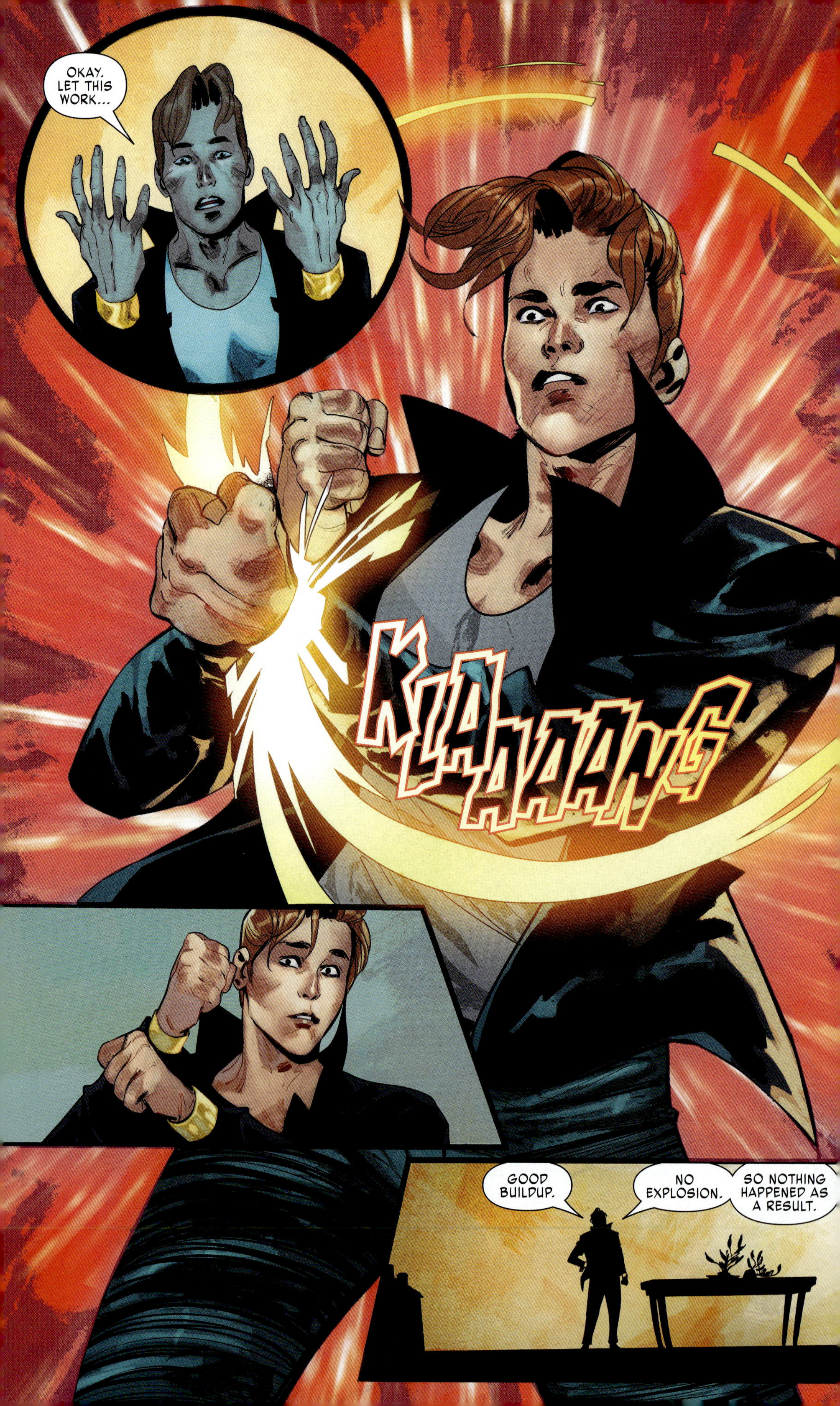
OKAY. LET THIS WORK...
KRAAAANG
GOOD BUILDUP.
NO EXPLOSION.
SO NOTHING HAPPENED AS A RESULT.

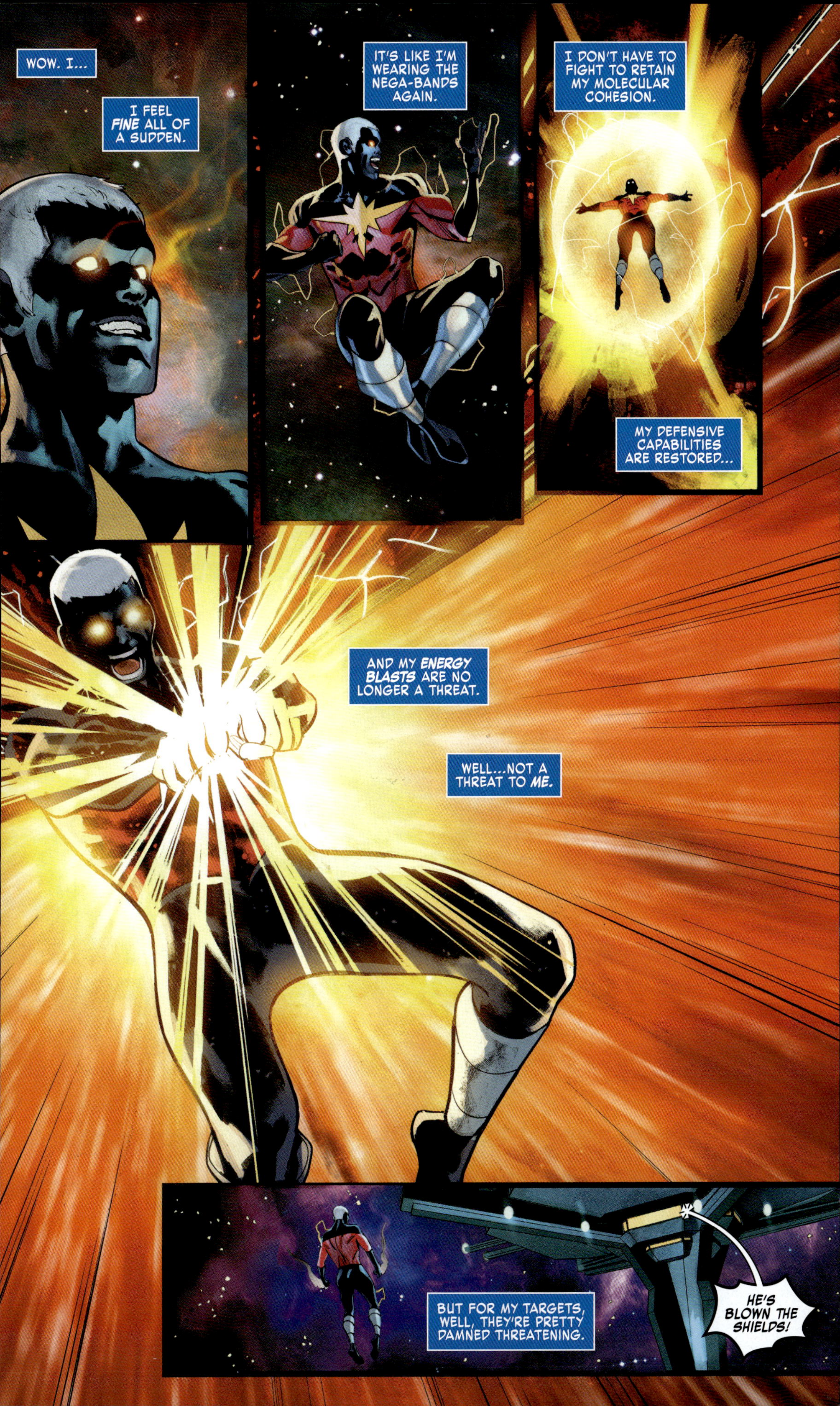
WOW. I...
I FEEL FINE ALL OF A SUDDEN.
IT'S LIKE I'M WEARING THE NEGA-BANDS AGAIN.
I DON'T HAVE TO FIGHT TO RETAIN MY MOLECULAR COHESION.
MY DEFENSIVE CAPABILITIES ARE RESTORED...
AND MY ENERGY BLASTS ARE NO LONGER A THREAT.
WELL...NOT A THREAT TO ME.
BUT FOR MY TARGETS, WELL, THEY'RE PRETTY DAMNED THREATENING.
HE'S BLOWN THE SHIELDS!

UHHHH...
PHYLA! ARE YOU OKAY?
CAROL DANVERS.
CURRENT CAPTAIN MARVEL.
SOMEONE BANGED NEGA-BANDS TOGETHER!
DO YOU NEED HELP?
I'VE GOT IT COVERED!
OOOKAY.

SHWAZAAAAK
THEIR WEAPONS ARE POWERFUL... NO DENYING IT...
GROZIT... IT'S BREAKING THROUGH... CAN'T HOLD MUCH LONGER...
PEW
PEW
PEW
PEW
YES! NICE MANEUVERING, JAZINDA!
WHO WANTS SOME?!
COME ON! BRING IT ON!

HULL BREACH ON LEVEL THREE!
SEAL IT UP AND FOCUS TORPEDO FIRE ON THE SKRULL SHIP!
HE'LL BREAK OFF TO PROTECT HER. I KNOW HIS TYPE.
WAIT... THEY'RE FIRING AT--
JAZINDA!
LOOK OUT!
RAKOVLAAM

OUCH.
SHIP. STATUS REPORT.
YOU ARE SEVERELY DAMAGED.
I MEANT *THE SHIP.*
LIKEWISE.
FANTASTIC. *SHIELDS?*
FUNCTIONING AT EIGHT PERCENT CAPACITY. THEY WILL NOT SURVIVE ANOTHER HIT.
GENIS... SAVE YOURSELF, FOR CRYING OUT LOUD...

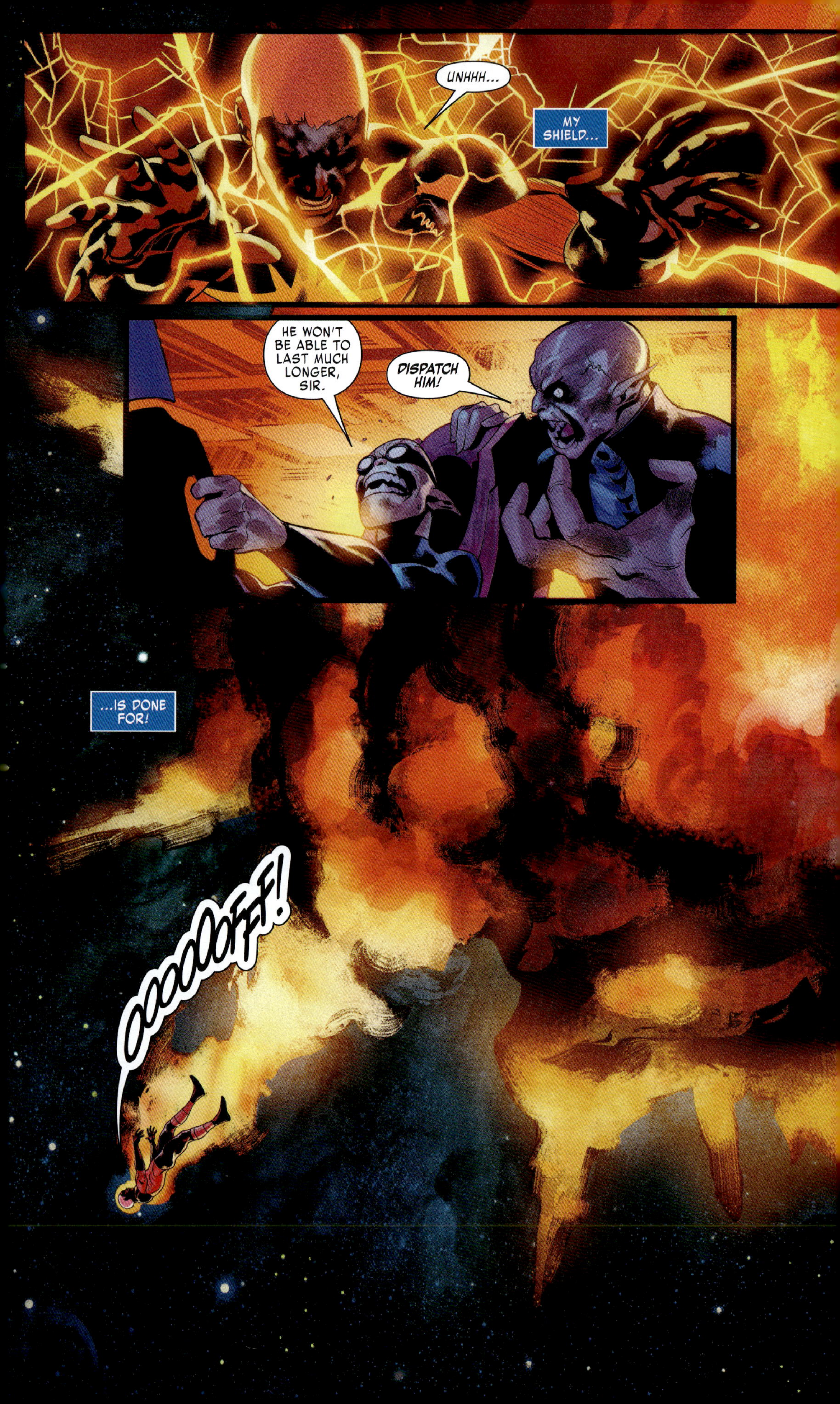
UNHHH...
MY SHIELD...
HE WON'T BE ABLE TO LAST MUCH LONGER, SIR.
DISPATCH HIM!
...IS DONE FOR!
OOOOOOFFF!

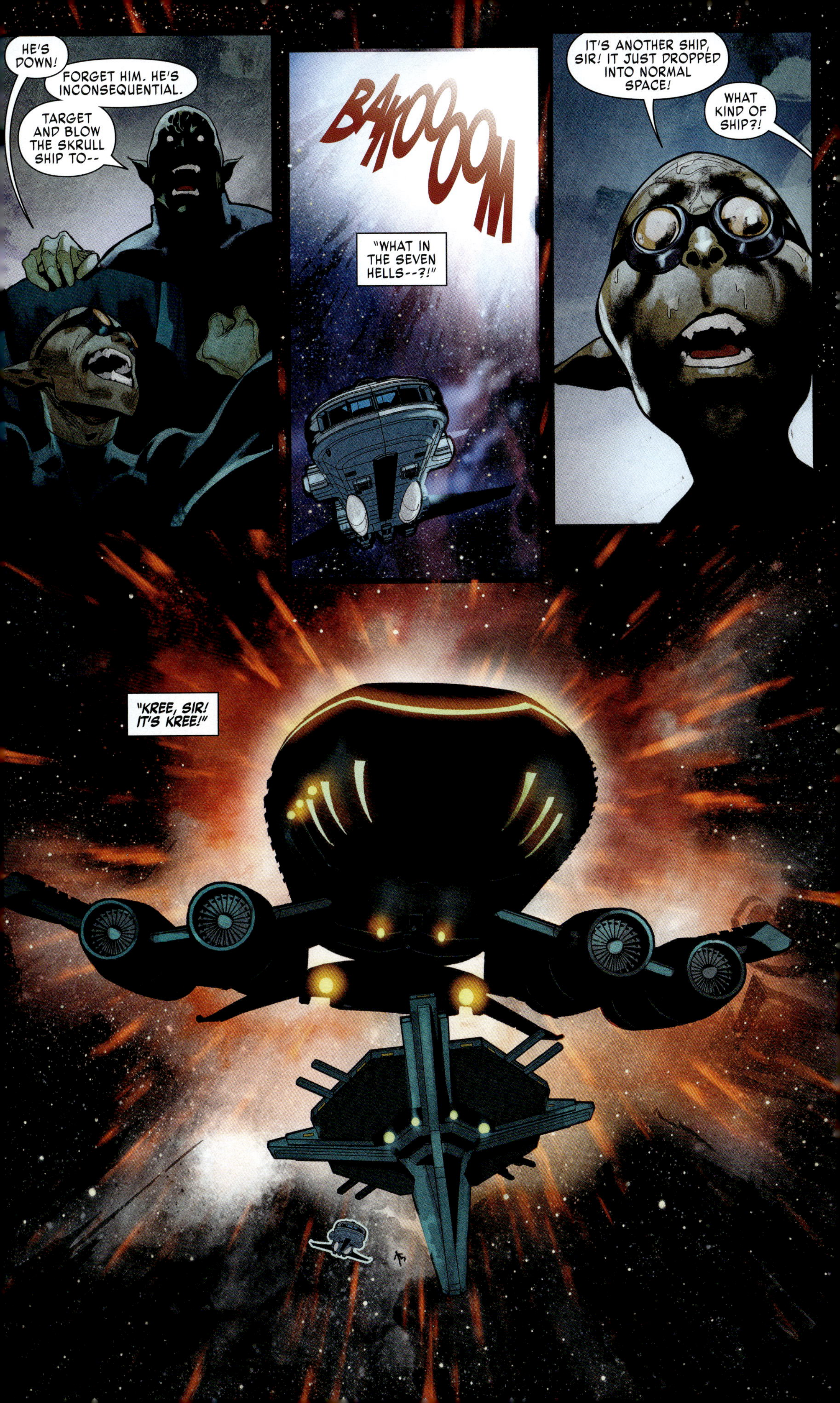
HE'S DOWN!
FORGET HIM. HE'S INCONSEQUENTIAL.
TARGET AND BLOW THE SKRULL SHIP TO--
BAKOOOOM
"WHAT IN THE SEVEN HELLS--?!"
IT'S ANOTHER SHIP, SIR! IT JUST DROPPED INTO NORMAL SPACE!
WHAT KIND OF SHIP?!
"KREE, SIR! IT'S KREE!"

WELL, COMMANDER?
YES, SIR. YOUR INFORMATION WAS CORRECT. GENIS WAS IN THIS AREA. WE FOUND HIM.
"WE" NEVER LOST HIM.
HIS ENERGY PATTERNS ARE REMARKABLY EASY TO TRACE. I'VE BEEN AWARE OF WHERE HE WAS THE ENTIRE TIME.
BRING HIM HERE TO NEW HALA, COMMANDER.
WHAT IF HE DOESN'T WANT TO COME, SIR?
YOU JUST SAVED HIS LIFE. TRUST ME, HE'LL COME. CONTACT ME WHEN YOU'RE APPROACHING.
SO...THE LATE VOX'S GREATEST CREATION WILL BE COMING HOME.
FORTUNATELY ENOUGH, THERE IS NOTHING HE CAN DO TO ME.
I MEAN, WHAT ACTION COULD HE TAKE AGAINST ME? TRY TO KILL ME?
I THINK HE WOULD FIND THAT RATHER DIFFICULT...

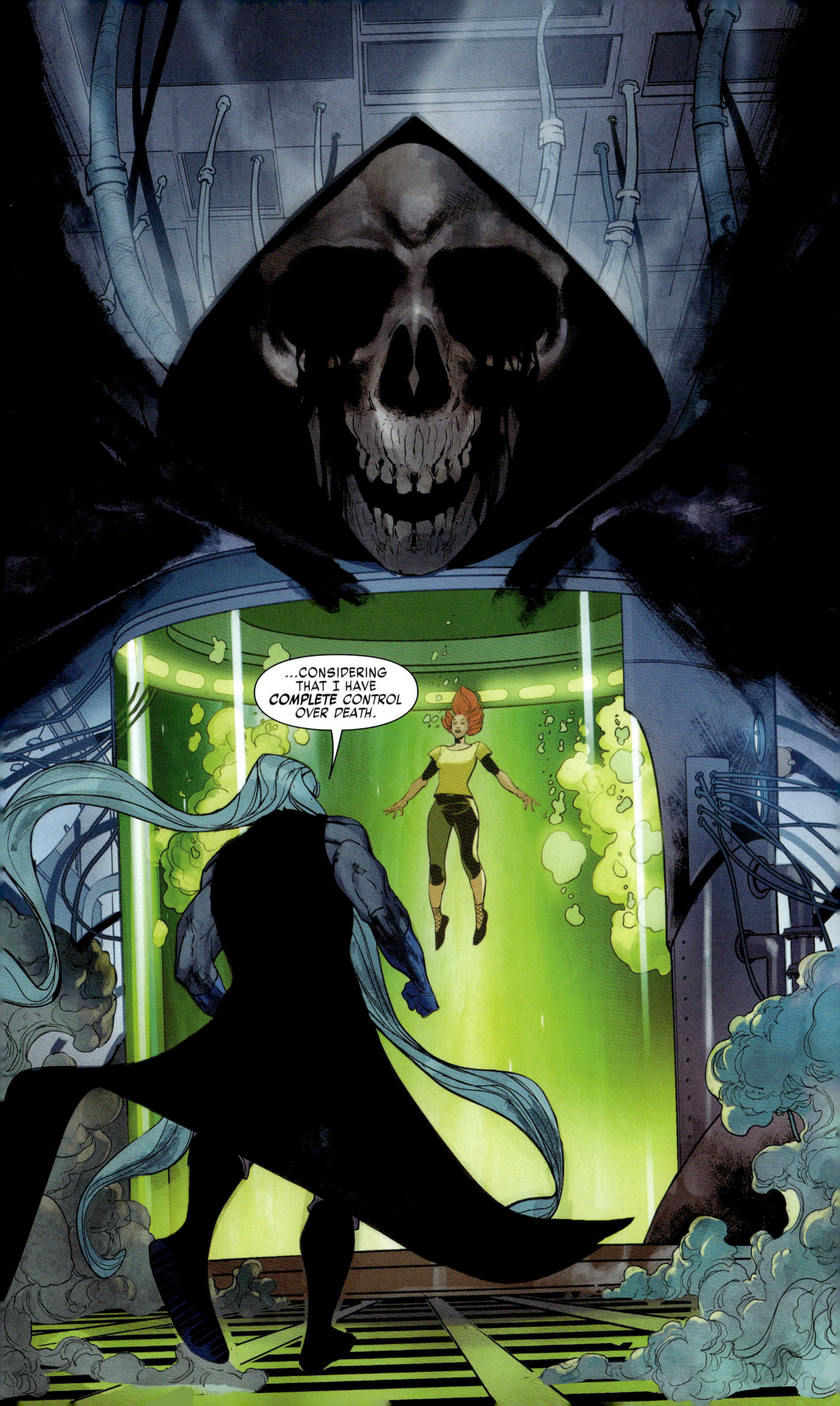
...CONSIDERING THAT I HAVE COMPLETE CONTROL OVER DEATH.

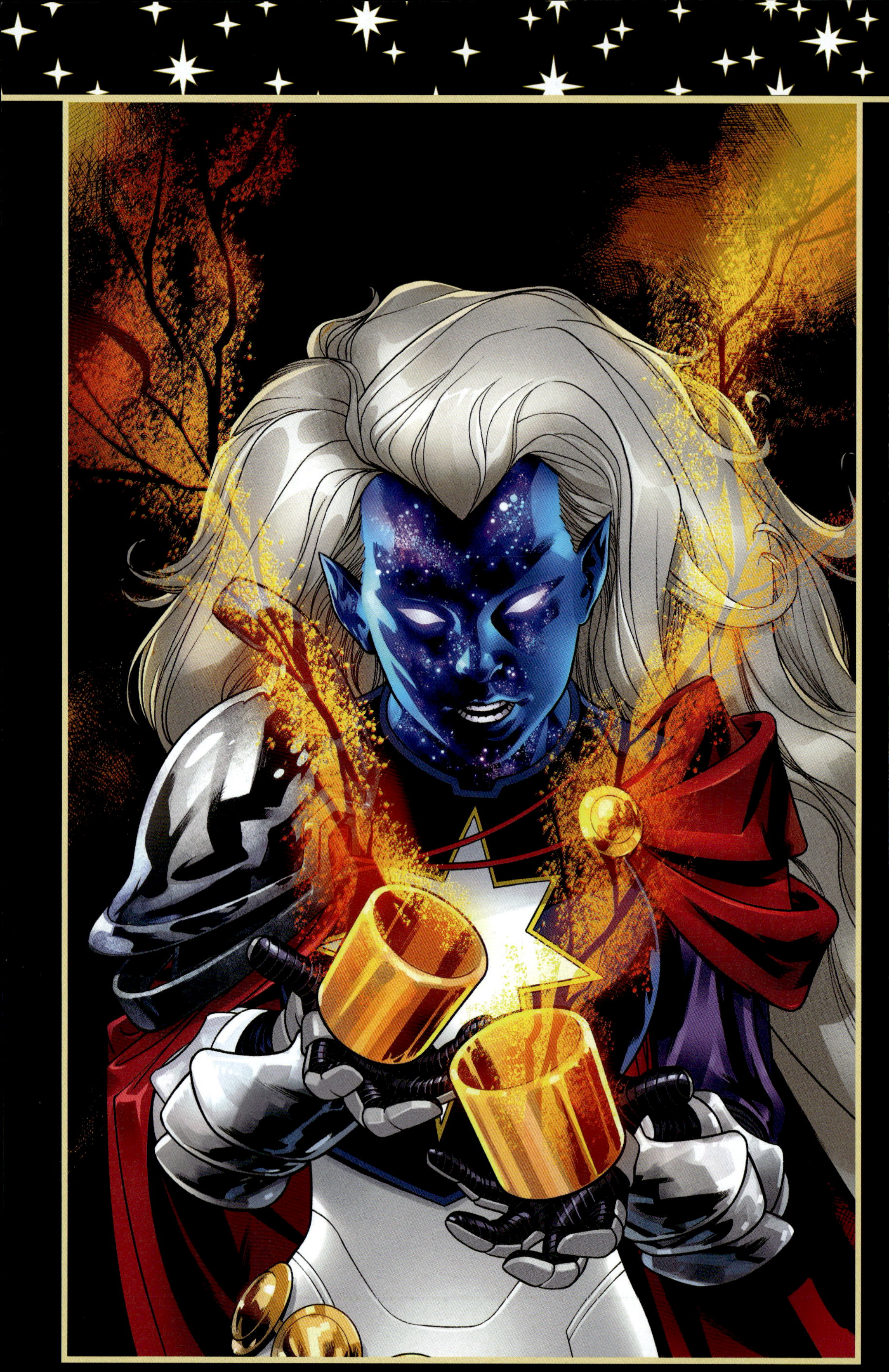

3

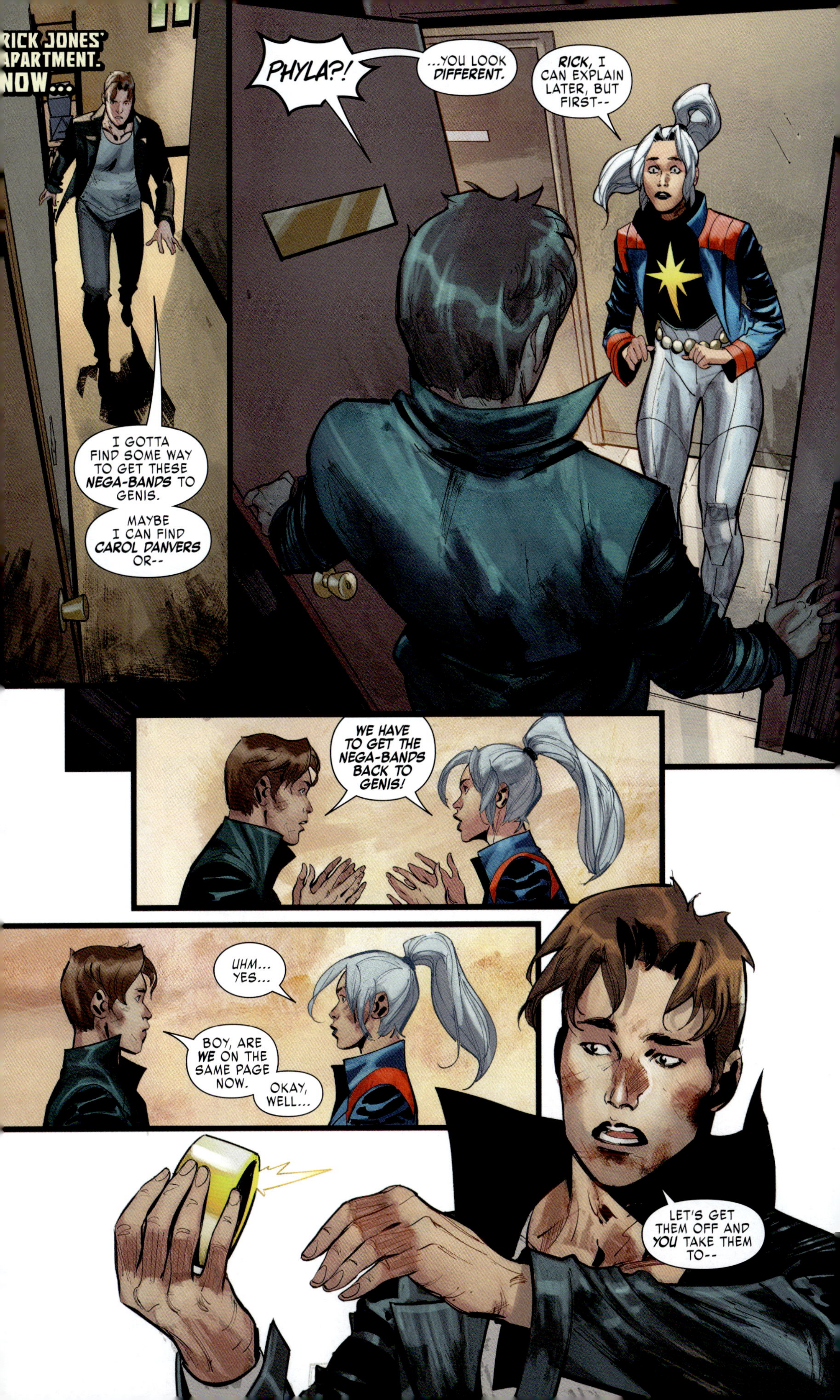
RICK JONES' APARTMENT. NOW...
I GOTTA FIND SOME WAY TO GET THESE NEGA-BANDS TO GENIS.
MAYBE I CAN FIND CAROL DANVERS OR--
PHYLA?!
...YOU LOOK DIFFERENT.
RICK, I CAN EXPLAIN LATER, BUT FIRST--
WE HAVE TO GET THE NEGA-BANDS BACK TO GENIS!
UHM... YES...
BOY, ARE WE ON THE SAME PAGE NOW.
OKAY, WELL...
LET'S GET THEM OFF AND YOU TAKE THEM TO--

HOLY--!
IT'S HAPPENING AGAIN!
THIS HAPPENED BEFORE?!
YES! QUICK! DO SOMETHING!
CLINK
CLANK
OH NO...IT'S HAPPENING AGAIN!
THE LIGHT IS OVERWHELMING MY BODY...
...AND I'VE NO WAY TO STOP IT!

REALLY DON'T LOVE BEING INTANGIBLE...
WELL, THEN...
...LET'S GET THESE BACK ON.
WHOA! THAT WAS...
WHOA!
GROZIT! I'M OKAY AGAIN!
EXCELLENT!
GOT TO CHECK IN ON JAZINDA. NOW THAT THE KREE SHIP HAS SCARED OFF THE BADOON...
...I'VE GOT TO MAKE SURE SHE'S OKAY.

JAZINDA? ARE YOU ALL RIGHT?
I'VE HAD BETTER DAYS.
THAT LOOKS AWFUL. CAN'T YOU JUST...I DON'T KNOW... SHAPE-SHIFT IT AWAY?
NO. CUTS AND BRUISES STAY, NO MATTER WHAT FORM I'M IN.
I CAN'T REBUILD SKIN THAT ISN'T THERE.
GENIS-VELL. ARE YOU READING ME?
I COPY, YES.
YOU ARE CORDIALLY INVITED TO NEW HALA. REN-VARR WISHES TO CATCH UP WITH YOU.
OH, DOES HE? WELL...THAT'S EXCELLENT.
I LOOK FORWARD TO HAVING A FEW WORDS WITH HIM.
THAT'S WHERE WE WERE HEADING ANYWAY.
YES, BUT IF WE TELL THEM THAT, THEY'LL ASK WHY AND THEY WON'T LIKE THE ANSWER.
FIRE UP THE ENGINES AND LET'S GO.

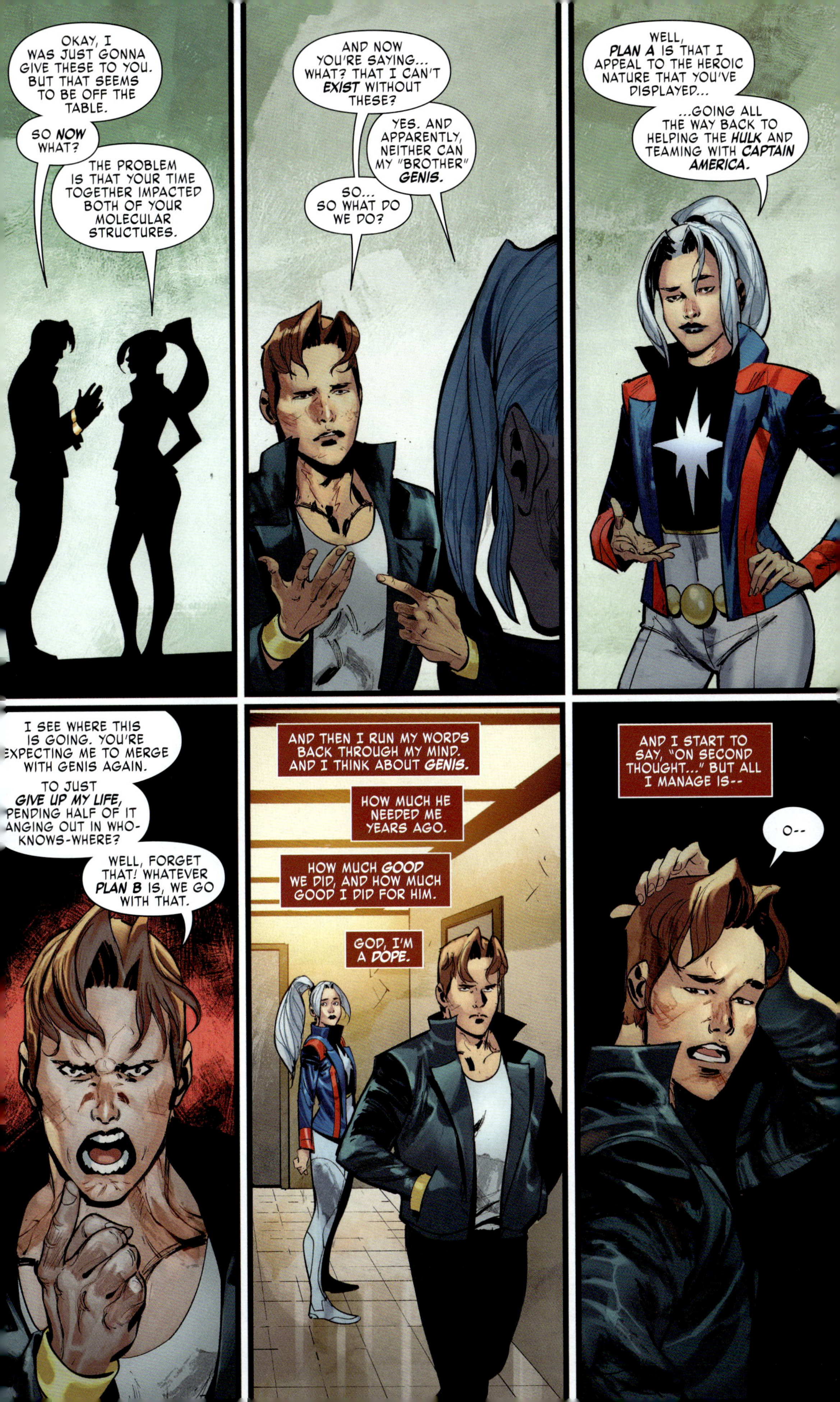

OKAY, I WAS JUST GONNA GIVE THESE TO YOU. BUT THAT SEEMS TO BE OFF THE TABLE.
SO NOW WHAT?
THE PROBLEM IS THAT YOUR TIME TOGETHER IMPACTED BOTH OF YOUR MOLECULAR STRUCTURES.
AND NOW YOU'RE SAYING... WHAT? THAT I CAN'T EXIST WITHOUT THESE?
YES. AND APPARENTLY, NEITHER CAN MY "BROTHER" GENIS.
SO... SO WHAT DO WE DO?
WELL, PLAN A IS THAT I APPEAL TO THE HEROIC NATURE THAT YOU'VE DISPLAYED...
...GOING ALL THE WAY BACK TO HELPING THE HULK AND TEAMING WITH CAPTAIN AMERICA.
I SEE WHERE THIS IS GOING. YOU'RE EXPECTING ME TO MERGE WITH GENIS AGAIN.
TO JUST GIVE UP MY LIFE, PENDING HALF OF IT ANGING OUT IN WHO-KNOWS-WHERE?
WELL, FORGET THAT! WHATEVER PLAN B IS, WE GO WITH THAT.
AND THEN I RUN MY WORDS BACK THROUGH MY MIND. AND I THINK ABOUT GENIS.
HOW MUCH HE NEEDED ME YEARS AGO.
HOW MUCH GOOD WE DID, AND HOW MUCH GOOD I DID FOR HIM.
GOD, I'M A DOPE.
AND I START TO SAY, "ON SECOND THOUGHT..." BUT ALL I MANAGE IS--
O--

PLAN B IT IS.
WAAAAM
THUUUUD
TOO BAD.
I THOUGHT BETTER OF YOU, RICK JONES OF EARTH-616.

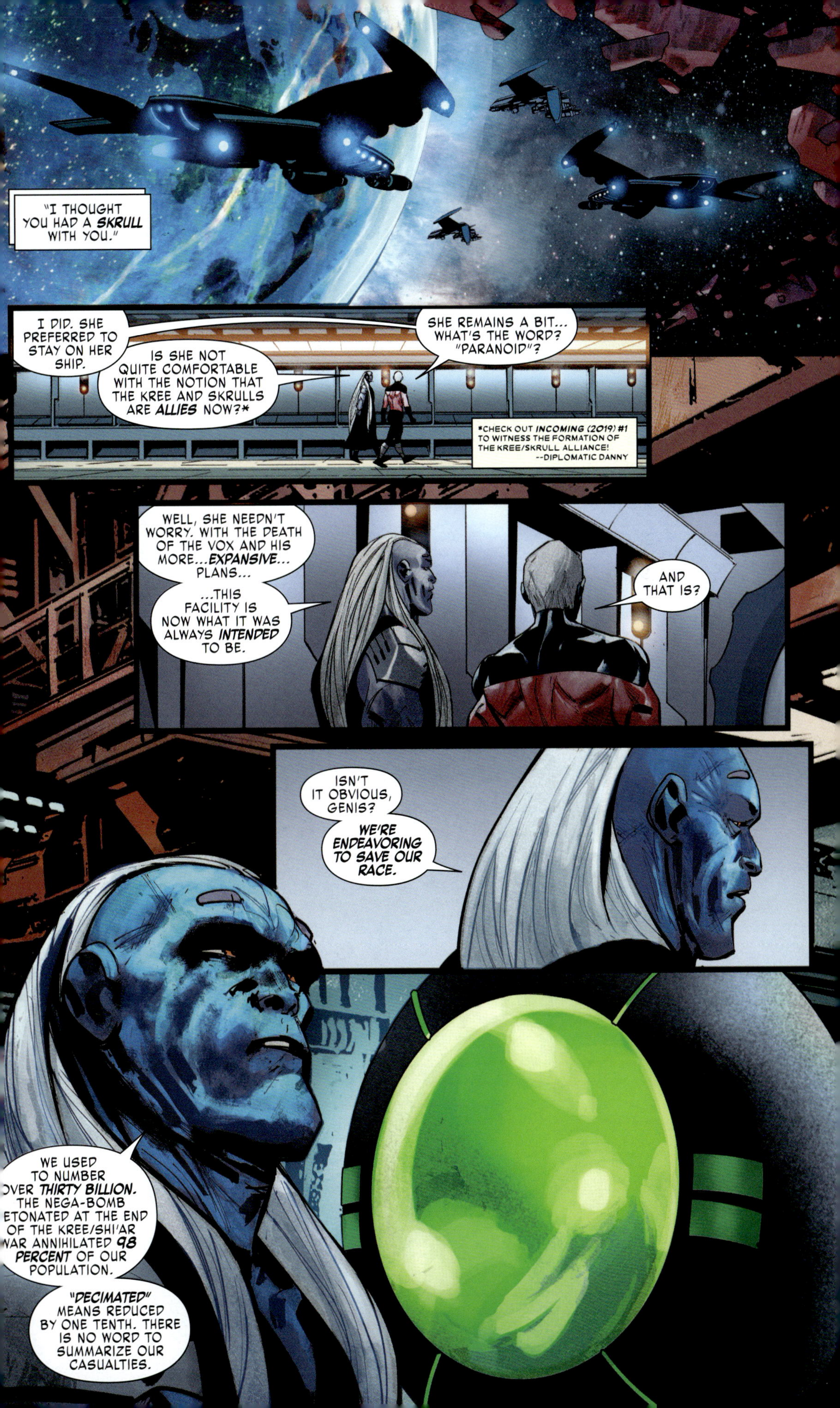
"I THOUGHT YOU HAD A SKRULL WITH YOU."
I DID. SHE PREFERRED TO STAY ON HER SHIP.
SHE REMAINS A BIT... WHAT'S THE WORD? "PARANOID"?
IS SHE NOT QUITE COMFORTABLE WITH THE NOTION THAT THE KREE AND SKRULLS ARE ALLIES NOW?*
*CHECK OUT INCOMING (2019) #1 TO WITNESS THE FORMATION OF THE KREE/SKRULL ALLIANCE! --DIPLOMATIC DANNY
WELL, SHE NEEDN'T WORRY. WITH THE DEATH OF THE VOX AND HIS MORE...EXPANSIVE... PLANS...
...THIS FACILITY IS NOW WHAT IT WAS ALWAYS INTENDED TO BE.
AND THAT IS?
ISN'T IT OBVIOUS, GENIS?
WE'RE ENDEAVORING TO SAVE OUR RACE.
WE USED TO NUMBER OVER THIRTY BILLION. THE NEGA-BOMB ETONATED AT THE END OF THE KREE/SHI'AR WAR ANNIHILATED 98 PERCENT OF OUR POPULATION.
"DECIMATED" MEANS REDUCED BY ONE TENTH. THERE IS NO WORD TO SUMMARIZE OUR CASUALTIES.

AND YOUR ANSWER TO THIS IS...?
WELL, IT SHOULD BE OBVIOUS. YOUR PRESENCE HERE ANSWERS THAT QUESTION.
REN-VARR, YOU MEAN...?
CLONING, YES. OBVIOUSLY.
THROUGH HERE.
MY GOD.
IMPRESSIVE, ISN'T IT?
WE ARE GROWING THEM IN REAL TIME, SINCE HASTENING THE PROCESS CAN HAVE UNEXPECTED AND EVEN DANGEROUS CONSEQUENCES...
...SOMETHING THAT I BELIEVE YOU YOURSELF ARE DISCOVERING.

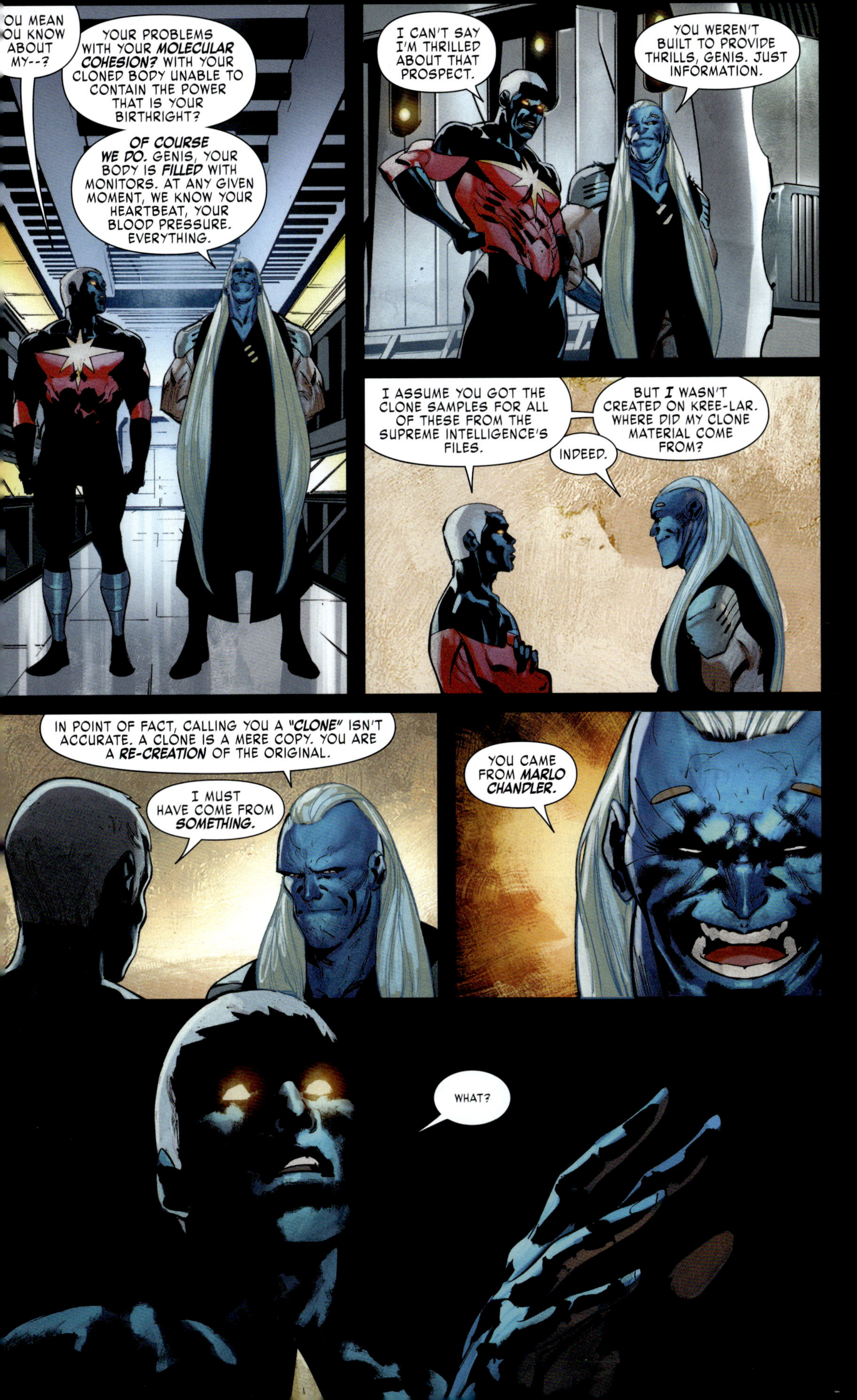
OU MEAN OU KNOW ABOUT MY--?
YOUR PROBLEMS WITH YOUR MOLECULAR COHESION? WITH YOUR CLONED BODY UNABLE TO CONTAIN THE POWER THAT IS YOUR BIRTHRIGHT?
OF COURSE WE DO. GENIS, YOUR BODY IS FILLED WITH MONITORS. AT ANY GIVEN MOMENT, WE KNOW YOUR HEARTBEAT, YOUR BLOOD PRESSURE. EVERYTHING.
I CAN'T SAY I'M THRILLED ABOUT THAT PROSPECT.
YOU WEREN'T BUILT TO PROVIDE THRILLS, GENIS. JUST INFORMATION.
I ASSUME YOU GOT THE CLONE SAMPLES FOR ALL OF THESE FROM THE SUPREME INTELLIGENCE'S FILES.
INDEED.
BUT I WASN'T CREATED ON KREE-LAR. WHERE DID MY CLONE MATERIAL COME FROM?
IN POINT OF FACT, CALLING YOU A "CLONE" ISN'T ACCURATE. A CLONE IS A MERE COPY. YOU ARE A RE-CREATION OF THE ORIGINAL.
I MUST HAVE COME FROM SOMETHING.
YOU CAME FROM MARLO CHANDLER.
WHAT?

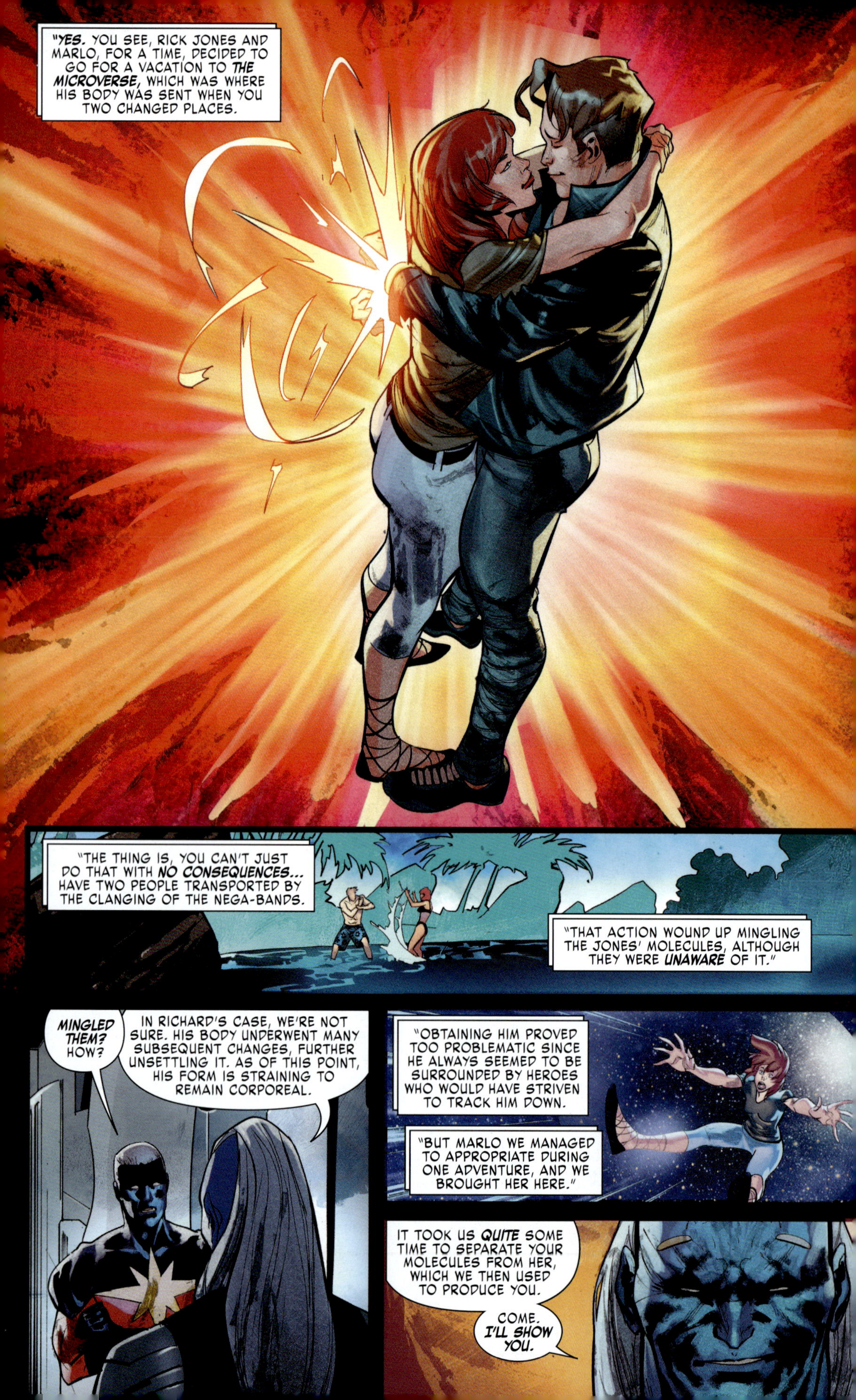
"YES. YOU SEE, RICK JONES AND MARLO, FOR A TIME, DECIDED TO GO FOR A VACATION TO THE MICROVERSE, WHICH WAS WHERE HIS BODY WAS SENT WHEN YOU TWO CHANGED PLACES.
"THE THING IS, YOU CAN'T JUST DO THAT WITH NO CONSEQUENCES... HAVE TWO PEOPLE TRANSPORTED BY THE CLANGING OF THE NEGA-BANDS.
"THAT ACTION WOUND UP MINGLING THE JONES' MOLECULES, ALTHOUGH THEY WERE UNAWARE OF IT."
MINGLED THEM? HOW?
IN RICHARD'S CASE, WE'RE NOT SURE. HIS BODY UNDERWENT MANY SUBSEQUENT CHANGES, FURTHER UNSETTLING IT. AS OF THIS POINT, HIS FORM IS STRAINING TO REMAIN CORPOREAL.
"OBTAINING HIM PROVED TOO PROBLEMATIC SINCE HE ALWAYS SEEMED TO BE SURROUNDED BY HEROES WHO WOULD HAVE STRIVEN TO TRACK HIM DOWN.
"BUT MARLO WE MANAGED TO APPROPRIATE DURING ONE ADVENTURE, AND WE BROUGHT HER HERE."
IT TOOK US QUITE SOME TIME TO SEPARATE YOUR MOLECULES FROM HER, WHICH WE THEN USED TO PRODUCE YOU.
COME. I'LL SHOW YOU.

UHH... WHAT...?
WHAT?!
WE'RE... THIS IS A QUINJET!
YES.
WHERE DID YOU GET A QUINJET?!
FROM THE AVENGERS.
HE AVENGERS OANED YOU A QUINJET?
YOU STOLE A QUINJET?
"LOANED" MIGHT NOT BE THE RIGHT WORD.
THAT'S SOMEWHAT CLOSER TO THE TRUTH, YES.
I NEED A DRINK.
THEY ONLY HAVE SODA-COLA ON THIS VEHICLE.
RIGHT, BECAUSE THEY TRY TO KEEP ALCOHOL AWAY FROM TONY. A COLA SOUNDS FINE.
THANKS. WHY THE HELL DID YOU KNOCK ME OUT?
BECAUSE YOU WEREN'T GOING TO COME WILLINGLY.

HOW ABOUT NEXT TIME YOU GIVE A GUY A COUPLE OF SECONDS TO CONSIDER WHAT YOU'RE SAYING AND MAYBE, Y'KNOW, **CHANGE HIS MIND?**
AND DID YOU? CHANGE YOUR MIND?
I GUESS. ALTHOUGH MY LIFE IS SUCH A FREAKING MESS...
...I DON'T KNOW WHY I EVEN **CARE** ANYMORE.
Y'KNOW, I **DIED.** FROM A **FIRING SQUAD.** AND PART OF ME...
PART OF ME WAS RELIEVED. I THOUGHT, "FINALLY. NO MORE GUILT. NO MORE INSANITY. I'M DONE. I'M JUST **DONE.**"
BUT NO. I FREAKING CAME BACK TO LIFE.
RICK...YOU GOT A **SECOND CHANCE.** THAT'S FANTASTIC.
IS IT? "REST IN PEACE." I COULD USE SOME PEACE, Y'KNOW? I--
AW **C'MON...** HERE WE GO **AGAIN...**
TELL GENIS I'M SORRY...

THERE SHE IS.
WHY DO YOU HAVE HER CONTAINED? FOR THAT MATTER...
...WHY DO YOU EVEN STILL HAVE HER HERE AT ALL? SHE'S SERVED HER PURPOSE.
WELL, THAT'S A BIT MORE COMPLICATED. I'M AFRAID YOU'RE NOT AUTHORIZED TO HEAR IT.
REN-VARR, I CAN'T SAY I APPRECIATE YOUR--
SHE'S AWAKE!
REN-VARR, GET HER OUTTA THERE!
IT'S NOT THAT SIMPLE. SHE--
GENIS? WHAT'S WR--?
YOU'RE NEEDED ELSEWHERE.

RICK, YOU CAN FIGHT THIS!
MAYBE... I'M SICK OF FIGHTING... MAYBE I'M...
...DONE...
HUH?
RICK, WE DON'T HAVE MUCH TIME...
THE HELL--?!
GENIS! WHERE ARE WE--?!
I'M REASONABLY SURE THIS IS THE MICROVERSE.
WAIT...YEAH... I REMEMBER THIS. MARLO AND I CAME TO THIS BEACH. HOW DID--?
THERE'S NO TIME TO EXPLAIN. RICK... YOU'RE DYING. YOU NEED TO STOP.

WHY? WHY SHOULD I?
MAYBE IT'LL TAKE THIS TIME. IF I'M LUCKY...
IF YOU'RE LUCKY?
RICK JONES...YOU ARE THE LUCKIEST INDIVIDUAL I'VE EVER KNOWN.
SUPER HEROES ATTENDED YOUR WEDDING! SUPER HEROES CONSIDER YOU ONE OF THEIR OWN.
YEAH? SO?
RICK... SUPER HEROES ARE THE BEST HUMANITY HAS TO OFFER.
THEY SELFLESSLY RISK THEIR LIVES IN ORDER TO HELP OTHERS, FOR NO PAY OR REWARD, AND OFTEN DESPITE TERRIBLE PERSONAL HARDSHIPS.
AND THEY CONSIDER YOU ONE OF THEIR OWN. THEY ALWAYS HAVE.
SO WHAT DOES THAT MEAN, GENIS?
IT MEANS THEY SEE THINGS IN YOU THAT YOU NEED TO RECOGNIZE. THINK OF THAT...
...AND THINK OF MARLO.
MARLO? MARLO'S DISAPPEARED...
NO, SHE'S ON NEW HALA. I'M STARING RIGHT AT HER.
WHAT?!

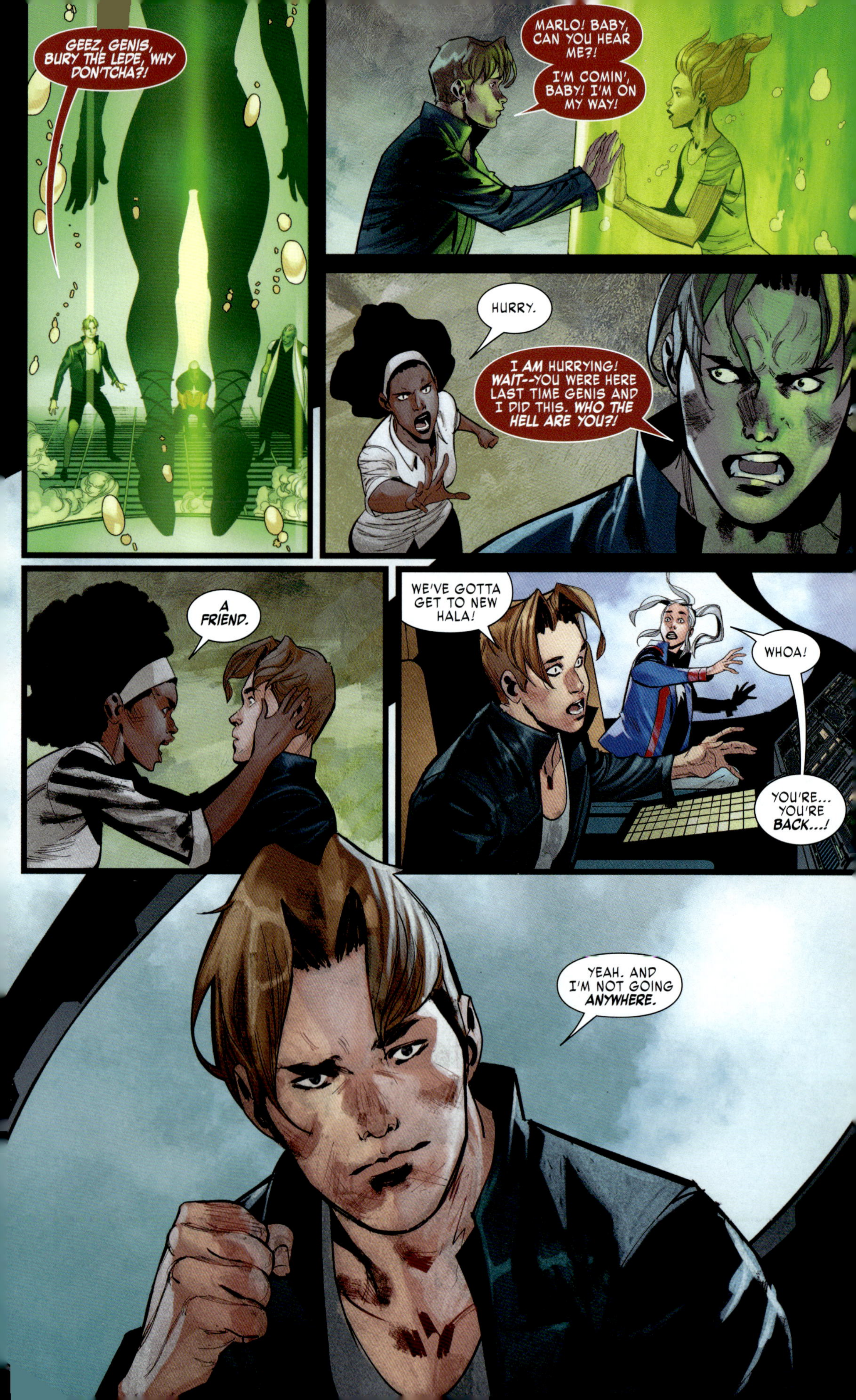
GEEZ, GENIS, BURY THE LEDE, WHY DON'TCHA?!
MARLO! BABY, CAN YOU HEAR ME?!
I'M COMIN', BABY! I'M ON MY WAY!
HURRY.
I AM HURRYING! WAIT--YOU WERE HERE LAST TIME GENIS AND I DID THIS. WHO THE HELL ARE YOU?!
A FRIEND.
WE'VE GOTTA GET TO NEW HALA!
WHOA!
YOU'RE... YOU'RE BACK...!
YEAH. AND I'M NOT GOING ANYWHERE.

PUT HER BACK UNDER! NOW!!!
UHHH...
LET HER OUT OF THERE! NOW!
I'M AFRAID NOT.
I'M AFRAID SO!
NO, DON'T! I'M WARNING Y--
SHHHWAAAAM

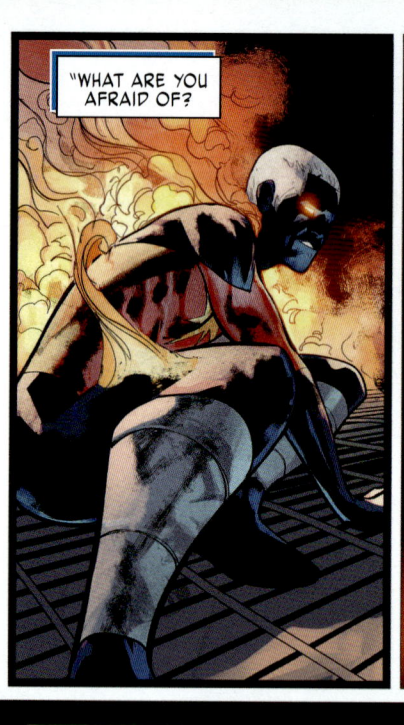

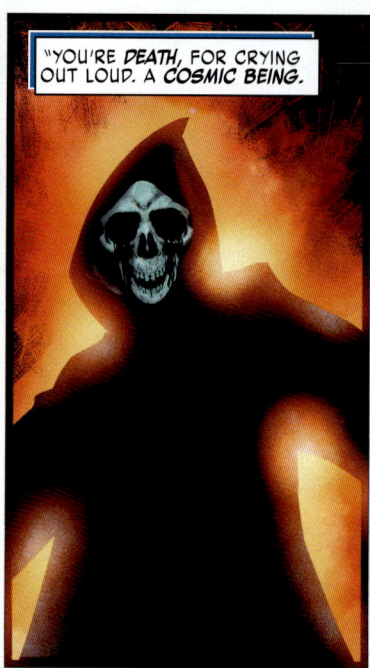

"WHAT ARE YOU AFRAID OF?

"YOU'RE *DEATH*, FOR CRYING OUT LOUD. A *COSMIC* BEING.

"WHAT COULD POSSIBLY SCARE YOU?

"WELL?"

HALVACENTER... THEN...

THE *SUPREME INTELLIGENCE*, IF YOU MUST KNOW.

THE SUPREME INTELLIGENCE? *WHY?*

HE FEARS HIS DEATH.

HE HAS BEEN RUNNING FUTURE SCENARIOS AND SEEMS TO BELIEVE HIS DEATH IS INEVITABLE.

AND HE BELIEVES IF HE CAN *CONTROL* DEATH, HE CAN *PREVENT* THAT?

YES.

WHOA!
SOMETHING SHOOK THE BUILDING!
ARE WE ON A FAULT LINE--?
SOMETHING OR SOMEONE?
SOMETHING IS COMING.
BOTH, I THINK.
MILADY DEATH!

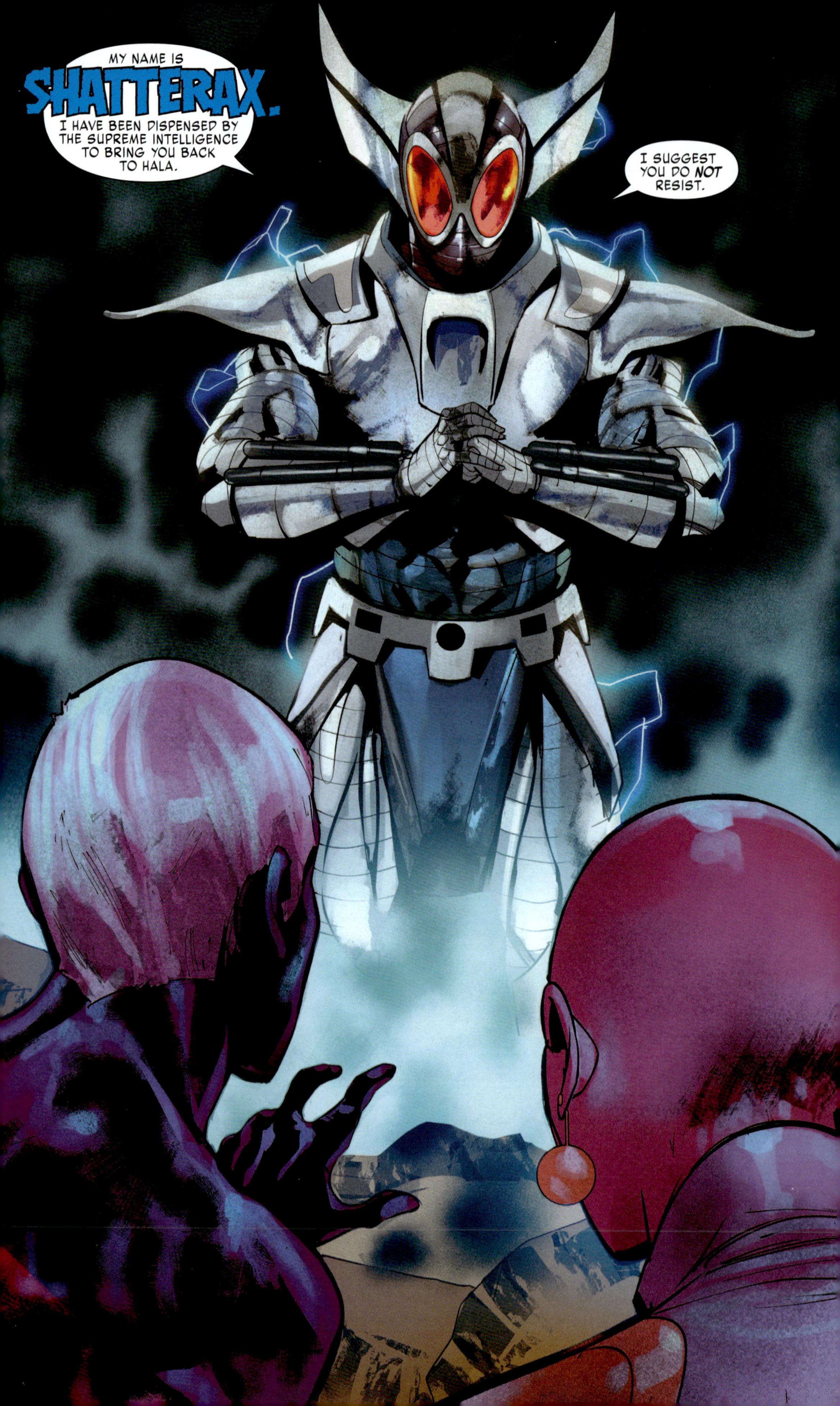
MY NAME IS
SHATTERAX.
I HAVE BEEN DISPENSED BY THE SUPREME INTELLIGENCE TO BRING YOU BACK TO HALA.
I SUGGEST YOU DO NOT RESIST.

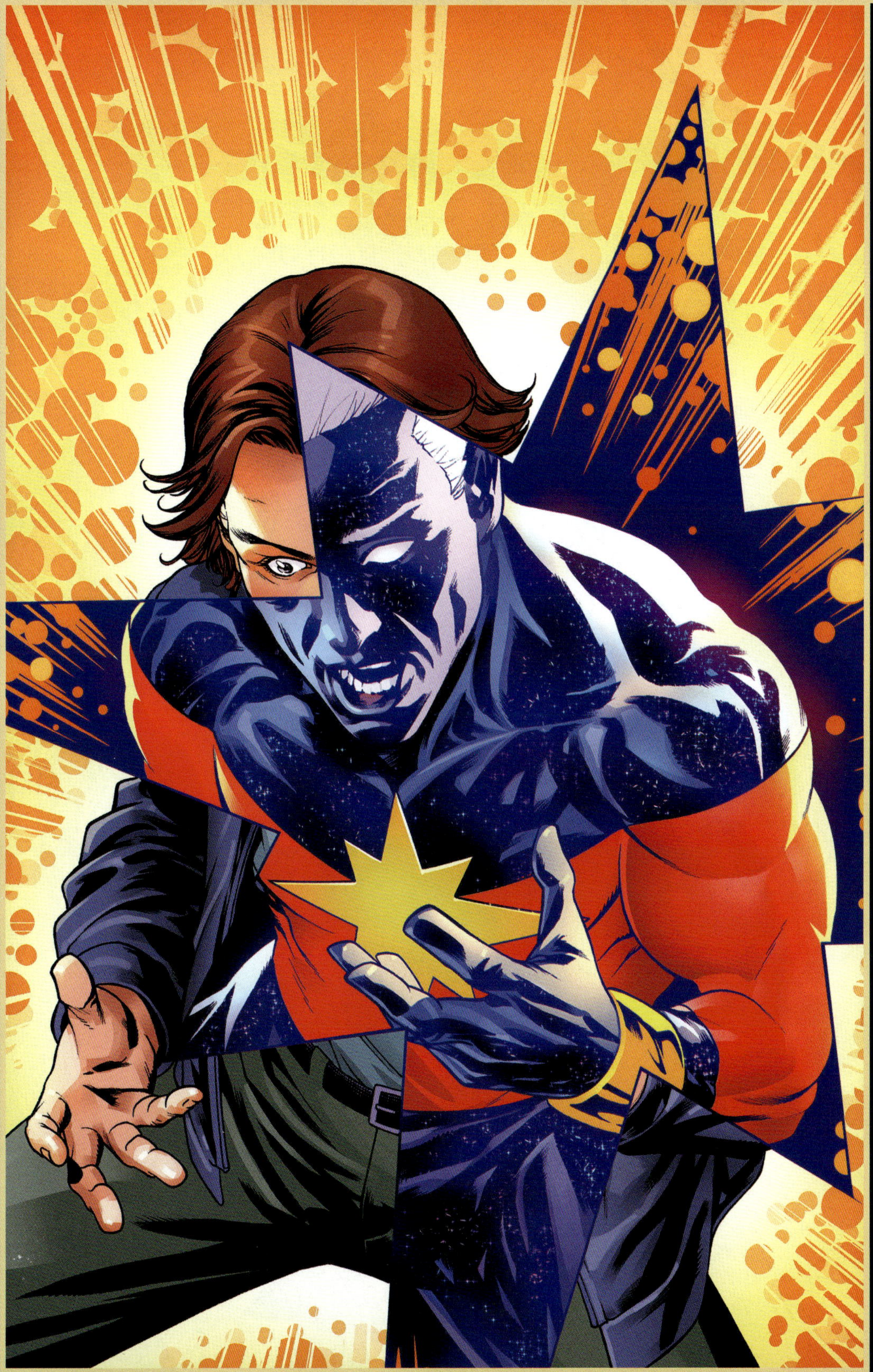

4

HALVACENTER. THEN...
BACK OFF, ROCO-BAI!
YOU... KNOW MY REAL NAME?
I WOULDN'T EXACTLY BE COSMICALLY AWARE IF I DIDN'T!

WELL, I HAVE NO IDEA WHO YOU ARE!
THEY CALL ME CAPTAIN MARVEL...
WHAT? NO, CAPTAIN MARVEL IS A FEMALE TERRAN.*
IT'S COMPLICATED.
*EDITOR'S NOTE: AT THIS POINT IN TIME, HE ACTUALLY MEANS MONICA RAMBEAU, NOT CAROL DANVERS! --DIFFERENTIATING DANNY
FORTUNATELY ENOUGH, I DON'T CARE, SO YOU NEEDN'T EXPLAIN IT.
ALL I KNOW IS THAT THE SUPREME INTELLIGENCE HAS BUSINESS WITH THE ONE CALLED DEATH, AND IT'S MY RESPONSIBILITY TO BRING HER TO HIM.
AND I TAKE MY RESPONSIBILITY...
...VERY SERIOUSLY!

THERE. THAT WASN'T MUCH OF A CHORE.
WHOEVER THIS SO-CALLED "CAPTAIN MARVEL" IS, HE DIDN'T PROVIDE MUCH OF A FI--
FWAZAAAAM
"FIGHT," I BELIEVE, IS THE WORD YOU WERE SEARCHING FOR.

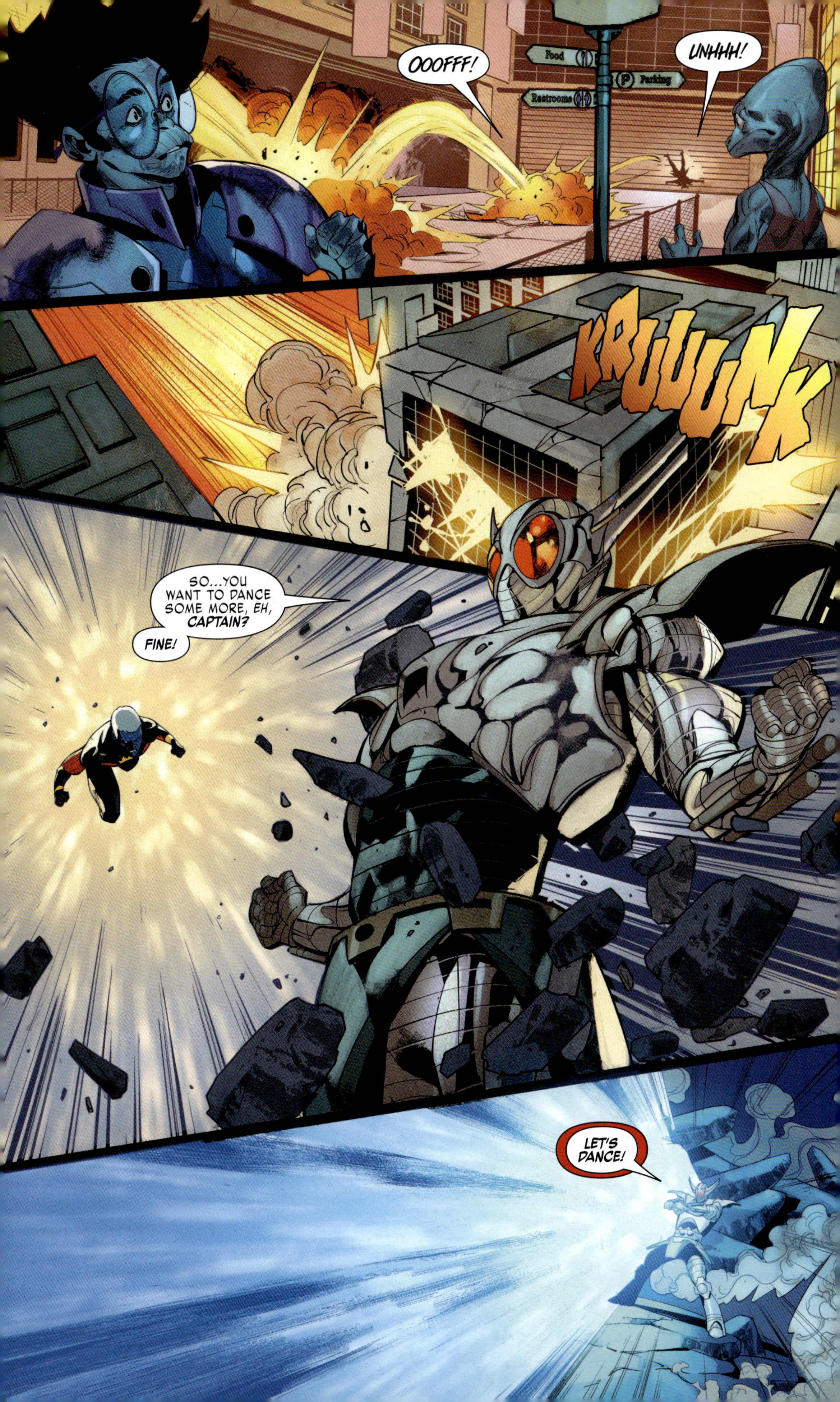
OOOFFF!
Food
Parking
Restrooms
UNHHH!
KRUUUNK
SO...YOU WANT TO DANCE SOME MORE, EH, CAPTAIN?
FINE!
LET'S DANCE!

UNFFFFF!
IS THAT... ALL YOU'VE GOT... SHATTERAX?
I'M AFRAID...
...YOU'LL NEED...
...MORE... THAN THAT!

RAKATHAM
IF A TACTIC ISN'T WORKING, SIMPLY CHANGE TACTICS. THAT'S JUST BASIC WARFARE.
YOUR SHIELDS MAY RESIST MY FORCE BEAMS, BUT THE GROUND YOU WERE STANDING ON? NOT SO MUCH!
HA!
WAM
WAM
WAM
WAM

COME ON! WE'VE GOT TO GET OUT OF HERE!
WHY? SO HE CAN PURSUE ME ALL ACROSS HALVACENTER?
I'M TIRED OF RUNNING.
I DO IT ALL THE TIME. IT'S FUN!
YOU'RE SWEET TO CARE ABOUT ME, MARLO.
WELL, OF COURSE I CARE! YOU HAVE THE HARDEST JOB IN THE UNIVERSE, DEATH.
YOU FEEL...SORRY FOR ME?
MOST BEINGS FEAR ME.
I GUESS I DID...AT FIRST. BUT I'VE HAD TIME TO THINK ABOUT IT.
AND NOW I...
...I FIGURE MAYBE YOU CAN USE A FRIEND.
I CAN.

THERE. THAT SEEMS TO HAVE DISPOSED OF HIM.
THE...THE OPERATIVE WORD...IS...
..."SEEMS"...
OOOOOFF!

WE COULD HAVE BEEN FRIENDS, ALLIES!
FOUGHT TOGETHER ON BEHALF OF THE KREE!
BUT NO! YOU HAVE TO GO WHEREVER THE INTELLIGENCE SENDS YOU, OBEY HIS INSTRUCTIONS BLINDLY!
OBVIOUSLY! BECAUSE THAT'S WHAT SOLDIERS DO!
SWAKAAAM
THWUUUUD
IF YOU TRULY BELIEVE WE COULD BE ALLIES, THEN GIVE UP, "CAPTAIN."
SURRENDER NOW!
NEVER!

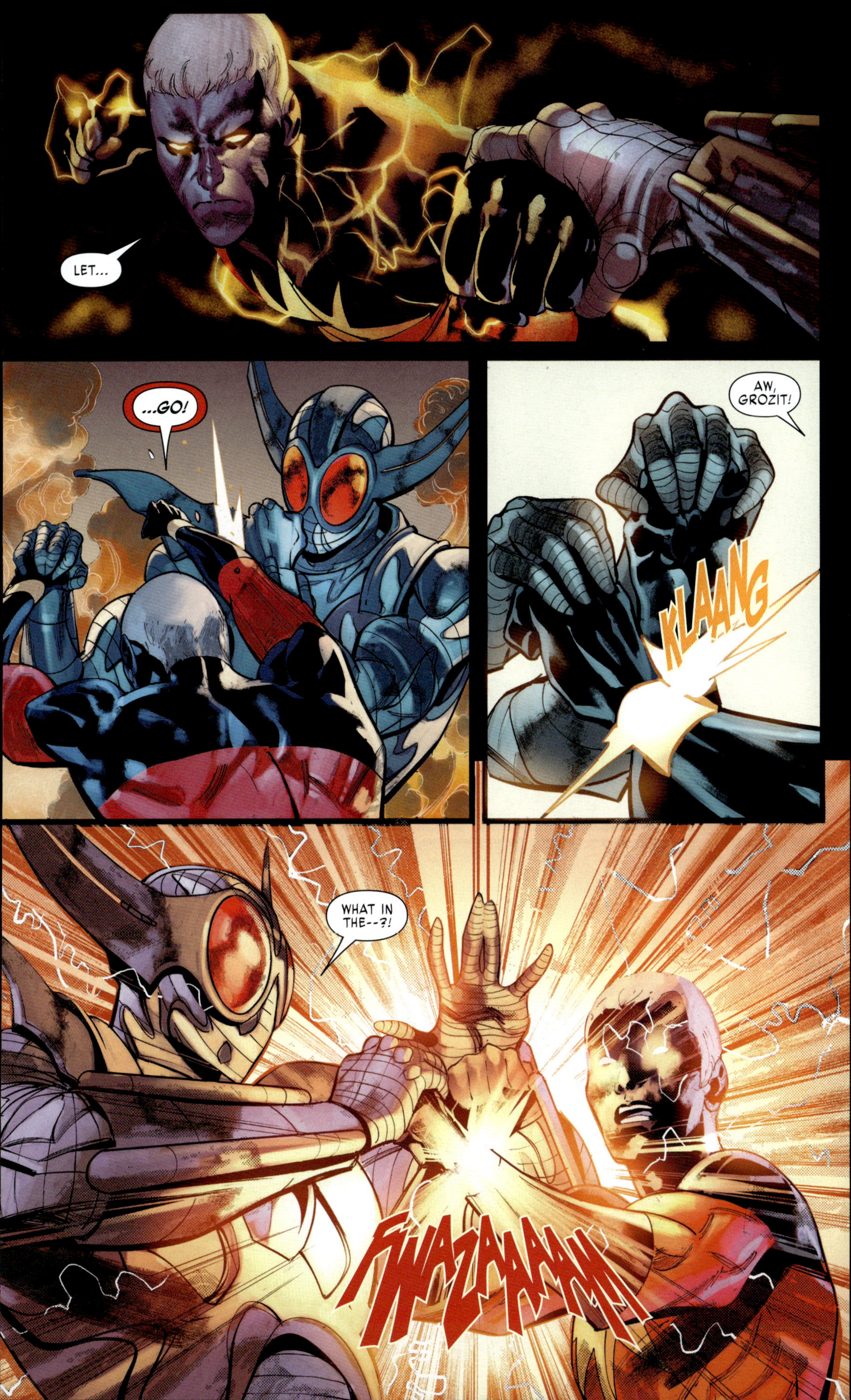
LET...
...GO!
AW, GROZIT!
KLAANG
WHAT IN THE--?!
FWAZAAAAM

UH...
HI.
HELLO.
SO, UH, HOW ABOUT YOU PUT ME DOWN AND WE WORK THIS WHOLE THING--?
KRAK
I COULD JUST KILL HIM NOW, I SUPPOSE.
HE CERTAINLY HAS BEEN ENOUGH OF A HASSLE.
BUT NO. HE IS A WARRIOR AT HEART.
ONE DOESN'T DISPOSE OF A WARRIOR IN HIS SLEEP. IT IS... UNWORTHY.
FAREWELL, "CAPTAIN." YOU CERTAINLY GAVE ME MORE OF A CHALLENGE THAN THE PREVIOUS HERO OF THAT NAME.

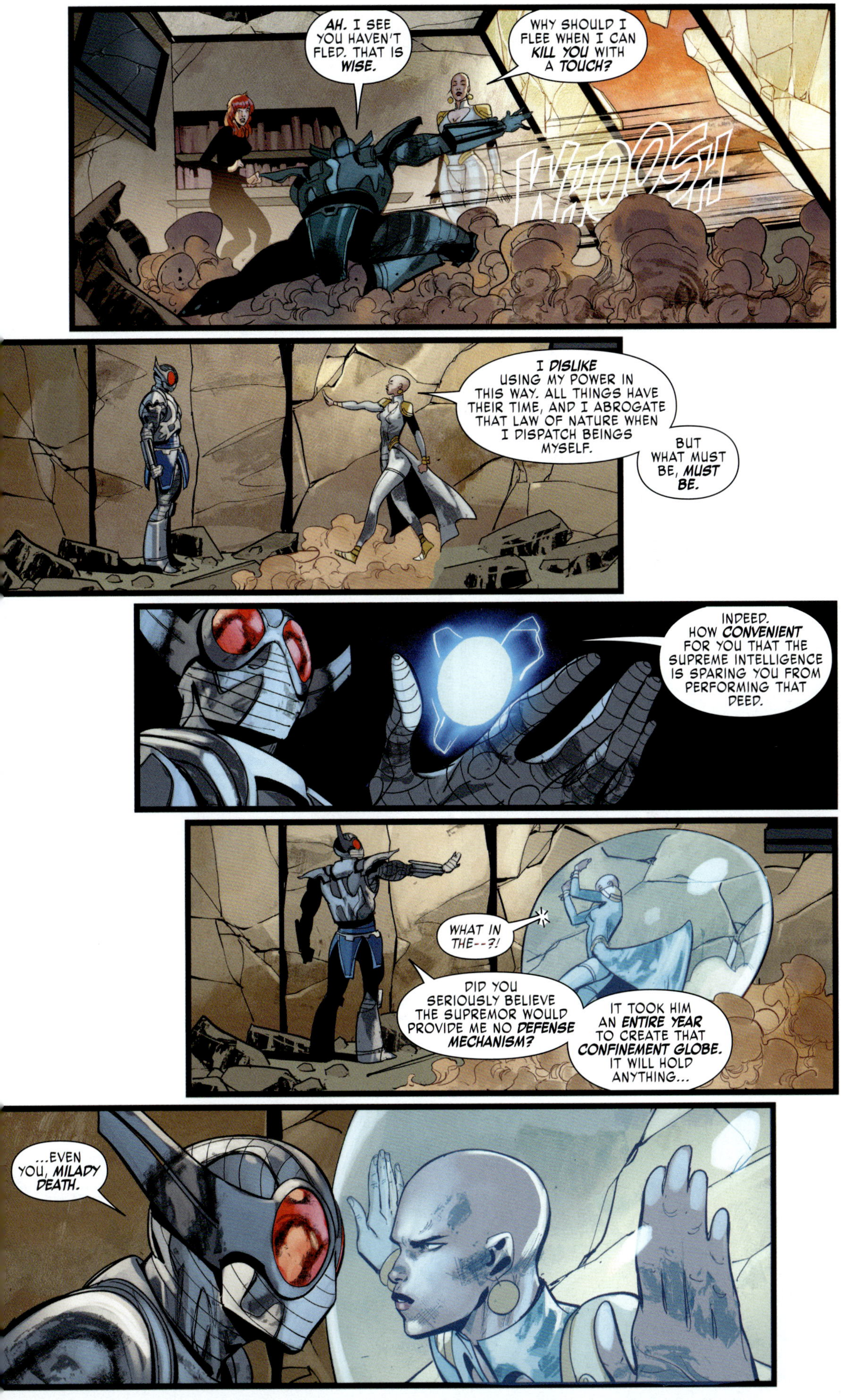
AH. I SEE YOU HAVEN'T FLED. THAT IS WISE.
WHY SHOULD I FLEE WHEN I CAN KILL YOU WITH A TOUCH?
WHOOSH
I DISLIKE USING MY POWER IN THIS WAY. ALL THINGS HAVE THEIR TIME, AND I ABROGATE THAT LAW OF NATURE WHEN I DISPATCH BEINGS MYSELF.
BUT WHAT MUST BE, MUST BE.
INDEED. HOW CONVENIENT FOR YOU THAT THE SUPREME INTELLIGENCE IS SPARING YOU FROM PERFORMING THAT DEED.
WHAT IN THE--?!
DID YOU SERIOUSLY BELIEVE THE SUPREMOR WOULD PROVIDE ME NO DEFENSE MECHANISM?
IT TOOK HIM AN ENTIRE YEAR TO CREATE THAT CONFINEMENT GLOBE. IT WILL HOLD ANYTHING...
...EVEN YOU, MILADY DEATH.

LET HER GO. NOW.
A WEAPON. BY ALL MEANS, FIRE IT, CHILD. IT WILL BE AMUSING.
DON'T DO IT, MARLO. IT WILL RICOCHET OFF HIM AND STRIKE YOU. YOU CAN'T WITHSTAND THE BLAST.
SO I JUST...WHAT? LET HIM TAKE YOU?
YOU HAVE NO CHOICE. NO FORCE IN THE UNIVERSE CAN PENETRATE THAT FIELD.
A PITY YOU DON'T HAVE A SECOND ONE.
EH?
GOODBYE.
SNAP
I SHOULD HAVE KNOWN.
KNOWN WHAT?! WHO THE HELL IS THIS?!

FASTER, GEN! WHO KNOWS HOW LONG WE WERE UNCONSCIOUS?!
SEVEN MINUTES, THIRTY-NINE SECONDS, RICK.
DO YOU KNOW HOW FAR HE COULD HAVE GOTTEN IN THAT TIME?!
FOUR HUNDRED FIFTY-NINE SECONDS AWAY.
NOT HELPING!
GENIS! OH, THANK GOD. I DIDN'T KNOW WHAT HE'D DONE TO YOU.
I'M FINE. ARE YOU OKAY?
GENIS? WHAT ARE YOU DOING HERE?
DON'T YOU REMEMBER?
REMEMBER WHAT?
WHERE'S SHATTERAX?
THAT BIG GUY WHO BUSTED IN HERE?
YES, OF COURSE!
WELL, HE CAME BACK HERE AND THEN... AND THEN...
AND THEN WHAT?
I...I DON'T REMEMBER.

NEW HALA. NOW...
REN-VARR, YOU HAVE AN EARTH BEING CONFINED IN THERE. LET HER GO.
SHE MAY LOOK LIKE AN EARTH BEING, BUT SHE IS FAR MORE THAN THAT.
I'M SORRY, BUT THAT'S ALL I'M AUTHORIZED TO S--
I'M AUTHORIZING YOU TO SAY MORE.
GUARDS!
I WOULDN'T.
GUARDS! STOP HIM!
DROP HIM, GENIS! NOW!
I THINK I'D RATHER DROP YOU.
FWZAAAK

I'VE LOST CONTACT WITH GENIS! CAN'T YOU MAKE THIS JET GO ANY FASTER, PHYLA?!
WE'RE MOVING AT THE VESSEL'S MAXIMUM SPEED.
CAN YOU GO ANY FASTER?
YOU MEAN I, MYSELF?
YEAH.
I DON'T NEED TO BE LIMITED TO FTL. ON MY OWN, I CAN WARP SPACE.
CREATE A SORT OF LOCALIZED WORMHOLE.
GREAT! LET'S DO THAT!
THE SHIP WON'T SURVIVE.
CAN YOU GIVE ME A RIDE?
I DON'T KNOW IF THE NEGA-BANDS WILL ENABLE YOU TO HANDLE DEEP SPACE.
WELL, LET'S FIND OUT. WORST THAT HAPPENS IS I DIE.
ALL RIGHT. LET'S SET THE SHIP TO RETURN AUTOMATICALLY AND--
YOU OKAY?
AWEEEEESOME...

ZWAOWWW
NOW! TELL ME WHAT--!
SSSSSS
KOFF
QUICKLY! DISPOSE OF HIM WHILE HE'S--
HOW ABOUT YOU ANSWER HIS QUESTION?
WHAT?! WHAT ARE YOU...?

WELL, SINCE YOU ASKED...
THE NAME'S JAZINDA, AND I'M A SKRULL.
I HEAR WE'RE ALLIES NOW, BUT SORRY, I'M KINDA OLD SCHOOL.
NOW... ANSWER HIS QUESTION...
...OR I'M GOING TO DECORATE THIS WALL WITH YOUR BRAINS IN FIVE SECONDS.
THAT WON'T BE NECESSARY, JAZINDA. IT SHOULD BE OBVIOUS.
SHE MAY LOOK LIKE MARLO, BUT WE BOTH KNOW WHO SHE IS.
SHE'S THE REASON YOU BROUGHT ME HERE.
MY GOD.
CLOSE.
DEATH.
THERE YOU GO.

ARE YOU OUT OF YOUR MIND, REN-VARR?
DO YOU HAVE ANY IDEA OF THE POWER YOU'VE GOT TRAPPED IN THERE?
OF COURSE I DO! I HAVE THE POWER TO UNDO THE ANNIHILATION OF THE KREE RACE!
WE DON'T HAVE TO CONTENT OURSELVES WITH THE ENDLESS CLONING OF SAMPLES FROM ANCIENT RECORDS! WHY REBUILD THE KREE...
...WHEN, WITH A SNAP OF HER FINGERS, SHE CAN BRING THEM ALL BACK TO LIFE!
AND WHAT OF YOU? YOU'VE SUFFERED YOUR OWN LOSSES...INCLUDING YOUR REVERED FATHER.
IMAGINE HER TRULY RETURNING HIM WITH THE MEREST BLINK OF HER EYES.
THINK OF ALL THE GOOD YOU CAN DO. YOU'D BE REVERED FOR YOUR SUCCESS IF YOU CAN MAKE HER COOPERATE.
YOU'LL BE A GOD.

GENIS...
SHUT UP.
O...OKAY, BUT...
NOT YOU, JAZINDA.
SHUT UP, REN-VARR.
YOU'RE GOING TO RELEASE HER IMMEDIATELY, OR THIS IS GOING TO GET VERY UGLY, VERY QUICKLY.
YOU HAVE NO IDEA HOW UGLY AND HOW QUICKLY.
OH NO.
ROUND TWO, GENIS.
AND THIS TIME, YOU WON'T BE ABLE TO TRICK YOUR WAY OUT OF DEFEAT.

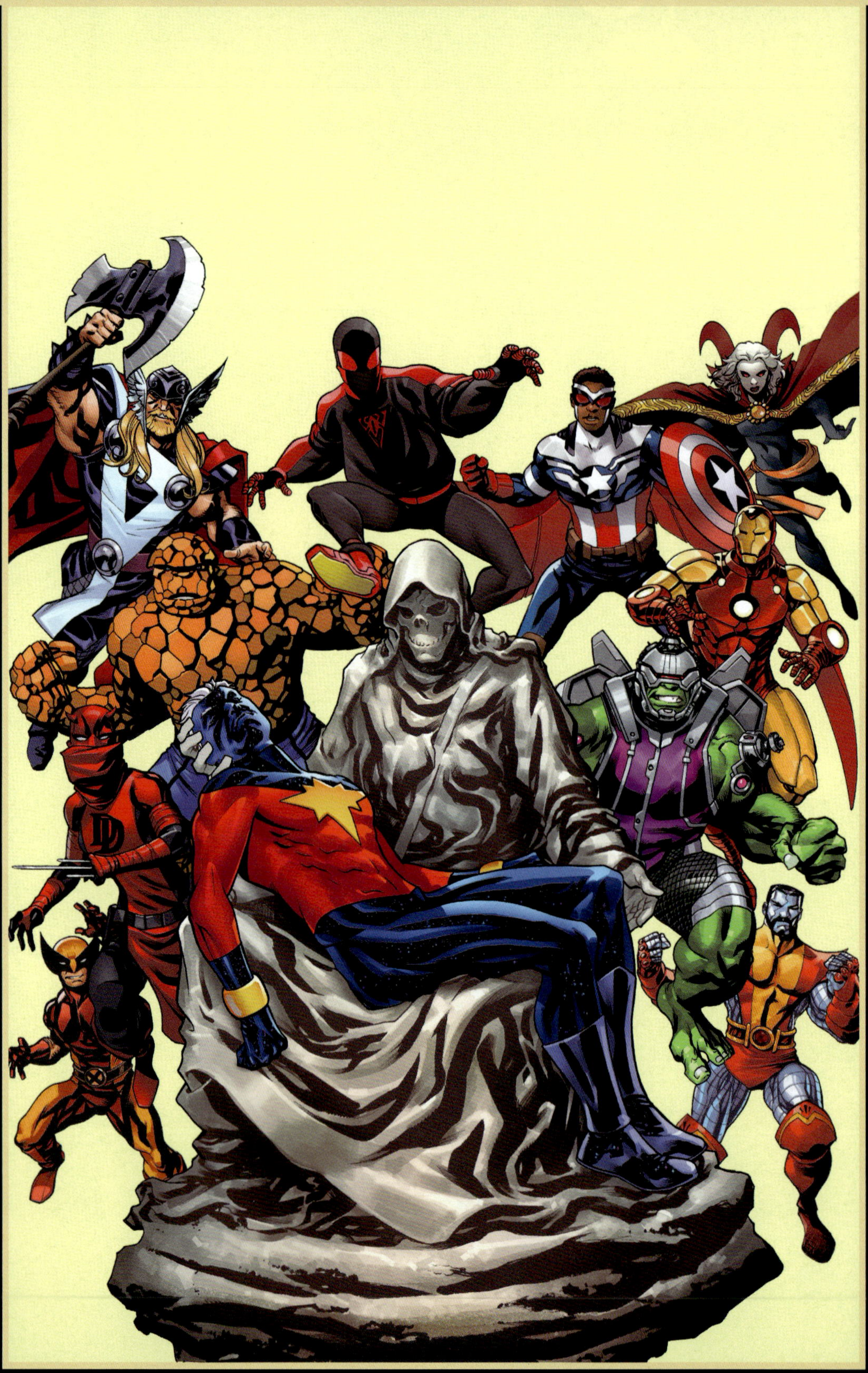

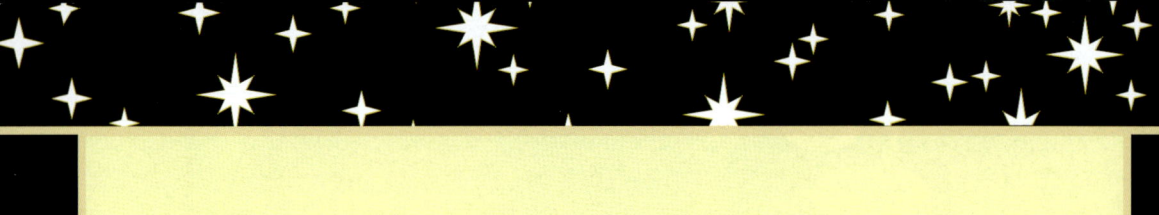

NEW HALA. NOW.
A UNIVERSAL WEAPON! YOU'VE UPGRADED, SHATTERAX.
I HAVE, INDEED.
YOU BARELY SURVIVED THE LAST TIME WE BATTLED, GENIS. THIS TIME...
...I DON'T EXPECT YOU TO LAST MORE THAN A COUPLE OF SECONDS!
BWAZAAAAAK

KRUUUNCH
SHWAKOWWW
STILL HAVE SOME **ENERGY** LEFT? SHOULDN'T TAKE LONG TO **DISPOSE** OF THAT.
ALL GUARDS! CONVERGE ON--

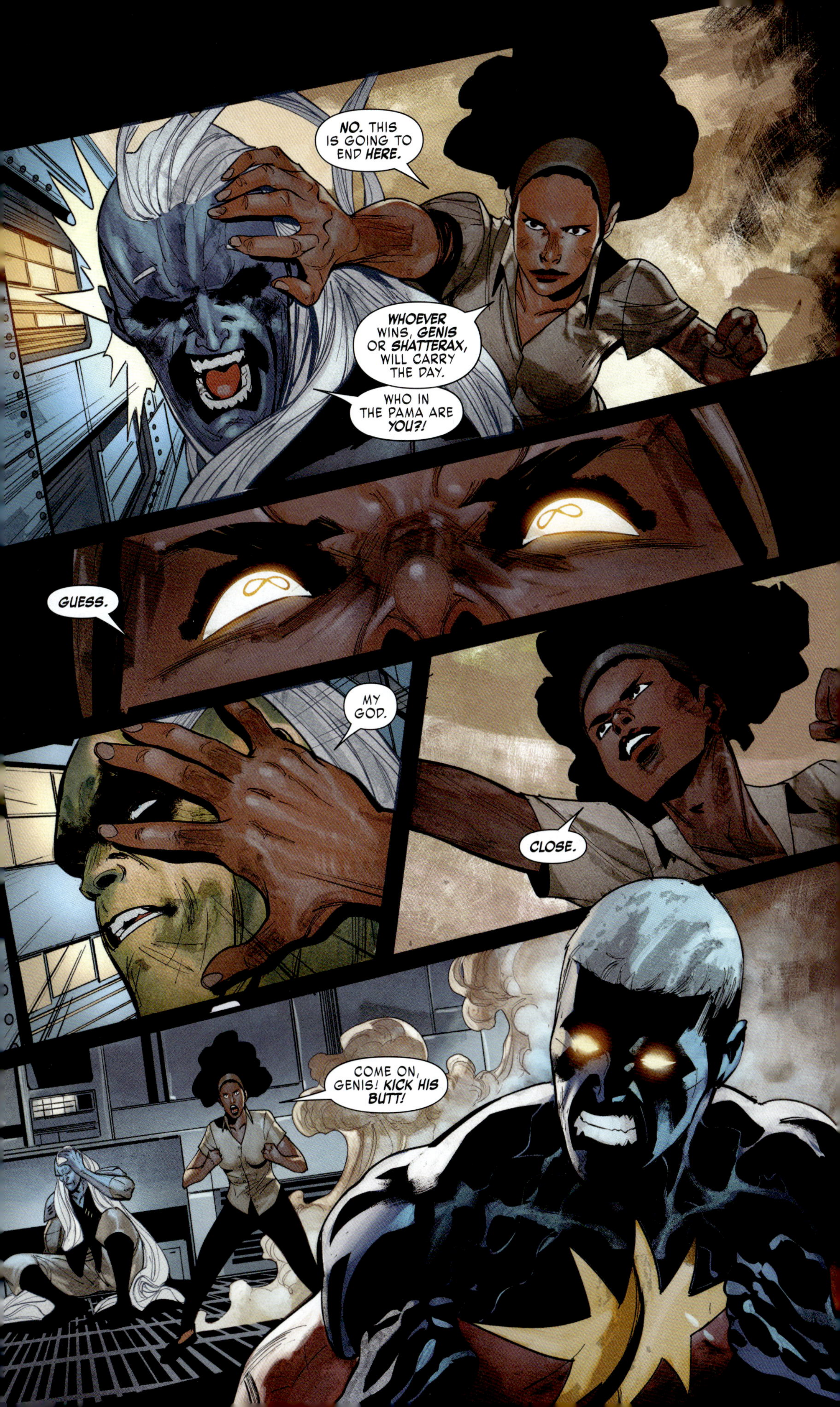

NO. THIS IS GOING TO END HERE.
WHOEVER WINS, GENIS OR SHATTERAX, WILL CARRY THE DAY.
WHO IN THE PAMA ARE YOU?!
GUESS.
MY GOD.
CLOSE.
COME ON, GENIS! KICK HIS BUTT!

WELL, THE NEGA-BANDS ARE CLEARLY PROTECTING YOU...
DEEP IN SPACE.
NO. SOMETHING'S WRONG.
WHAT--?
I'M STARTING TO MARTY McFLY AGAIN.
I DON'T KNOW WHO THAT IS.
I'M BEGINNING TO FADE OUT AGAIN...
"GENIS MUST BE USING HIS COSMIC ENERGY IN BATTLE, BIG TIME.
"AND HE'S PROBABLY BURNING THROUGH IT, AND HIMSELF, PRETTY DAMNED QUICKLY."
YOU'VE GOTTEN...STRONGER... IN THE PAST YEARS... GENIS...

YOU'RE MISTAKING *MERCY* FOR *WEAKNESS*, SHATTERAX!
I COULD *KILL YOU* WITH A SINGLE BLOW!
BUT I CHOOSE *COMPASSION!*
SOMETHING THAT YOU COULDN'T *POSSIBLY* UNDERSTAND!
YOU MAY HAVE A POINT ABOUT THAT.

KRUNCH
YOU SO-CALLED HEROES. YOU ALL MAKE ME SICK.
YOU FANCY YOURSELVES SO SUPERIOR TO SIMPLE WARRIORS.
YOU'RE SUPERIOR TO NO ONE!
I SEE IT DIFFERENTLY.
SHWAZAKK
IS THAT ALL YOU'VE GOT?

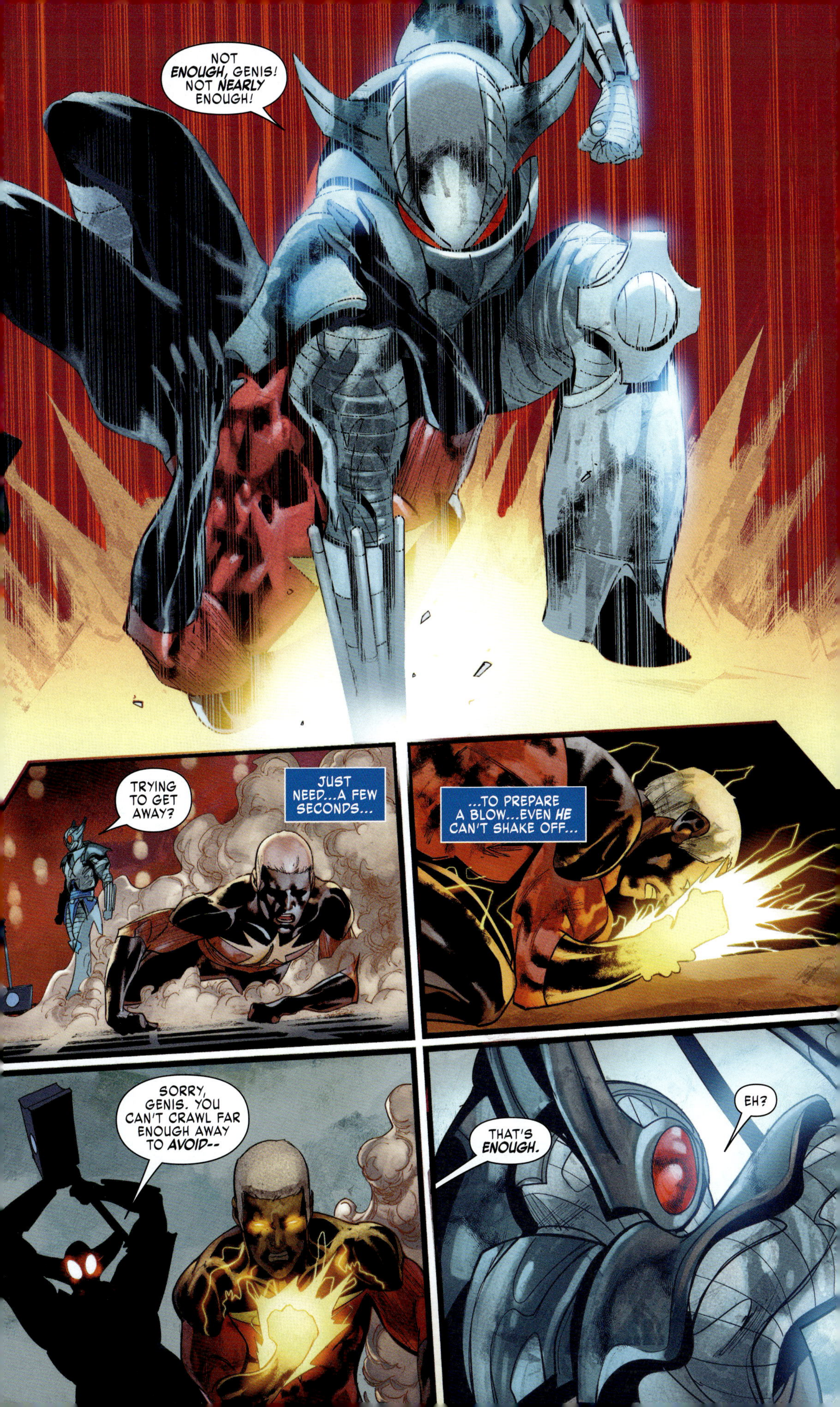
NOT ENOUGH, GENIS! NOT NEARLY ENOUGH!
TRYING TO GET AWAY?
JUST NEED...A FEW SECONDS...
...TO PREPARE A BLOW...EVEN HE CAN'T SHAKE OFF...
SORRY, GENIS. YOU CAN'T CRAWL FAR ENOUGH AWAY TO AVOID--
EH?
THAT'S ENOUGH.

I SAID THAT'S QUITE ENOUGH.
WHAT IN THE--?!
RONAN? RONAN THE ACCUSER!
YOU DARE ADDRESS ME WHILE STANDING, AS IF WE ARE EQUALS?
I...I APOLOGIZE, MY LORD.
GIVE ME YOUR WEAPON.
YES, OF COURSE, I...
WAIT...WHERE IS YOUR UNIVERSAL WEAPON? AND...
...AREN'T YOU DEAD?

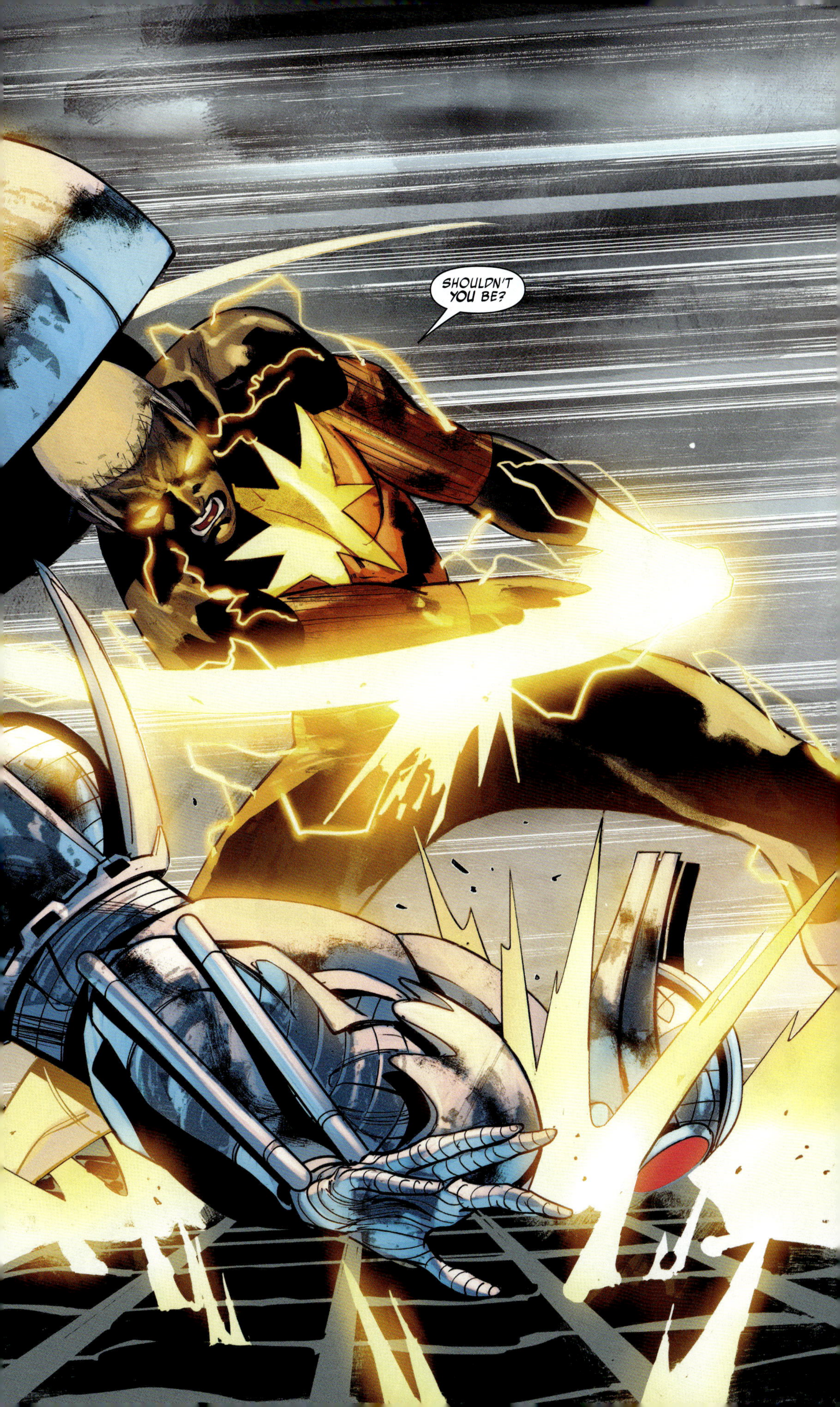
SHOULDN'T YOU BE?

I THINK THAT DID IT, GEN--
STAY BACK, JAZINDA! I'M... I'M OVERLOADING! AND...
AND THIS TIME...I CAN'T TAMP IT BACK DOWN! CLEAR THE AREA BEFORE I EXPLODE!
GEN! HOLD ON!
I'M COMING, BUDDY!

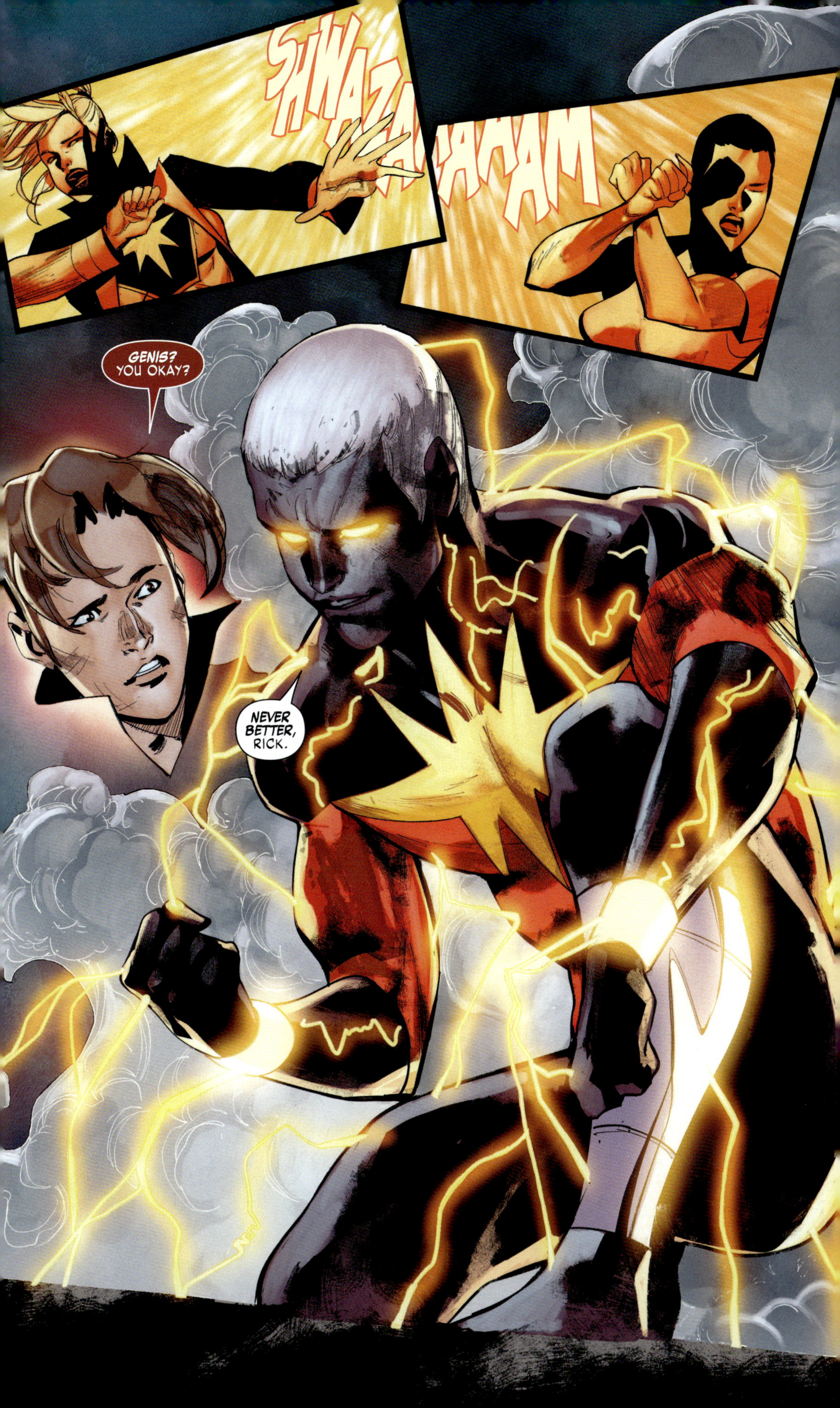
SHWAZAAAAAAM
GENIS? YOU OKAY?
NEVER BETTER, RICK.

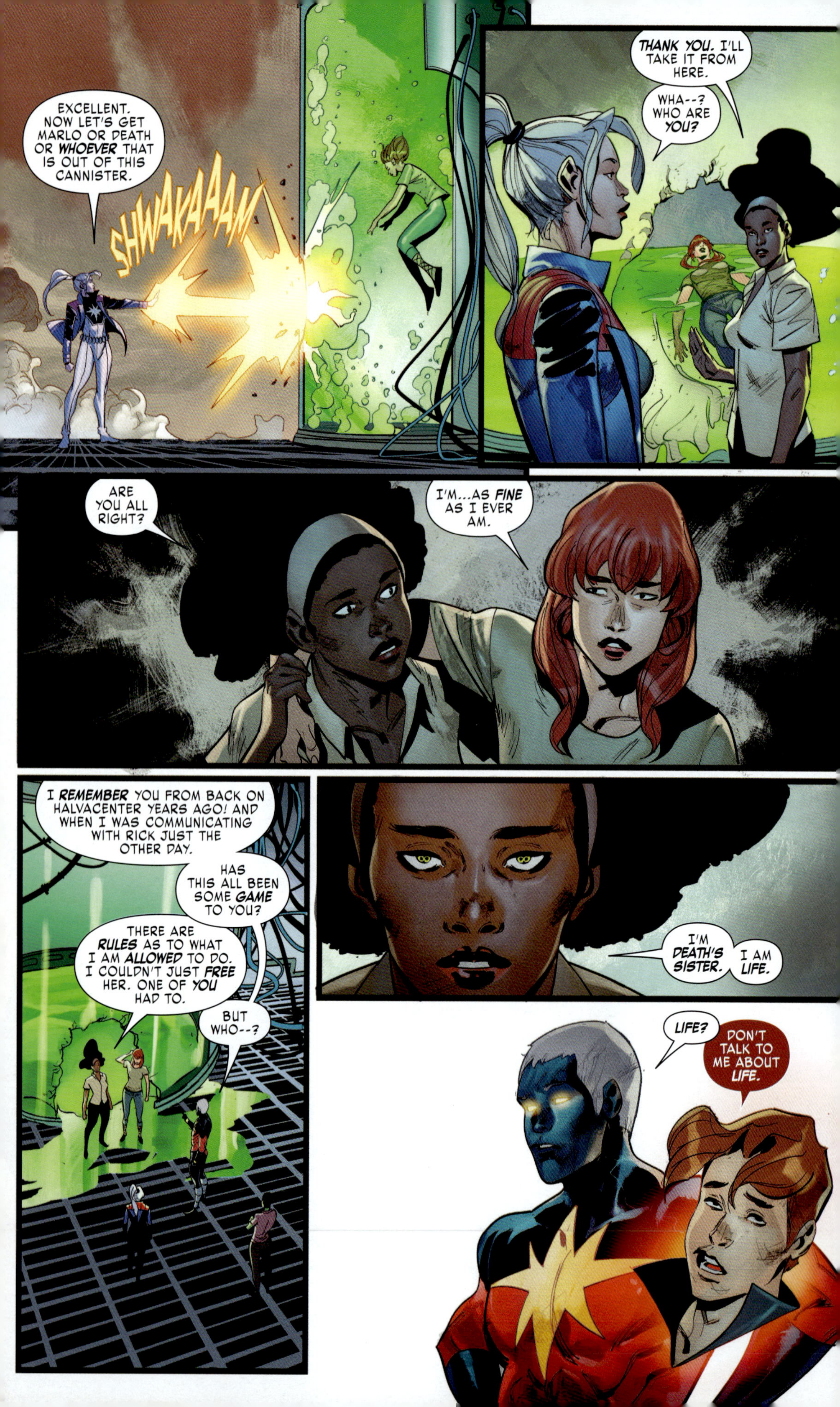
EXCELLENT. NOW LET'S GET MARLO OR DEATH OR WHOEVER THAT IS OUT OF THIS CANNISTER.
SHWAKAAAM
THANK YOU. I'LL TAKE IT FROM HERE.
WHA--? WHO ARE YOU?
ARE YOU ALL RIGHT?
I'M...AS FINE AS I EVER AM.
I REMEMBER YOU FROM BACK ON HALVACENTER YEARS AGO! AND WHEN I WAS COMMUNICATING WITH RICK JUST THE OTHER DAY.
HAS THIS ALL BEEN SOME GAME TO YOU?
THERE ARE RULES AS TO WHAT I AM ALLOWED TO DO. I COULDN'T JUST FREE HER. ONE OF YOU HAD TO.
BUT WHO--?
I'M DEATH'S SISTER.
I AM LIFE.
LIFE?
DON'T TALK TO ME ABOUT LIFE.

LET ME GET THIS STRAIGHT. YOU'RE LIFE... *PERSONIFIED?*
WHY ARE YOU SO *SURPRISED?* IS MY EXISTENCE ANY MORE *DOUBTFUL* THAN THAT OF MY SISTER'S?
COME, SISTER. JOIN US.
THE THREAT IS ENDED.
IT TOOK YOU LONG ENOUGH.
THAT'S ALL YOU HAVE TO SAY? HOW ABOUT "THANK YOU"?
*WHAT*EVER.
GENIS. LET ME OUT. I *GOTTA* TALK TO MARLO.
WHY?
SHE'S *MY WIFE,* FOR GOD'S SAKE! JUST *DO IT!*
SHAZAAAK

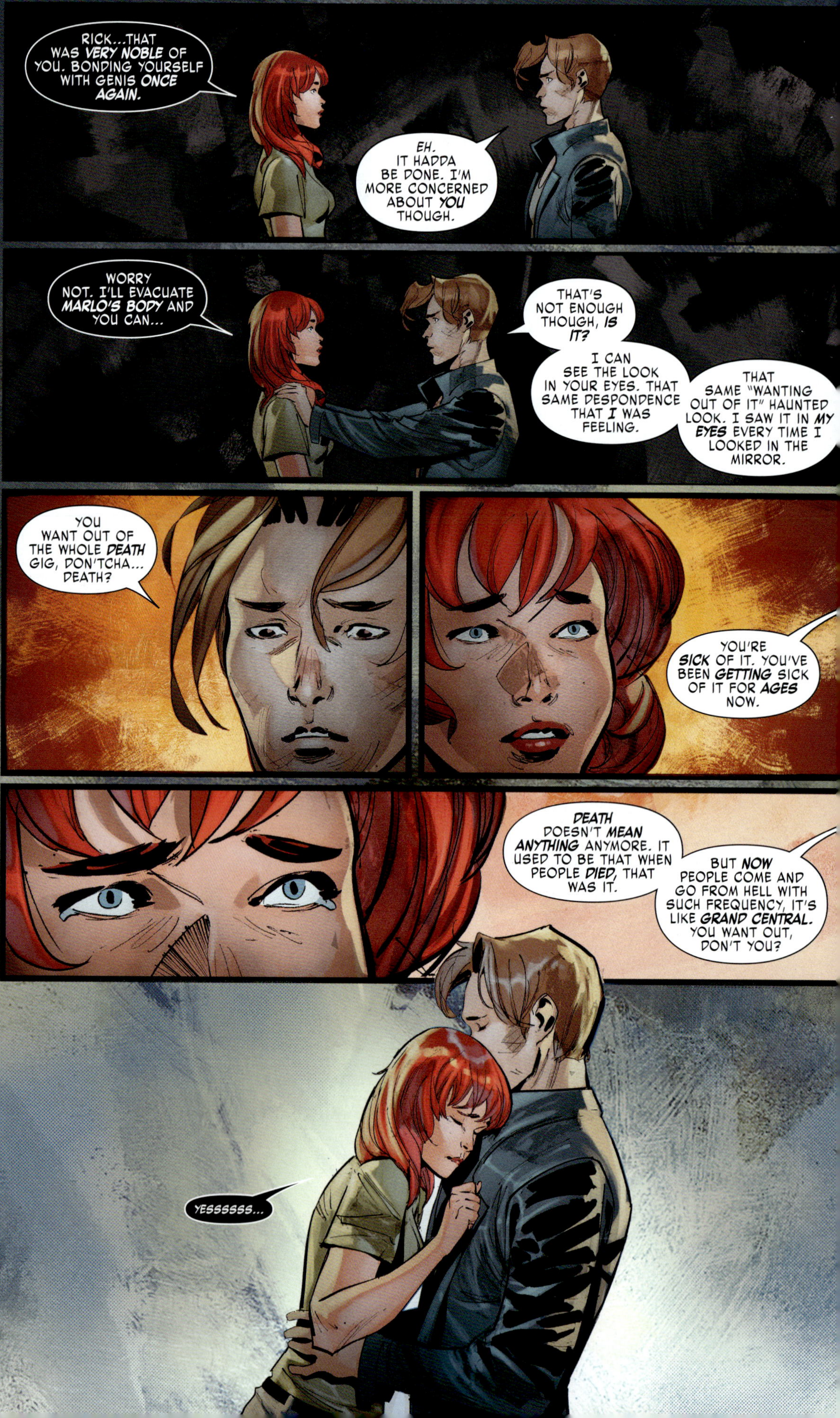

RICK...THAT WAS VERY NOBLE OF YOU. BONDING YOURSELF WITH GENIS ONCE AGAIN.
EH. IT HADDA BE DONE. I'M MORE CONCERNED ABOUT YOU THOUGH.
WORRY NOT. I'LL EVACUATE MARLO'S BODY AND YOU CAN...
THAT'S NOT ENOUGH THOUGH, IS IT?
I CAN SEE THE LOOK IN YOUR EYES. THAT SAME DESPONDENCE THAT I WAS FEELING.
THAT SAME "WANTING OUT OF IT" HAUNTED LOOK. I SAW IT IN MY EYES EVERY TIME I LOOKED IN THE MIRROR.
YOU WANT OUT OF THE WHOLE DEATH GIG, DON'TCHA... DEATH?
YOU'RE SICK OF IT. YOU'VE BEEN GETTING SICK OF IT FOR AGES NOW.
DEATH DOESN'T MEAN ANYTHING ANYMORE. IT USED TO BE THAT WHEN PEOPLE DIED, THAT WAS IT.
BUT NOW PEOPLE COME AND GO FROM HELL WITH SUCH FREQUENCY, IT'S LIKE GRAND CENTRAL. YOU WANT OUT, DON'T YOU?
YESSSSSS...

YOU WANT... OUT...? I...I DON'T UNDERSTAND.
OF COURSE YOU DON'T! EVERYONE CELEBRATES LIFE! BUT THEY FEAR DEATH!
AND I'M JUST EXHAUSTED. HAVING TO OVERSEE EVERYTHING FROM GENOCIDAL WARS TO DISEASES THAT KILL MILLIONS...
IT WASN'T SO BAD WHEN LIFE WAS JUST BEGINNING, BUT NOW EARTH ALONE HAS SEVEN BILLION AND...
...I'VE BEEN LETTING THE REINS SLIP FOR YEARS NOW.
I DON'T WANT TO BE IN CHARGE OF DEATH ANYMORE.
THERE CAN'T BE NOBODY IN CHARGE. SOMEONE MUST BE THE COURT OF LAST RESORT. SOMEONE HAS TO BE RESPONSIBLE.
DEATH...?

"I'LL DO IT."

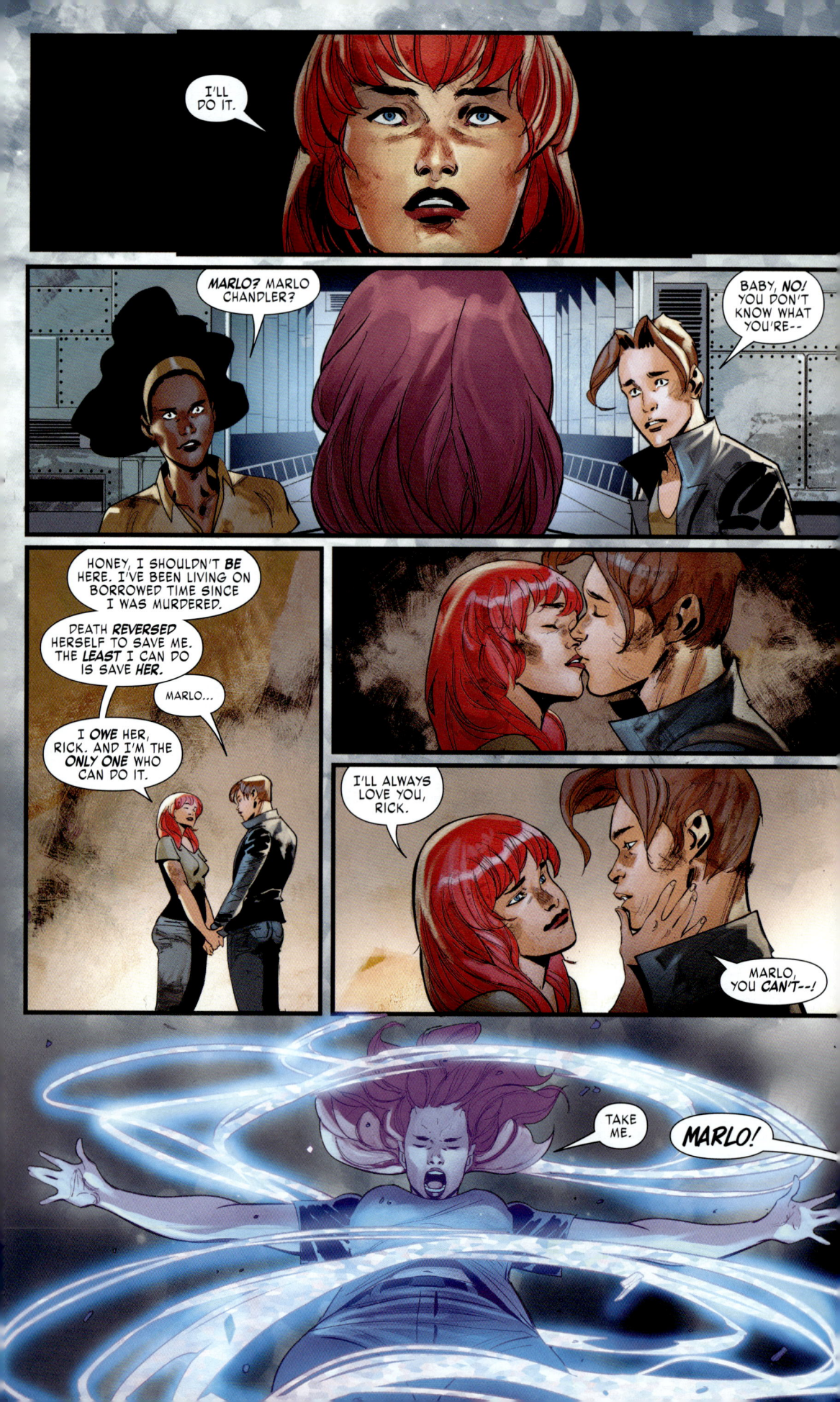

"MARLO? MARLO CHANDLER?"

"BABY, NO! YOU DON'T KNOW WHAT YOU'RE--"

"HONEY, I SHOULDN'T BE HERE. I'VE BEEN LIVING ON BORROWED TIME SINCE I WAS MURDERED.

DEATH REVERSED HERSELF TO SAVE ME. THE LEAST I CAN DO IS SAVE HER."

"MARLO..."

"I OWE HER, RICK. AND I'M THE ONLY ONE WHO CAN DO IT."

"I'LL ALWAYS LOVE YOU, RICK."

"MARLO, YOU CAN'T--!"

"TAKE ME."

"MARLO!"

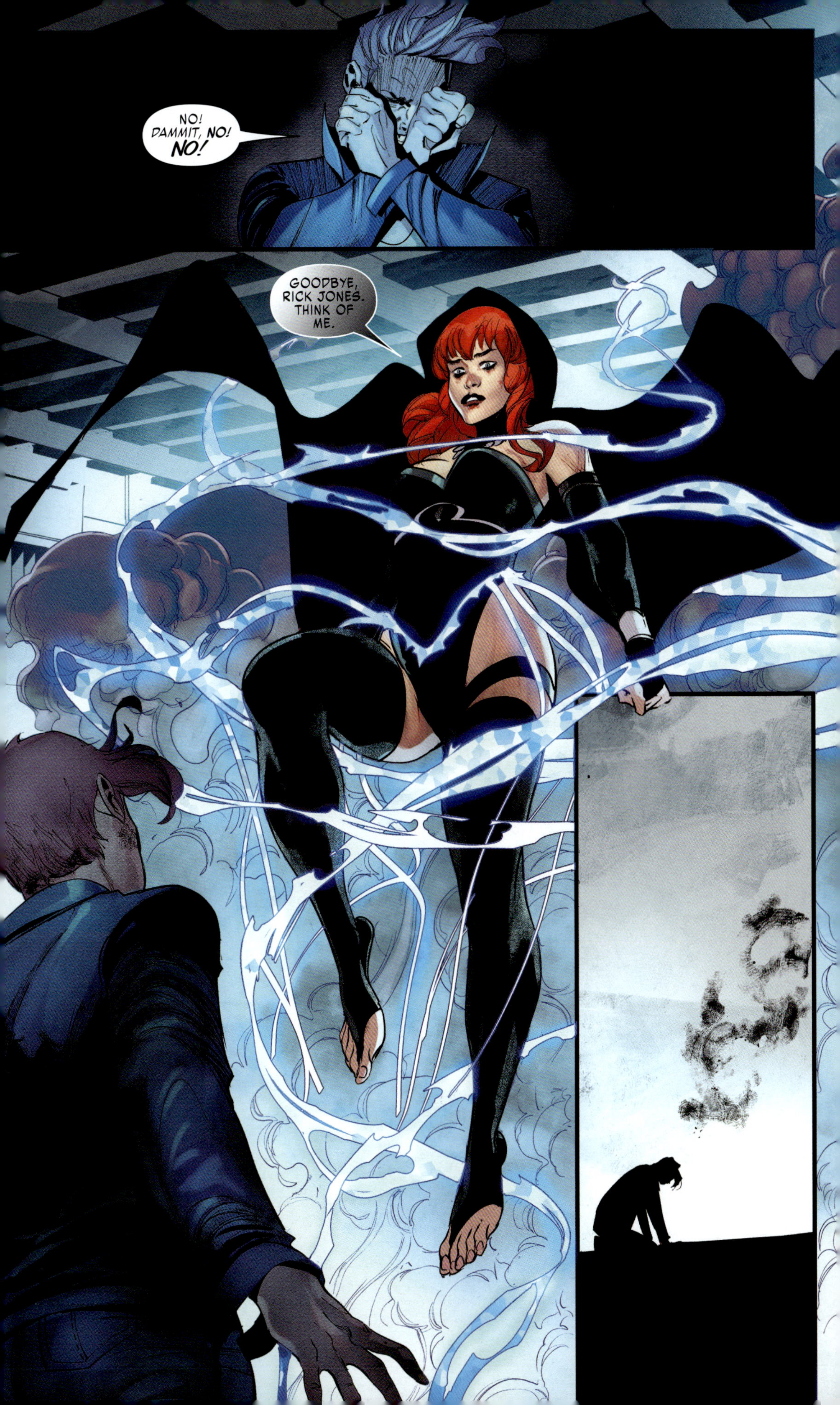
NO! DAMMIT, NO! NO!
GOODBYE, RICK JONES. THINK OF ME.

SHE'S GONE, RICK.
LIFE TOO.
SHE...SHE *HAD* TO HELP. SHE *ALWAYS* HAS TO HELP...
I HOPE YOU'RE *SATISFIED*, JONES. YOU LET MY SUBJECT GET AWAY.
HER *VALUE* IN MY EXPERIMENTS WAS--
WAAAM
WAAM WAAM WAAM
YOU SHOULD TAKE HIM *HOME* WHEN HE'S DONE.
YEAH, THAT COULD BE A WHILE.

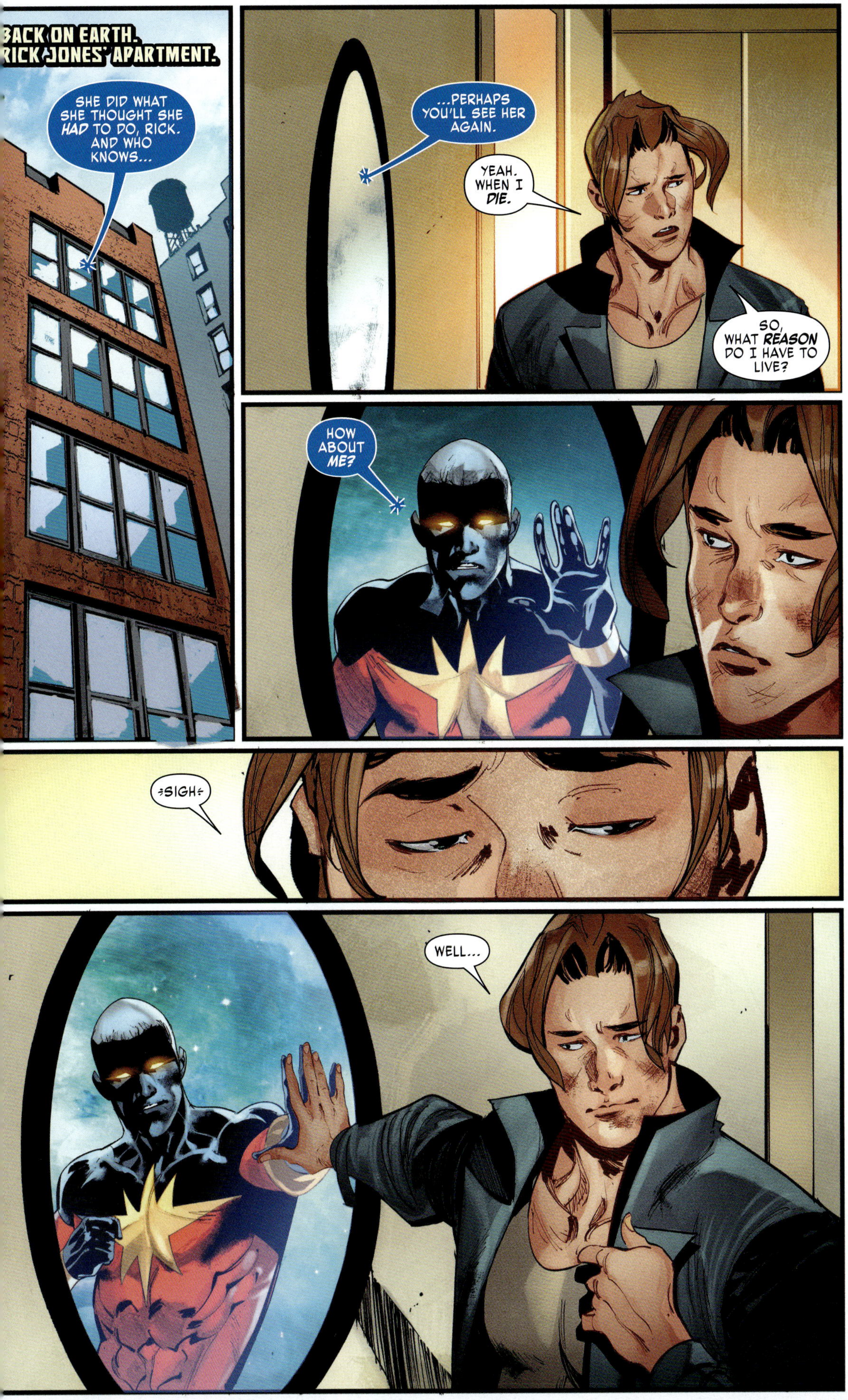
BACK ON EARTH.
RICK JONES' APARTMENT.
SHE DID WHAT SHE THOUGHT SHE HAD TO DO, RICK. AND WHO KNOWS...
...PERHAPS YOU'LL SEE HER AGAIN.
YEAH. WHEN I DIE.
SO, WHAT REASON DO I HAVE TO LIVE?
HOW ABOUT ME?
SIGH
WELL...

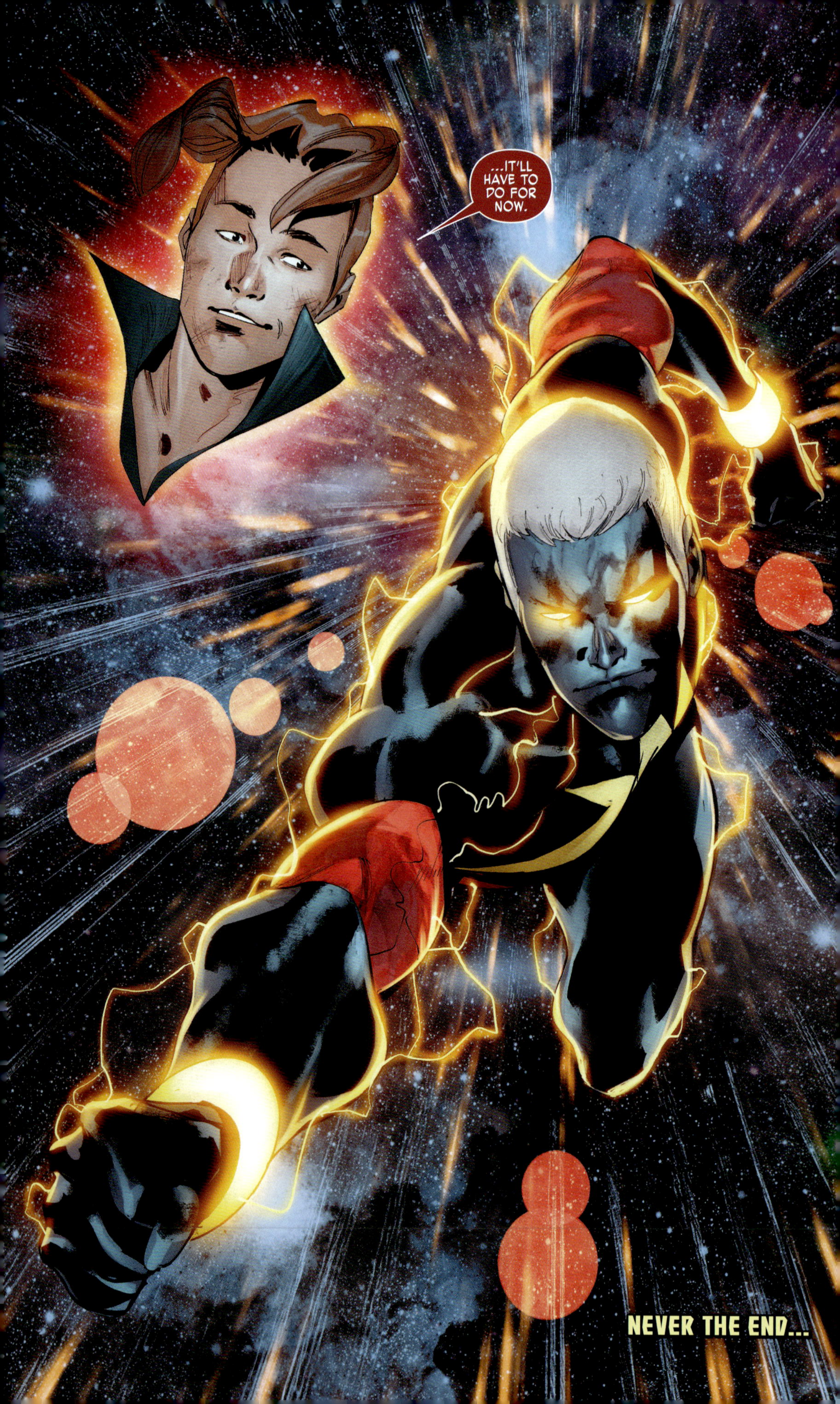
...IT'LL HAVE TO DO FOR NOW.
NEVER THE END...

SHARING SPACE

Thank you all for joining us on this ride through the cosmos, past and present, with Rick and Genis! Everyone had a blast working on this series, and I hope y'all had just as much--if not more!--fun reading it. For those deep-diving readers out there, here are some notes from the first three issues of this book!

ISSUE #1

Page 7 — Tony Stark mentions both Bruce Banner and Jen Walters, Hulk and She-Hulk, who were both part of the incredible IMMORTAL HULK run by Al Ewing and crew!

Page 8 — That hairbrush was actually given to Marlo Chandler in the classic INCREDIBLE HULK #418, which featured the wedding of Rick Jones and Marlo!

Page 25 — This dreamscape is emulating the fateful scene in INCREDIBLE HULK #1 where Rick was saved from the gamma bomb that created the original Bruce Banner HULK!

ISSUE #2

Page 3 — Jazinda first appeared in the pages of SHE-HULK (Vol. 2) #22 right before the events of the Skrull-focused event, Secret Invasion!

Page 6 — We learn of Jazinda swallowing the gem of Sy-Torak in SHE-HULK (Vol. 2) #33 after she's caught stealing it by the Kree! Also in that issue, she's being hunted by her own father, Kl'rt the Super-Skrull!

Page 8 — The Badoon first appeared aaaaaaaall the way back in the classic SILVER SURFER (Vol. 1) #2 from 1968! One issue before the infamous debut of MEPHISTO!

ISSUE #3

Page 1 — This Phyla-Vell is actually from Earth-18897 as the Earth-616 Phyla died back in GUARDIANS OF THE GALAXY (Vol. 2) #24.

Page 5 — As you may already know, Rick was with Bruce/Hulk from day one in HULK #1 (1962) but did you know that not only did he help form the Avengers in AVENGERS (Vol. 1) #1 but then also became Captain America's sidekick? Check out AVENGERS (Vol. 1) #4!

Page 7 — The Nega-Bomb was detonated toward the end of the Galactic Storm storyline in WONDER MAN (Vol. 2) #9.

Page 10 — Rick and Marlo ran off into the Microverse back in CAPTAIN MARVEL (Vol. 3) #32 right before they took a break.

Page 12 — Poor Rick was indeed killed by firing squad in the pages of SECRET EMPIRE #1 as he cried out "AVENGERS ASSEMBLE!"

Page 20 — SHATTERAX! A.K.A. Roco-Bai, first appeared in IRON MAN (Vol. 1) #278.

One last thing: Did you notice the cover to issue #5 was an homage to THE DEATH OF CAPTAIN MARVEL? See that cover below and compare where our heroes were in 1982 to forty years later in 2022!

MARVEL GRAPHIC NOVEL
THE DEATH OF
CAPTAIN MARVEL
by JIM STARLIN

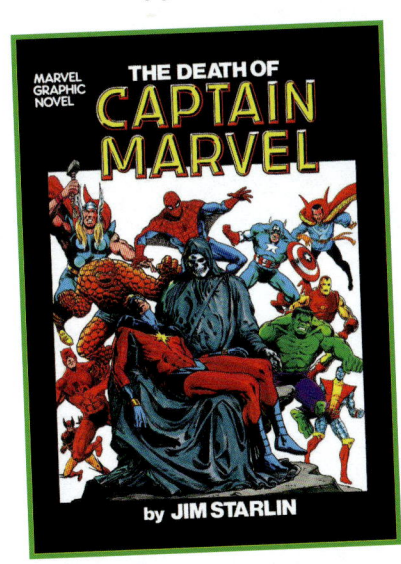

Thanks for all the love, gang. Keep your eyes peeled for where Genis & Rick will pop up next--until next time!

-- Danny Khazem

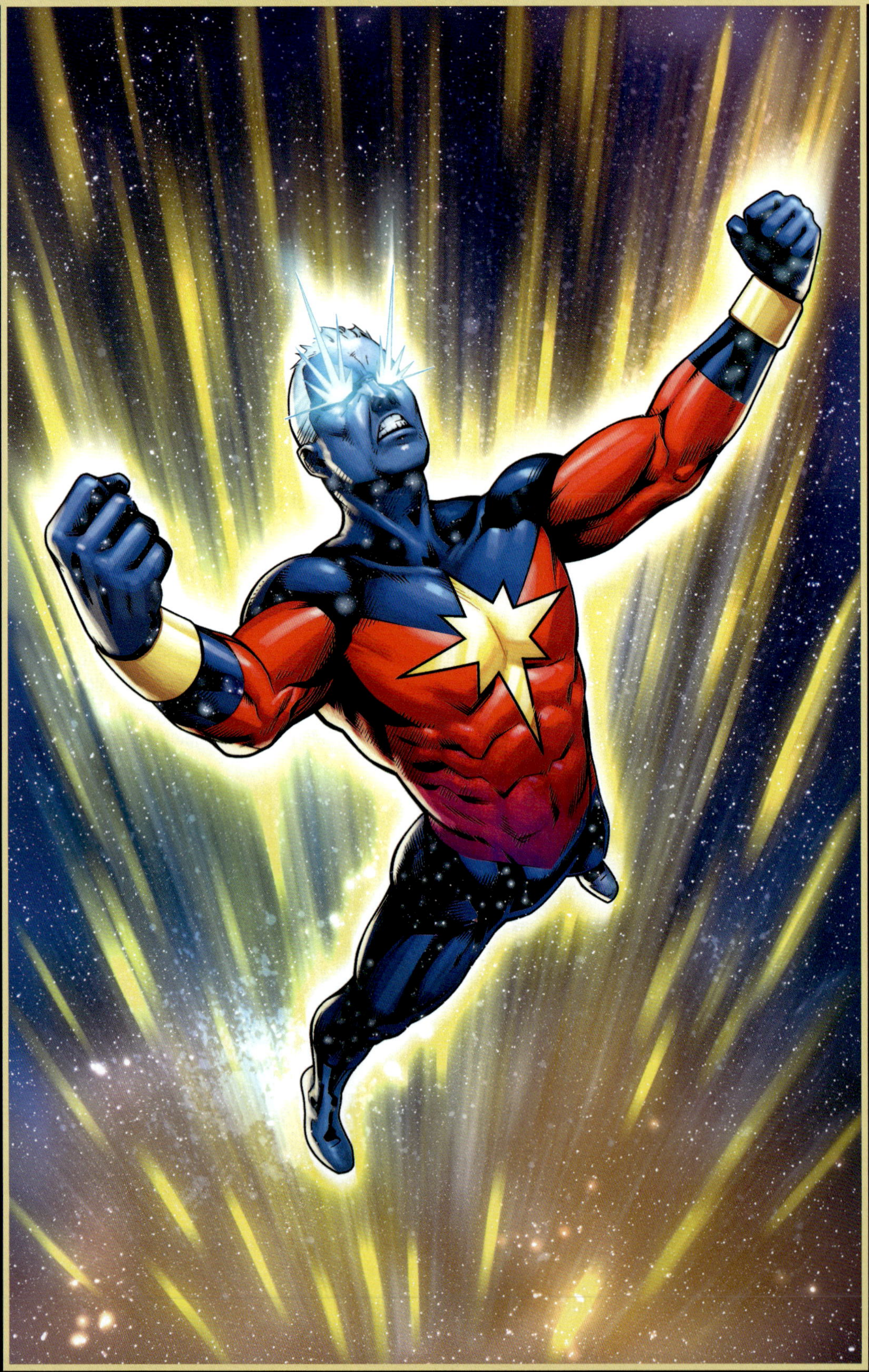

JUANN CABAL & EDGAR DELGADO
#1 Stormbreakers variant

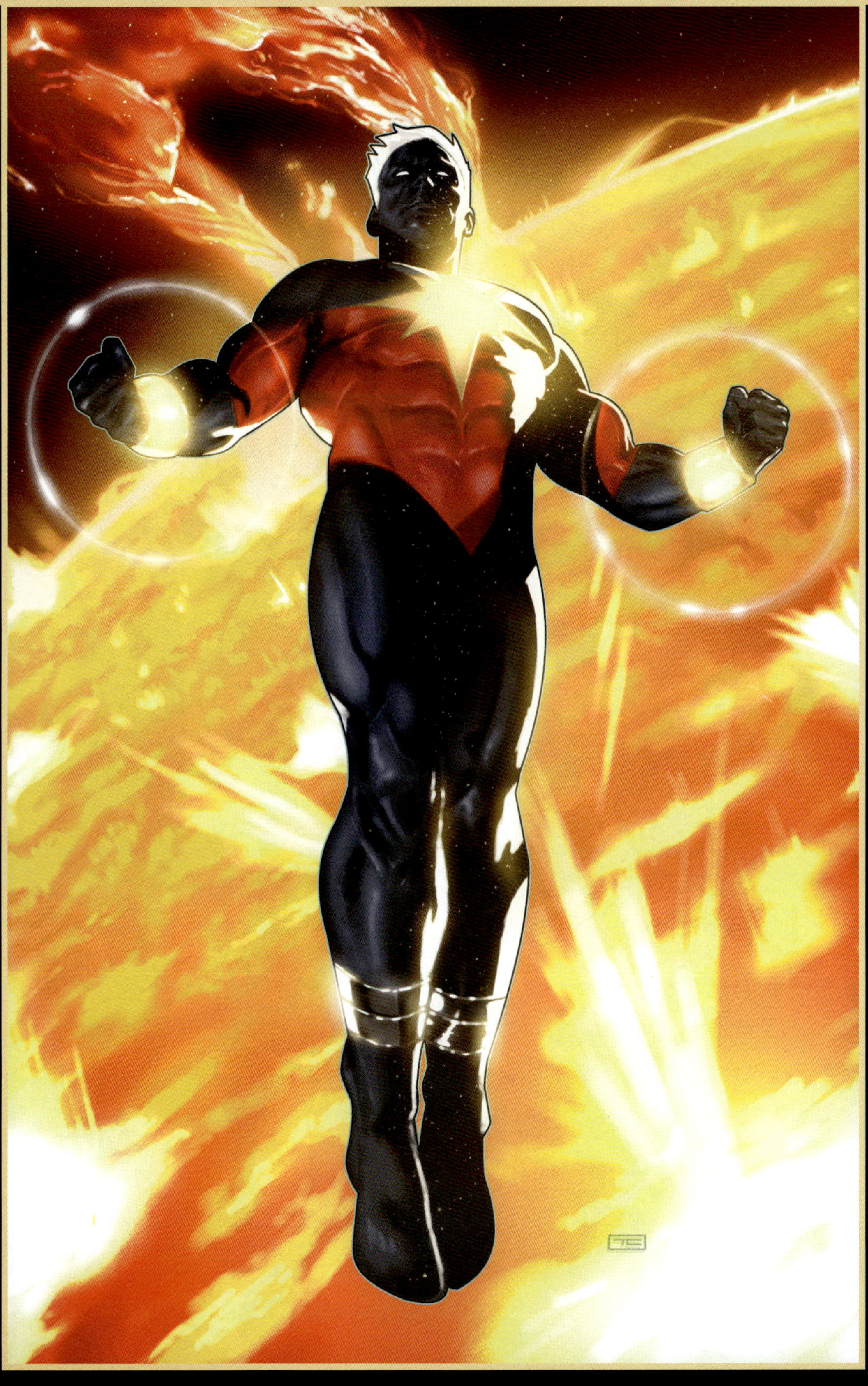

TAURIN CLARKE
#1 variant

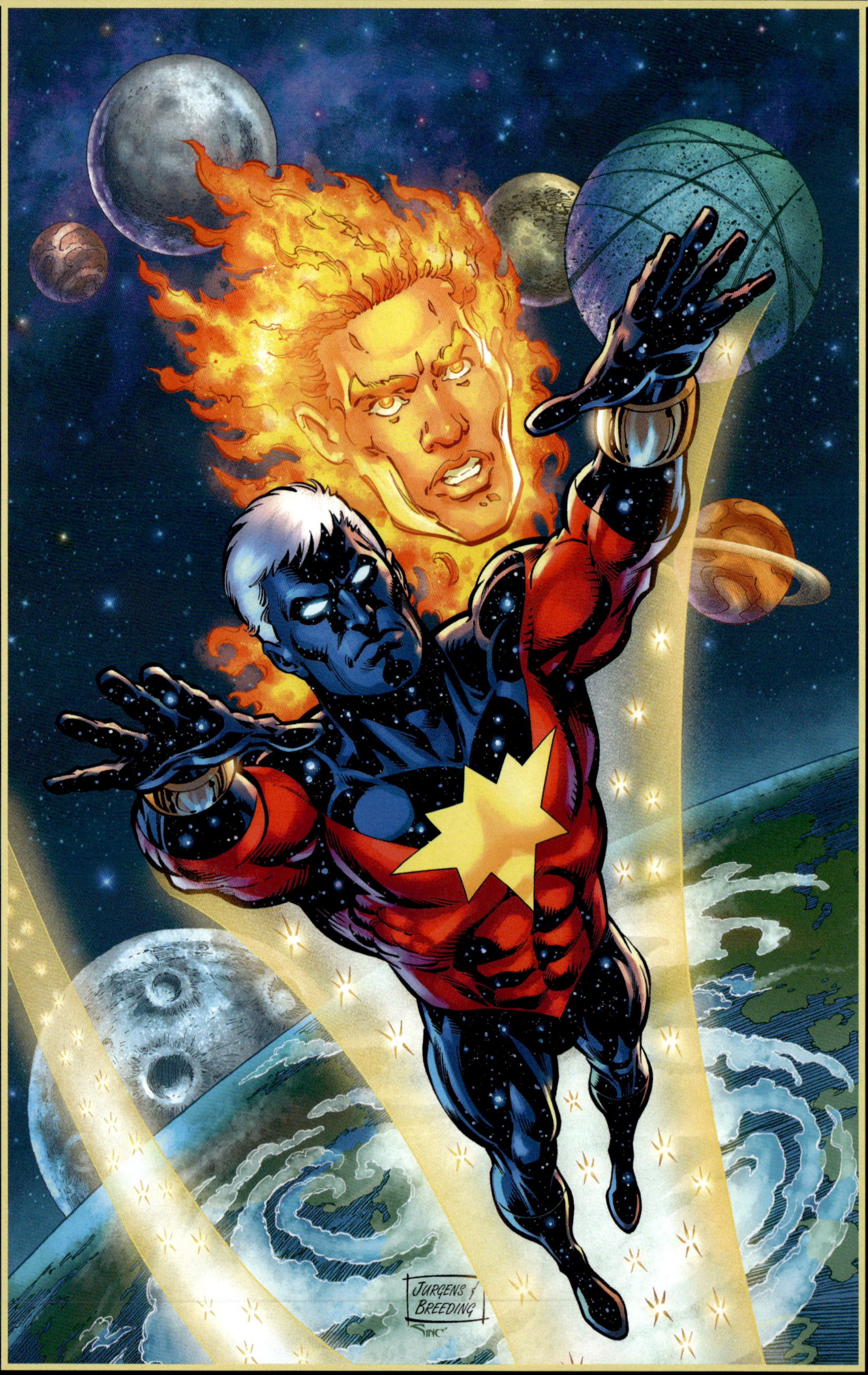
JURGENS &
BREEDING
SINC

DAN JURGENS, BRETT BREEDING & ALEX SINCLAIR
#1 variant

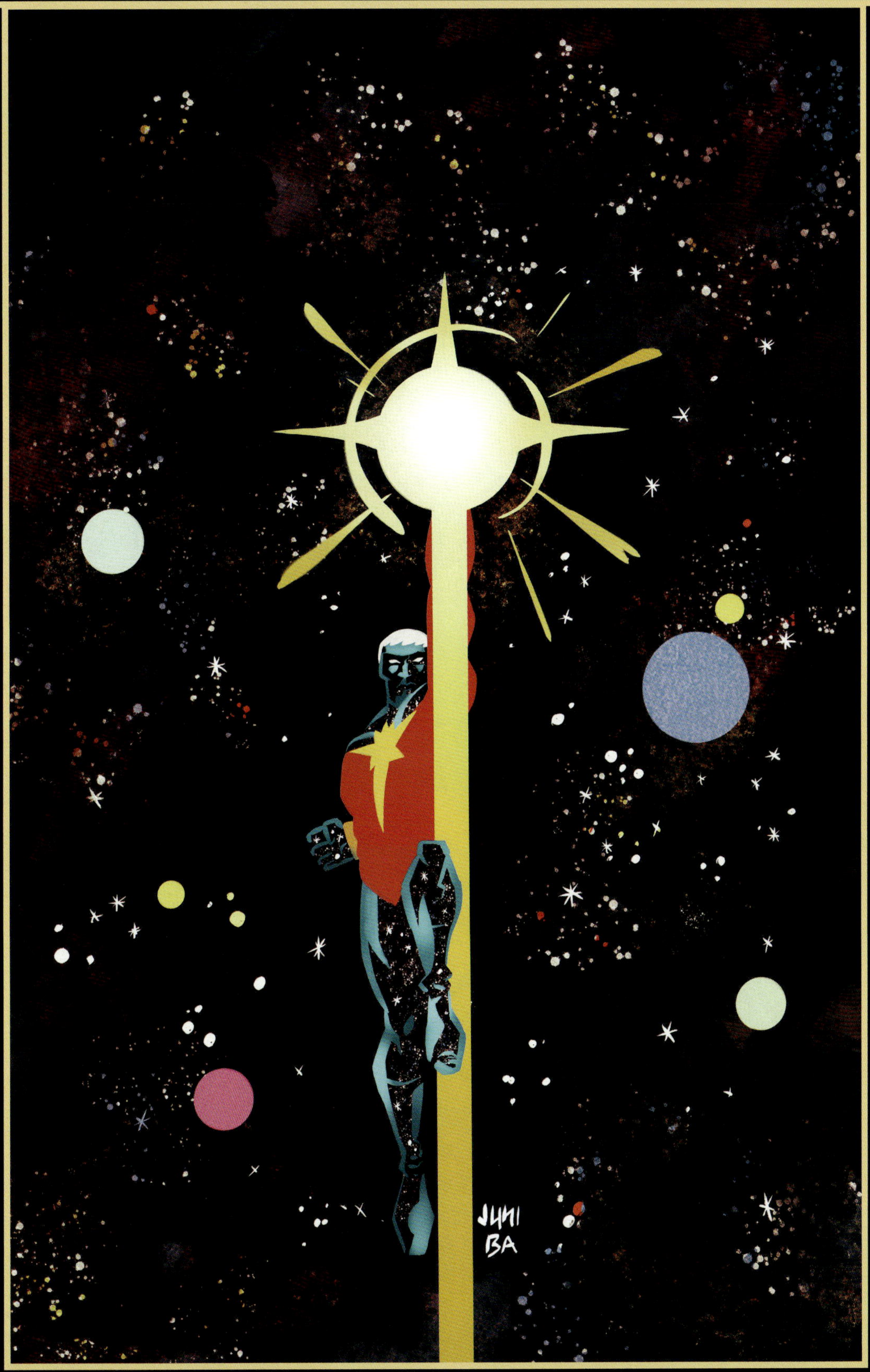
JUNI
BA

JUNI BA
#1 variant

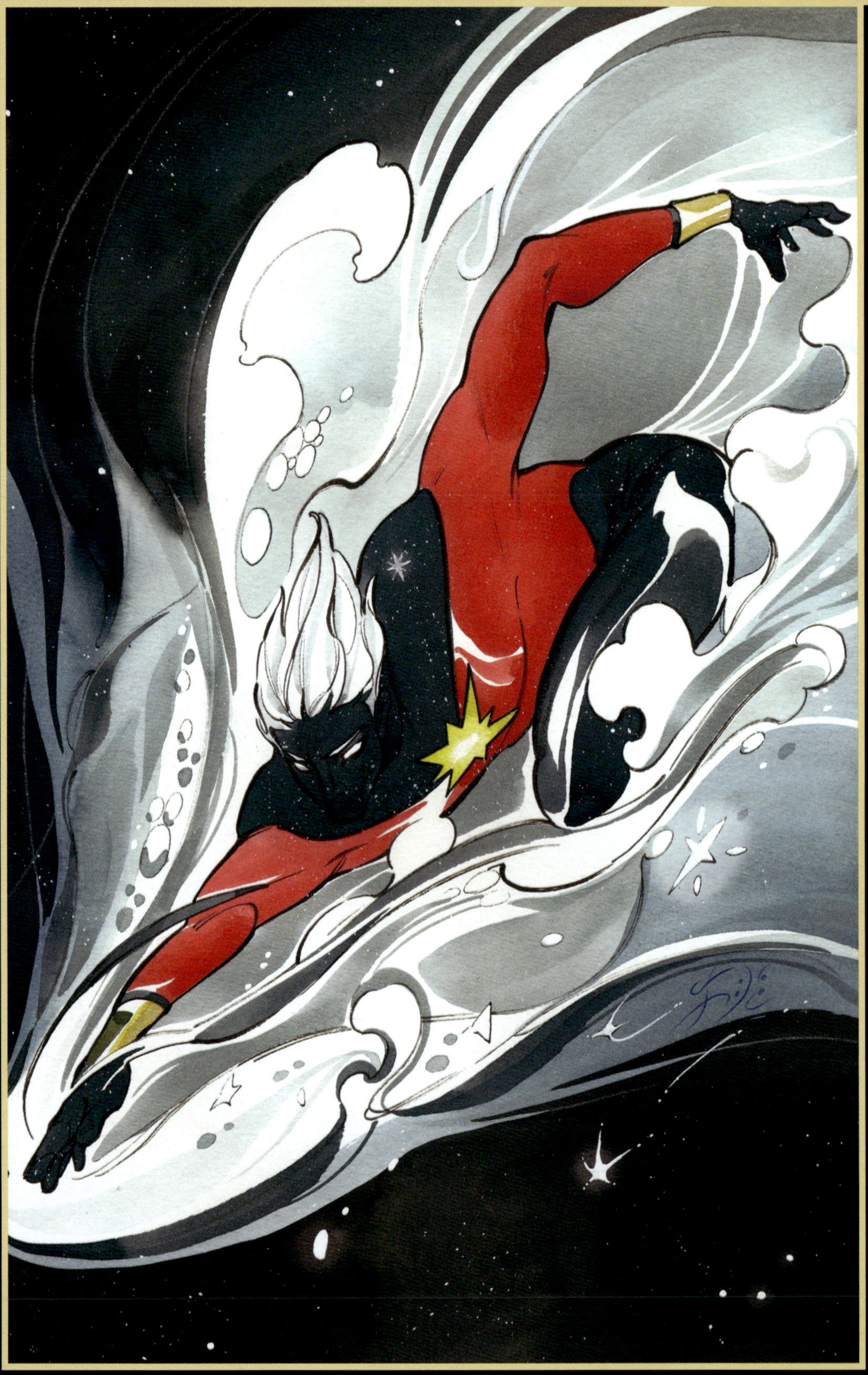

PEACH MOMOKO
#1 variant

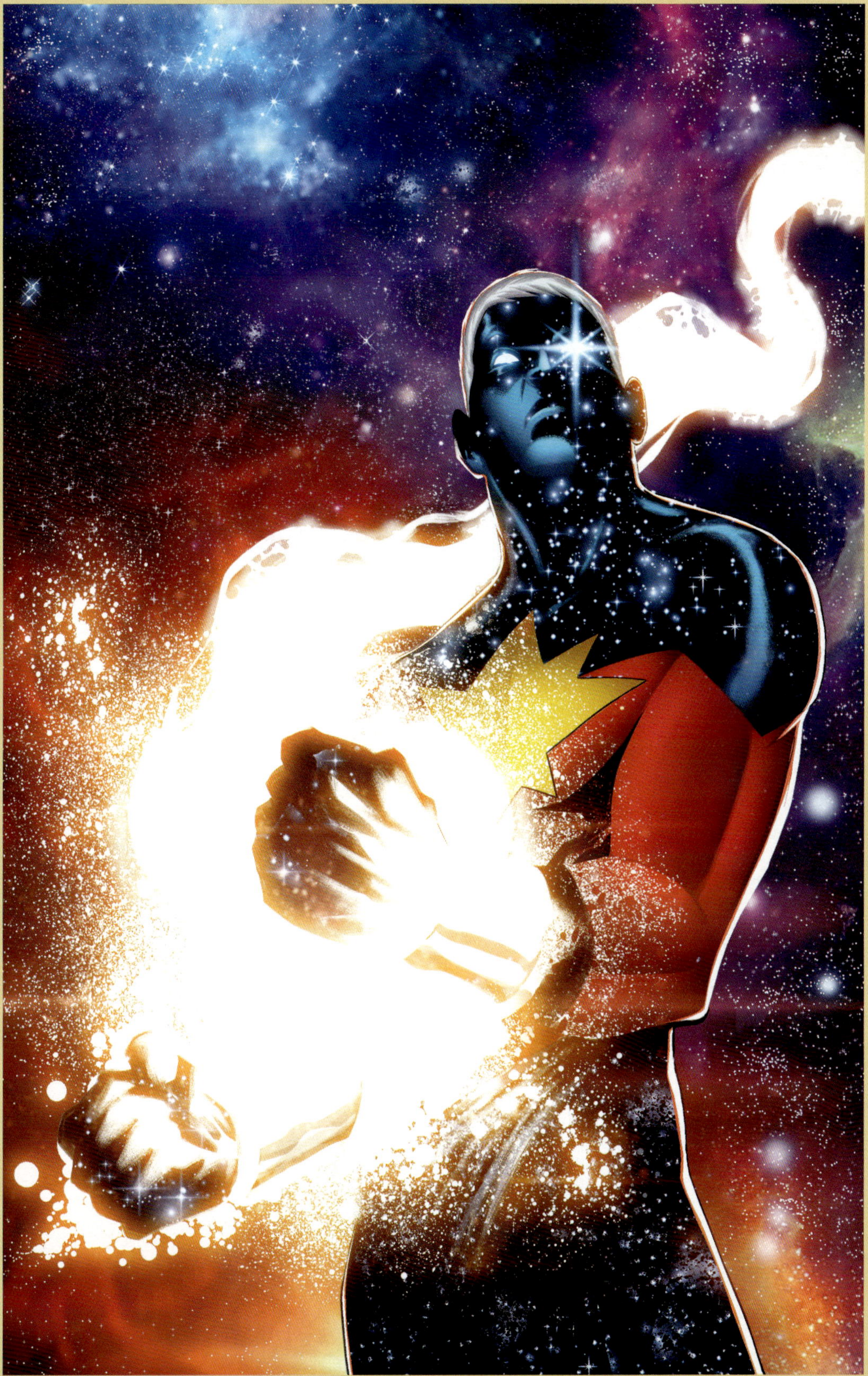

DAVID BALDÉON
#1 variant

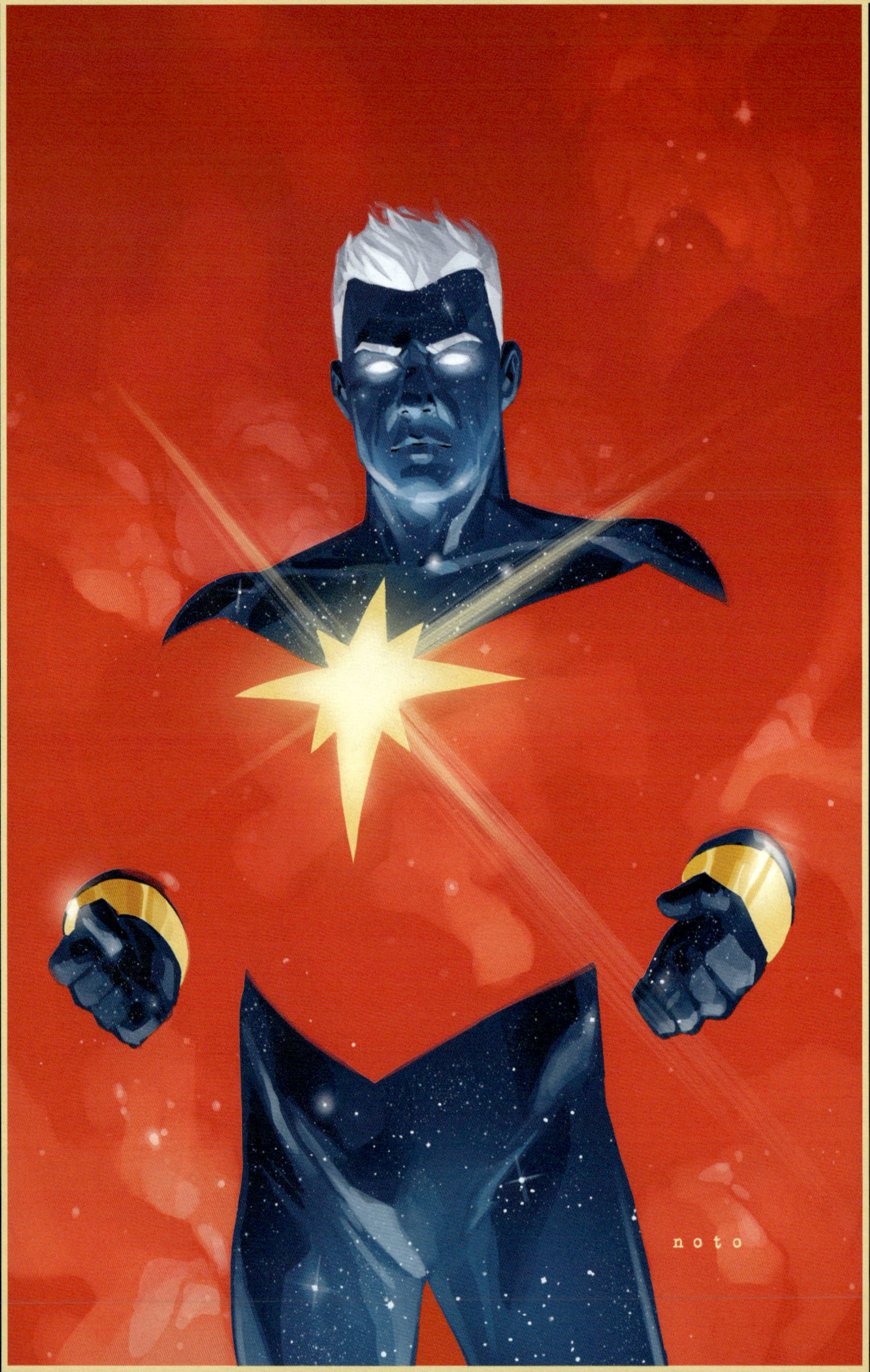
noto

PHIL NOTO
#2 variant

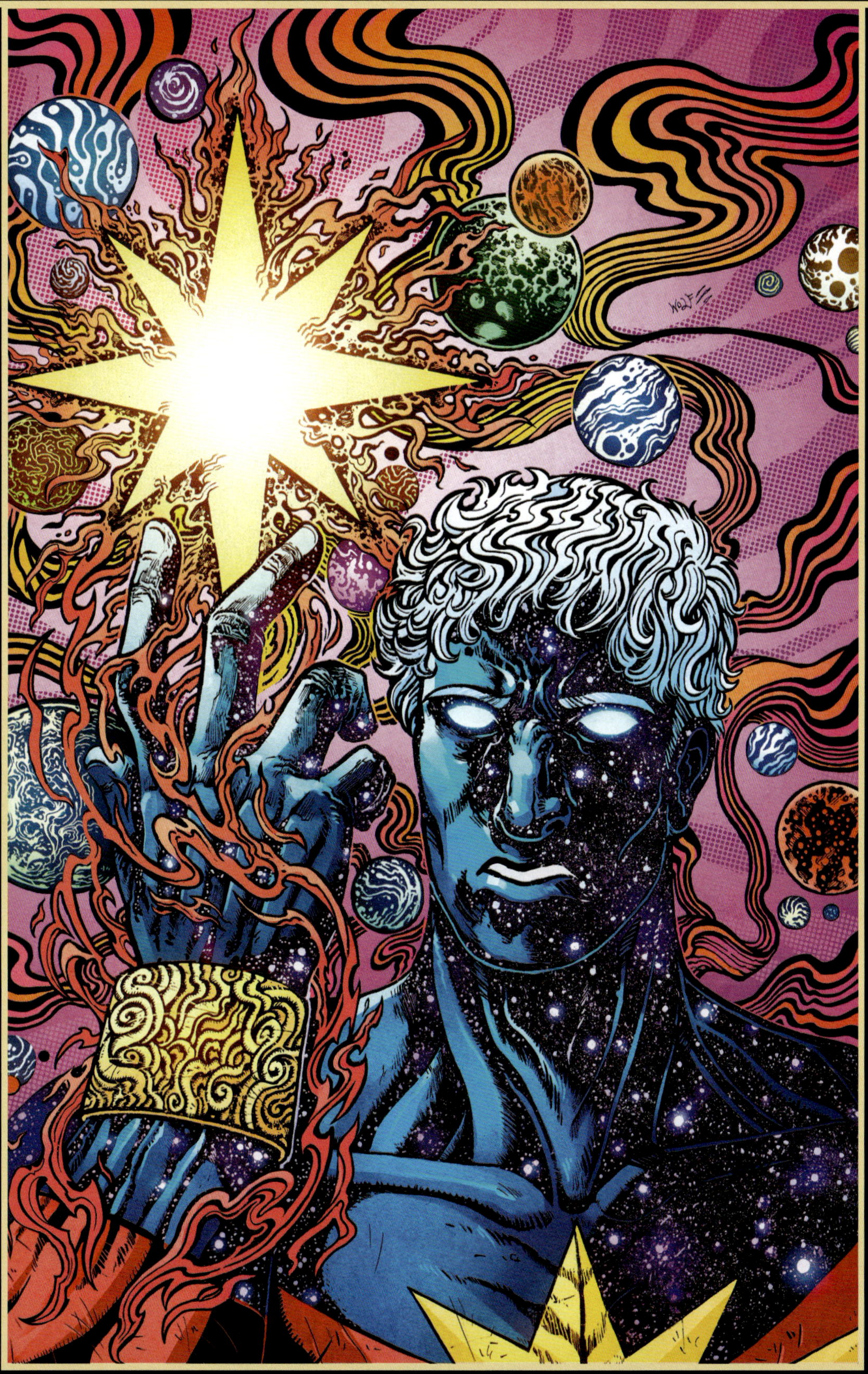

MARIA WOLF & MIKE SPICER
#3 variant

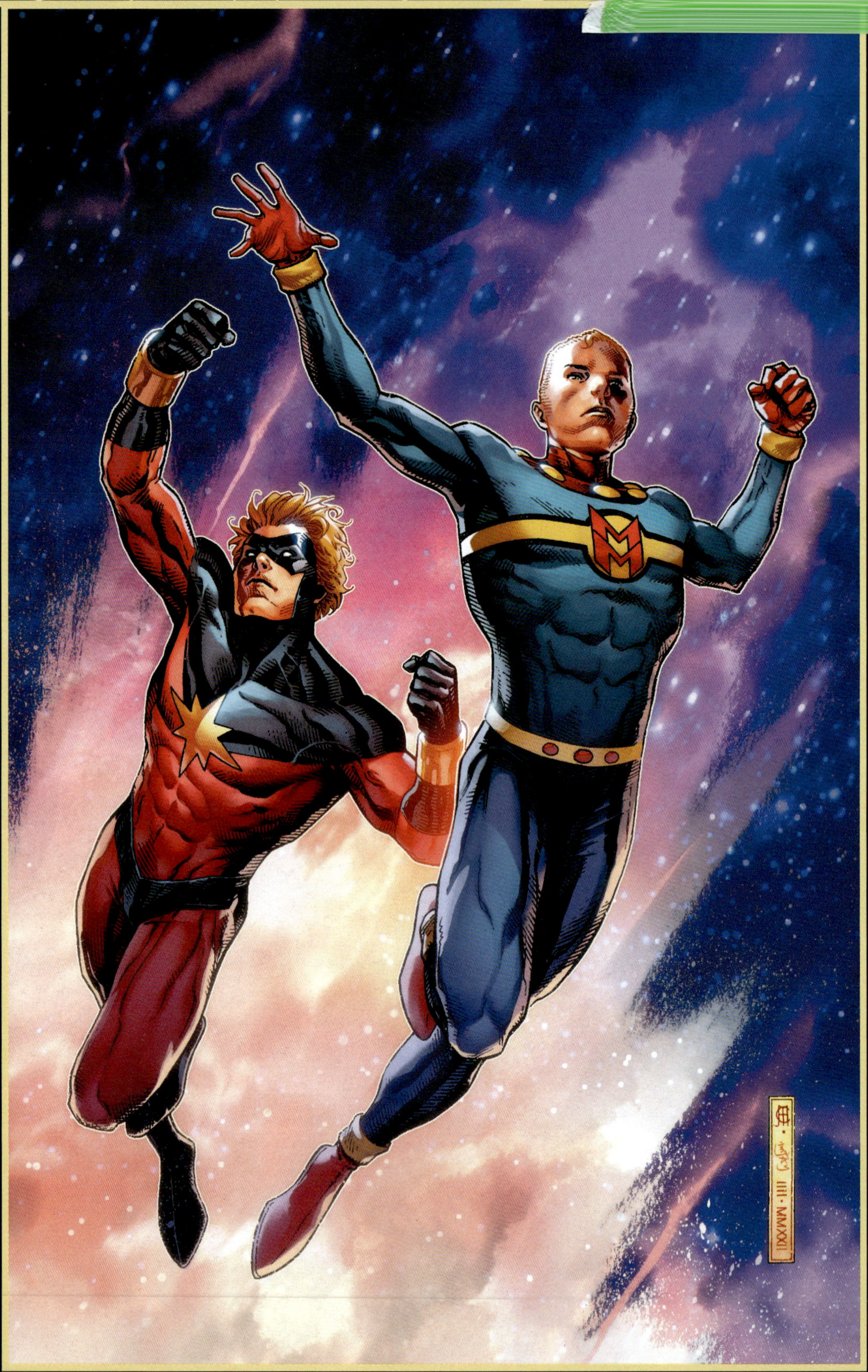

JIM CHEUNG & JAY DAVID RAMOS
#4 Miracleman variant